HOT COURAGE

Hostile Operations Team® - Strike Team 2

LYNN RAYE HARRIS

The Hostile Operations Team® and Lynn Raye Harris® are
trademarks of H.O.T. Publishing, LLC.

Printed in the United States of America

First Printing, 2022

For rights inquires, visit www.LynnRayeHarris.com

HOT Courage
Copyright © 2022 by Lynn Raye Harris
Cover Design Copyright © 2022 Croco Designs

ISBN: 978-1-941002-78-0

Chapter One

Noah "Easy" Cross sat at a table in the Early Bird Diner, waiting for the attorney who'd called him yesterday to arrive. He had a cup of coffee that he hadn't sipped from and a knot in his gut.

The knot had been there since a different attorney had informed him a week ago that his estranged sister had died recently. He'd been out of the country on a mission when it'd happened. He'd missed the funeral, and he had no desire to travel to North Carolina right now when there was nothing he could do. Maybe later, once the pain lessened.

The attorney meeting him today, a Ms. Lillian Calvert, wasn't with the law firm in North Carolina. She was a DC lawyer who was coming to deliver something from Sally. Perhaps it was Sally's cremated remains. She'd always said she wanted to be cremated, and it'd be like her to send him the urn.

Jesus.

Noah raked a hand through his hair and frowned at

the cars going by outside. Sally wasn't his sister by blood or marriage, but she was the closest thing to family he'd had in this world.

He'd *had*. He didn't miss the significance of the past tense or the hollow way it made him feel.

Sally had been his family, and he couldn't save her. He'd tried. God knew, he'd tried. But being fostered by the Parkers had been worse on her than it had on him. It hadn't been easy on him either, but at least he was male and big enough to fight back.

The door opened and a woman in a tailored suit walked inside carrying a cute little girl with blond pigtails. The pigtails bounced as the woman strode across the floor. The little girl held a stuffed animal in one hand, and her other hand curled into the woman's jacket.

Noah frowned as the woman's gaze landed on him. Something flared in that gaze before she started in his direction.

"Noah Cross?" she asked as she stopped at the table.

He frowned up at her. "Yeah."

She stuck out a hand. "I'm Lillian Calvert."

He shook her hand quickly. A waitress hurried over and asked, "Do you need a high chair?"

"Thank you, yes," Lillian said, her tone brisk.

Noah wanted to ask her to get on with it so he could go, but apparently she'd had trouble getting childcare that day and he was going to have to wait until she settled the toddler first. He felt a little guilty for refusing to go to her office now, but it was too late for that.

"Mama," the little girl said as Lillian put her into the high chair and collapsed onto the seat.

"Mama's not here, sweetie," Lillian said softly. "Would you like to color?"

She put the placemat with the picture and a crayon the waitress had given her onto the table where the little girl could scribble. The child took the crayon and started coloring big swaths across the paper.

Lillian blew out a breath and rummaged around in the giant satchel she'd set onto the booth seat. Noah had a million questions, but he bit them back and waited.

"Mr. Cross," she finally said as she pulled out a folder from her bag and placed it on the table. "I'm very sorry for your loss. Your sister left a will, and in it she named you Alice's guardian."

Alarm bells clanged deep inside.

What the fuck?

Noah looked at the child. Really looked at her. He could see Sally's nose, and the hair was one hundred percent hers. Anger flared, along with a sharp sense of betrayal. Why hadn't Sally told him she'd had a kid? Why hadn't she gotten in touch instead of ghosting him for the past three years? And what the fuck had she been thinking to leave him in charge of her kid? Not only that, but *why* hadn't he gone after her sooner and *made* her talk to him?

Fucking hell!

He resisted the urge to blurt that Sally wasn't really his sister and there was no way he could take her kid. From the time they'd been young adults making their way in the world, they'd listed each other as next of kin on any and all paperwork.

Someone now wanting to give him a child because of that was an outcome he couldn't have imagined.

"It's not possible," Noah said, his voice feeling as if it belonged to someone else. Dry. Cracked. Rusty.

Lillian blinked at him. "I assure you it is. There are no other living relatives."

Noah felt as if steel bands were tightening around his chest. "My sister and I were estranged. I didn't even know she *had* a child, and now I'm her legal guardian?" He shook his head. "What about the father? Won't he have something to say about that?"

Lillian scraped a fingernail along the edge of the folder. "According to the information I was given, he's a married man who wanted her to have an abortion. Sally refused. He's not named on the birth certificate and hasn't been involved in Alice's life."

Noah looked at the little girl again. She was adorable, but there was no way he could take her. Not even for Sally.

"It's impossible for me to be her guardian," he stated numbly. "I'm in the military and I don't get to choose when or if I have to travel. It could be tomorrow, or it could be next week. That's no life for a kid."

Travel was the vague way of saying that he didn't get to choose when it was time to board a plane and drop into a hostile war zone in order to kick terrorist ass, or rescue hostages, or any number of dangerous missions that could end up with him very dead and not coming back again.

"Yes, but you have a support structure," Lillian said. "The military is very good at providing for dependent family members. I've had military clients before."

She smiled at him as if it was simple. As if he just needed to waltz into HOT HQ tomorrow and inform General Mendez and Colonel Bishop that he'd acquired a pint-sized dependent.

"It's not that easy."

He could have laughed at the word. *Easy.* His call sign. Because everything was easier than the shithole life he'd come from. Compared to being a foster kid in the system, at least for him, the military was as easy as a picnic on a lazy Sunday afternoon.

"Perhaps not, but you're resourceful, Mr. Cross."

"Sergeant," he said. "Sergeant Cross."

"Very well, Sergeant Cross." She turned her head a fraction. "This is Alice. Your niece."

———

JENNA LANE PULLED her blond hair into a ponytail, swiped on mascara and some lip gloss, and went to retrieve her purse so she could head into work. Her roommate was sitting on the couch, smoke circling her head. Jenna coughed and waved her hand, trying to dissipate the smell of burning grass that emanated from the joint.

"I thought you were going to take that stuff outside from now on," she said.

Tami looked at her with glassy eyes. "Still daylight. Someone might see."

Jenna snatched her purse up and dug for her car keys. "At least open a window, then."

"Say hi to Allison for me," Tami said, ignoring the instruction and naming the diner owner they both worked for. "No, say *fuck you* for me."

Jenna grumbled a reply and headed for the door, knowing nothing she said would get through to Tami when she was high. As soon as Jenna stepped outside, she took a deep breath and blew it out again. She'd been in Mystic Cove for two months now, and other than living with a pothead, working for a boss who gave Jekyll and Hyde a run for the money, and wondering if the floor was finally going to drop out of the trailer whenever Tami brought home some random guy to fuck, life was just peachy.

Peachy.

Jenna opened the door of her beat-up Toyota Corolla, dropped her purse onto the passenger seat, and shoved the key into the ignition. She turned it—and nothing happened.

"No," she muttered. "No, no, no. Come on, Lola," she begged as she turned the key again. There was nothing but a clicking sound. *Stupid car.* She missed the Nissan Armada SUV she used to drive. So much. But keeping the vehicle, and the car payments, hadn't been an option when she'd fled Las Vegas five months ago. Fastest way to get found was to leave a trail someone could follow.

"Sounds like you got a dead battery, honey," someone called.

Jenna looked up to see Mrs. Hanley on the front

porch of her trailer, rocking back and forth on a rocker with a cigarette dangling from one hand and a book in the other. She put the book down and stood. Jenna rolled the window down.

"Hi, Mrs. Hanley. Do you have cables? Can you give me a jump?"

She still had twenty minutes before she had to be to work, which was ten minutes away, but every second counted. Allison didn't appreciate lateness for any reason. And Jenna had already been late twice this month. Once there'd been an accident blocking the road, and the other time Tami had gotten high and "misplaced" Jenna's keys. Not that she'd been able to tell Allison that.

"Sorry, hon, I ain't got any." She nodded her head toward a house nearby. "Mr. Pruitt might have some."

"Thanks," Jenna called as she shoved the door open and headed for Mr. Pruitt's. He did indeed have cables and a truck to give her a jump, but he was at least eighty if he was a day and didn't move as fast as she might like. She had to wait for him to locate his keys, start the truck, and drive it over to park near Lola, all the while eyeing her phone and worrying about the time.

But he *did* help and she *was* grateful when Lola turned over.

"You might need to get a new battery, kiddo," Mr. Pruitt said as he unhooked the cables. "They wear out, you know."

Jenna removed the support bar from the hole so she could close the hood. "Yes, thank you, Mr. Pruitt. I'll check into it."

"Go to Tiny's Garage. He'll do you a turn better than that parts place over there on Main where they'll try to sell you something you don't need because you're a lady."

"I'll remember that. Thanks so much."

Mr. Pruitt waved as she got into Lola and put her in reverse. Ten minutes later, Jenna was walking through the back door of the Early Bird Diner and racing for her time card. She was fifteen minutes late, but Allison wasn't there which meant she might not notice until she did payroll. Jenna could hope.

"Hey," Vicki said with a grin as Jenna tied on her apron. "That hunky soldier you like is here. He's not alone, though. I've been waiting on them, but I'm not quite sure what's going on."

Jenna's heart beat a little faster at the mention of Noah Cross. He was a regular, and sometimes he brought other Army guys with him who called him Easy instead of Noah. She'd finally figured out that it was a code name or something, but he'd told her to call him Noah, so she did.

The entire lot of them were attractive in that alpha male warrior way, but Noah was the one who set her pulse skipping. The way he smiled at her... Lord, he was handsome. Too handsome to be interested in her, but that didn't mean she couldn't dream.

"What did they order?" she asked.

"Coffee for him. Nothing for the lady. A juice box for the kid."

"Kid?"

Vicki nodded. "Yep. Cute little thing."

Jenna peered through the opening between the kitchen and the counter area. Noah was in jeans and a black T-shirt, and the woman wore a suit. The little girl had two short pigtails on her head that bounced every time she moved.

"He was here first, then she came in about fifteen minutes later. He hasn't smiled at her once. She's done a lot of the talking so far, and he mostly frowns."

"You're late, Jenna."

Jenna whirled to find Allison with hands on hips and brows drawn low.

"I'm sorry but my car was dead. I had to get a jump."

"That's the third time this month. If you can't get here on time, then I can't serve my customers the way they deserve to be served. It's almost time for the dinner rush, and I can't be short-handed."

"I know. I'm sorry. I got here as soon as I could."

"If you can't do the job, then I need to find someone who can."

"I can do it, Allison. It's only fifteen minutes. The rush hasn't even started yet."

Allison's eyes narrowed. "Only fifteen minutes. Said like someone who doesn't give a shit about other people's time."

Jenna was about to say something else when Vicki jabbed an elbow in her back. She swallowed her retort instead.

Allison turned to go back to the small office at the rear of the diner. "We'll talk about this later," she threw over her shoulder. "For now, get to work."

Jenna snatched up her order pad and pen and stuck out her tongue. Vicki was shaking her head. "Girl, no use arguing with her. You won't win, and she'll dock your pay even more."

"I know. Thanks for the jab. I just—I hate that she treats us like we're the enemy, you know?"

"I know. It was better when her daddy ran the place, but he had to go and retire. Like Florida has better beaches than the Chesapeake or something."

Jenna snorted a laugh. "Um, I think they probably *do*."

Vicki grinned. "I know. I just wanted to make you laugh. You gotta admit that living this close to the bay is nice though. Fresh seafood and a small beach that's sorta like a real one. Plus all the boats and the tourists. Makes for good tips when it's high season, which it is."

Jenna nodded. She liked Mystic Cove. A lot. It was small, picturesque with its view of the water and the sailboats stacked side by side in the marina, and it was affordable. She'd tried a few places since leaving Vegas, and this one was the prettiest. The exact opposite of what she'd come from, which was good. It was also about a three hour drive away from Aunt Maggie in Delaware, but she didn't want to go to Aunt Maggie and potentially put her in danger, too.

Mystic Cove wasn't the kind of place the Flanagans would think to send an assassin. If she was lucky, they weren't even looking for her. The man who'd killed her boss had ended up in prison for a different crime, so it shouldn't even matter what she'd heard that night. In fact, she didn't even *know* if anyone knew she'd heard a thing. She'd assumed they had which was why she'd run. But what if she was wrong?

You willing to risk your life on that, Jenna?

"Welp," Vicki said, "I better get out there and see if your boyfriend wants anything else. Or would you like to do it?"

Jenna felt a flash of heat in her cheeks. "Stop that, Vic."

Vicki snorted. "Go on. Go see what they need." She peered out the service window and then tilted her head as if surprised. "The woman left, but the kid's still there. You going or am I?"

Jenna cursed beneath her breath as she said, "I'll go, evil wench. You fill the salt shakers."

Vicki snorted a laugh. "That's gratitude for ya."

Jenna ignored her as she pushed the kitchen door open and grabbed the coffee pot before heading for Noah's table.

Chapter Two

NOAH STARED AT THE CHILD IN THE HIGH CHAIR. *ALICE.* She was staring in the direction Lillian Calvert had gone and her chin was starting to quiver.

"Mama?" she asked before turning wide blue eyes onto Noah.

His gut twisted. *What the fuck was he supposed to do now?* Fucking Sally. Fucking Lillian Calvert, who'd shown him the documents, went to her car to fetch a small suitcase and a car seat, wished him good luck, and left him sitting in a diner with a toddler.

"More coffee?"

Noah jerked his gaze to the waitress who'd appeared at the table. Jenna. She smiled at him and he swallowed because he was at a loss. A big fucking loss.

She glanced at Alice. Alice turned big eyes on her. "Want Mama," the little girl said. Or at least that's what he thought she said because he wasn't so good at understanding the kid-speak.

Before Noah could formulate an answer, Alice burst into tears. "Mama," she wailed. "Mama."

Jenna looked at him, but he couldn't move. Couldn't respond. Didn't know what to fucking do. Jenna's expression changed from sympathetic to alarmed in a heartbeat. She set the coffee pot down and leaned over to hug the child. "Oh, honey, I'm sure she'll be back soon. Are you hungry? Do you want some cheese? How about a cracker? Would that help?"

"Mama," Alice wailed. But she clung to Jenna, who tugged her up and into her arms.

"Sorry," she mouthed to him.

"It's okay," he said, forcing the words past the giant knot in his throat. "Thank you for helping."

He didn't know why she was apologizing to him. He was grateful that somebody knew what to do.

"Hey, sweetie, do you want to see what's behind the counter? Let's go have a look over there, okay?"

Noah watched Jenna bounce Alice as she carried her over to the counter and started pointing at things, naming them as she went. He knew he should be the one holding the little girl, soothing her, but he didn't have a fucking clue how to do it. He was utterly numb. How the hell could Sally have left him her kid? And how could a lawyer waltz in and hand the child off to him as if he was qualified to take her?

Hell, he'd never even had a puppy, much less a kid. What was he supposed to do with her? He'd asked Lillian Calvert that, but she'd reiterated that he needed to rely on the support he'd get from the military for a dependent child. Except Alice wasn't his dependent, and he was pretty sure the military wasn't going to make her so without a formal adoption.

Noah raked both hands through his hair and stared at the tabletop, trying to make sense of everything that'd happened. He needed to call his team leader, Cade "Saint" Rodgers, and tell him everything. Saint would know the steps to take next.

Noah couldn't keep the kid. No matter that she was Sally's, he couldn't do it. His life wasn't made for being a parent. Hell, he wasn't so sure *he* was made for being a parent.

"If you want to give her up for adoption, you can do that," Lillian had said. *"She'll be adopted quickly because of her age, but she's also going to be in foster care for a little while first."*

The words had sent a chill through him. *Foster care.* Exactly what Sally would never want for her baby. The thing that had messed up Sally's life was not something she would have wanted for Alice.

Jenna came back over with Alice in her arms. The kid clutched a cookie and wasn't crying. Jenna shrugged apologetically as she tried to put Alice into her high chair. But Alice clung to her and made sniffling noises, so Jenna stopped trying to put the child down.

"I'm so sorry," she said to him. "She seems to want me to hold her. I should have asked you about the cookie, but I couldn't think of anything else."

"It's okay. Thanks for helping."

Jenna glanced toward the door. She was pretty in that plain way some women had. Her long blond hair was scraped back into a ponytail, and she wore minimal makeup. She wasn't especially curvy, or especially thin. She was something in between. Average, he guessed.

Right now, she was anything but average to him. She was holding Alice and she'd managed to soothe her. That was everything.

"Is she coming back? Your, er, the mother?"

Noah blinked in confusion. But then understanding dawned. "That was a lawyer. My sister died three weeks ago in a car accident. Alice is her child."

"Oh." Jenna nibbled her lip. "I'm so, so sorry." She put a hand up to cover the child's ear. The other was against her shoulder. "Poor little girl. Does she cry for her mother often?"

Noah felt like the worst kind of person at that moment. "I don't know. I… I just met her. I didn't know about her until today. My sister and I were estranged," he finished quietly.

Jenna looked as if she understood, though how could anybody understand this nightmare? He certainly didn't.

"Are you used to having a child around?" she asked.

He shook his head. "I don't know what to do. I've never… I'm not prepared for this, but here she is and I don't have a clue."

Jenna glanced down at the toddler's blond head. Alice's eyes were drooping. "She's been through a lot, I assume."

"Yeah." He blew out a breath. "I need to call my team leader, and I need to arrange child care. Can you watch her while I go out to my Jeep and make some calls in private?"

She didn't hesitate. "I can do that. I'm so sorry for your loss, Noah."

He stared at her holding Alice and his belly tightened. He didn't spend any time examining why. He got to his feet. "Thanks. I appreciate it. I'll be back in a few minutes."

She waved him off. "It's okay. Do what you need to do. We'll be fine. The dinner rush doesn't start for another hour."

———

JENNA LET Alice sleep on her shoulder as she took over the task of filling salt shakers from Vicki. It wasn't easy with the child, but she managed it while Vic took care of the customers. Allison emerged from the back, saw Jenna, and stalked over to her.

"Whose kid is that? You know I don't allow children at work."

Jenna shifted Alice and poured salt into a shaker. "She belongs to a patron."

Allison scanned the restaurant. "Which one?"

"He's outside, making a phone call. He needed help and she likes me."

Allison frowned. "Get rid of her as soon as you can and get back to work. This isn't a free babysitting service for Christ's sake."

"I'll hand her over as soon as he comes back in. Promise."

Allison didn't reply as she sailed into the kitchen and

disappeared to her office again. Vicki swung by, a look of concern on her face. "You okay?"

"I'm fine. Allison isn't happy, but the child belongs to a customer so she can't exactly complain about me not being helpful, right?"

"Allison's panties are on too tight, if you ask me," Vicki muttered. "It's that wedgie up her ass that makes her such a bitch."

Jenna snorted. God love Vicki. She told it like it was, and she was pretty much immune to Allison. Allison didn't bother her because she'd been a fixture at the Early Bird for almost two decades.

"I can take her for a few minutes if you like," Vicki said. "She's cute as a button, isn't she? Reminds me of my granddaughter."

"I'm good. She's sleeping pretty soundly anyway. I'd hate to wake her."

"All right, hon. Let me know if you need me to spot you." Vicki disappeared with the coffee pot and a pitcher of iced tea, and Jenna kept working on the shakers.

It'd been a couple of years since she'd worked at the day care center, but she hadn't forgotten how to soothe a child. She'd been working there and saving money to go back to college when she'd gotten the receptionist job at Sam Baxter's law office. The pay had been better, so she'd left the day care center. Besides, working with kids wasn't the easiest thing in the world. And it wasn't always the kids who were the problem either. Sometimes it was the parents. More than sometimes, really. Dealing with parents had been exhausting, which made answering phones and typing seem like a breeze.

And yet, answering phones and typing had landed her in far hotter water than dealing with an irate parent's complaint ever had. If she'd never left day care, she'd still be wiping snotty noses and leading craft sessions—and she'd be safe. She wouldn't have to constantly look over her shoulder for danger.

The bell over the door tinkled, and she looked up to see Noah striding toward her. He still had that shell-shocked look of disbelief, but he seemed marginally calmer than he had before he'd gone outside. Poor guy, losing his sister and gaining custody of a kid all at once. No wonder he'd been nothing like his usual self when she'd gone to fill his coffee cup.

"Everything taken care of?" she asked as he reached the table where she worked.

He nodded as he shoved his hands into his pockets. Almost as if he didn't want her to hand Alice over. The booth he'd been sitting at still had the papers he'd left, plus a car seat and a small suitcase that presumably contained Alice's clothes. He ignored it all for the moment. It was safe enough there, but maybe he just didn't want to face what looking at those things meant.

"Help is on the way. For now, I mean."

Jenna smiled up at him. "You'll figure it out. You seem pretty competent."

He snorted. "You can't know that. What if I'm highly incompetent at everything except ordering food and eating it?"

"The military must think you know how to do

*some*thing, right?" She offered him a smile, and he nodded more seriously than she would have expected.

"Yeah, I'm good at the job. But the job doesn't involve children."

"I worked in a day care once, so let me give you a tip; kids can scent fear. Don't wallow in your belief you're incompetent when it comes to her, and don't let her know you haven't a clue what you're doing sometimes. It'll be fine. These days, you have the entire world at your fingertips. Need to know how to change a diaper? Google. Want to know if she can eat a steak at her age? Google." She shrugged. "The internet is your friend."

He slid into the seat opposite her and unscrewed caps from the salt shakers she still had left. "You're right. I'll get it worked out. It'd be easier if I had your experience."

Jenna couldn't help but smile. "You'll get there pretty quickly. Kids are trial by fire."

"Jesus," he muttered as he stared at the salt shaker in his hand. "I didn't even know she had a kid."

Her heart squeezed with sympathy. "I'm really sorry, Noah. It has to be hard to find out she's gone and that she had a child you didn't know about."

"Yeah." He picked up the salt and filled a shaker. "Sally had some issues. I tried to help her get clean, but it wasn't what she wanted at the time. She stopped calling me about three years ago. I tried to call her, but she never responded so I stopped."

His jaw tightened with emotion. "I should have kept trying."

"You can't force someone to talk to you."

"I know. But I think maybe she thought I'd given up on her." He focused on Alice. "I wish she'd called and told me she had a baby. I'd have helped her if she needed it."

Jenna didn't know what to say so she didn't say anything. He didn't seem to expect her to anyway. Perhaps it was simply his way of working it through in his mind.

"What do I say when she asks for her mama again?" His voice sounded strangled with emotion.

Jenna reached out with her free hand and touched his. A zing of electricity zapped through her. He looked at their hands for a long moment and then lifted his head to gaze at her expectantly.

"You have to tell her the truth. Not the literal truth, because she's too little, but tell her that her mama went to heaven and she can't come back. If you don't believe in God, then tell her something else, but make it clear that her mother can't come back. She's very young and doesn't really understand death. She's going to get past this faster than you think, though she'll likely be clingy for a while. To her, the most significant person in her life is gone. She needs understanding and stability most of all right now."

"I don't know how I'm supposed to give her that. I deploy often, and I can be gone for weeks. *Shit*."

"You could hire a nanny. Someone to live with you both and help out with childcare. You have to realize that little Alice will bond to that person too, but it might be the best solution you have right now."

He blinked as if considering. "What about you? You said you worked in a day care, and she clearly likes you."

Jenna's heart thumped. "I have a job and a room-mate. I can't quit and I can't bail on her."

As much as she might like to. Living without the smell of pot in her life every day might be nice for a change. And it wasn't like she owed Tami. If anything, Tami owed her.

He nodded. "I get it. You have other responsibilities."

"I'm sorry, but yes, I do. You can find reputable nanny placement services online, though. This close to DC, there are bound to be a lot of them."

Allison poked her head out of the kitchen door, glaring daggers at Jenna.

"Speaking of jobs," she said, "I need to start taking orders. The dinner crowd is beginning to trickle in."

"Right. Of course."

Jenna eased from the booth and stood. Noah stood too. He was tall and so damned good looking. Brown hair, blue eyes, and the kind of jawline that could make Hollywood sigh. It definitely made her sigh. Made other parts of her take notice, too. It'd been a long time since she'd been on a date with anyone. A long damned time.

"You'll have to take her," she said softly. "We can do this quietly so as not to wake her."

Noah swallowed. "Okay."

"Hold your arms open."

He did as she said and she stepped into them, easing Alice off her shoulder and onto Noah's. He was quite a bit taller than she was, but she managed it. Their bodies didn't quite touch, but they were close enough she could feel his heat as he moved. He closed his arms around Alice, shifting her gently, and Jenna took a step back.

Her heart pounded much harder than it should, and her throat felt dry. "I, um, I have to go. I'll swing by your table in a few minutes and refill your drink. Do you want to order anything else?"

He shook his head. "It's okay. Someone will be here soon and I'll have to go. Thanks for everything, Jenna. I appreciate it."

"You're welcome," she said, ducking her head before scurrying away to help Vicki with seating new customers and taking orders.

It was a good thirty minutes before she had a free moment to take a breath. She looked in Noah's direction, but there was nothing to look at.

Noah and Alice were gone.

Chapter Three

ONE WEEK LATER...

NOAH TURNED his Jeep into Saint and Brooke's driveway and shut off the engine. He stared at the house, guilt swirling inside.

He couldn't keep doing this. He couldn't let others take care of Alice for him. It'd only been a week, but he was still fucking figuring it out. That first night—Jesus, it'd been tough. Alice had cried and clung to him, and he'd abused Brooke's kindness by texting her at the drop of a hat.

She'd never complained, and neither had Saint. They didn't have kids—yet—but they were planning on it. Brooke's best friend, Grace Spencer, had a baby that Brooke watched from time to time. She was the most experienced person in his inner circle at this point. Between her and Google, he was figuring some things out.

But he was still at a loss, still felt like the whole thing was a bad dream and he'd wake up any minute. Except he didn't wake up. The nightmare kept going.

He hadn't been to the Early Bird Diner in a week, but he kept seeing Jenna's face when he closed his eyes. Kept hearing her tell him matter-of-factly to use Google to find out what he needed to know. He'd taken her advice immediately, and while it wasn't perfect, it helped. Though not everything was on Google. Like when Alice cried for three hours straight and he never did figure it out. She hadn't been hungry, or tired, or wet, or sick. She'd just been cranky. He'd walked around with her in his arms, rocking her almost frantically until she went to sleep.

The next day he'd had bags under his eyes and she'd been as fresh as a flower. He'd dragged through the day, then picked up a boisterous Alice from the babysitter. When they'd gotten home, there'd been a repeat performance—though Alice thankfully tired out after only two hours that time.

He couldn't keep going like this. He had to find a nanny ASAP.

Noah went to the front door and knocked. Max, Brooke's German Shepherd, barked once before someone must have shushed him. Brooke answered a few moments later, looking petite and pretty, and he felt a little pang of envy for his team leader. Saint was happy, and it showed nearly all the time.

"She's napping. She was such a good little girl today," Brooke said, opening the door wide. Max stood there with his tail wagging back and forth. "Come on in.

Did you eat? We're having tacos. I'd be happy to set a place for you."

Saint emerged from the back of the house, grinning when he saw Noah. "Yeah, man, stay for dinner. Brooke always fixes enough for an army when it's her turn to cook."

Brooke snorted and rolled her eyes. "Listen to you. *You* always fix enough for ten armies, mister. That's why I keep freezing leftovers."

He snaked an arm around her and kissed her temple. "Gotta feed my woman."

"I've imposed enough," Noah said, scratching Max's ear. The dog tilted his head for more.

"Not at all," Brooke replied instantly. "Alice isn't any trouble."

He appreciated how quickly she said that. Made him think she meant it, which was good. Plus, he was too damned tired to figure out what to get for dinner anyway. "I could eat a taco or two," he admitted, because he was getting sick of takeout and leftover takeout.

"Then come on into the kitchen and help me get it on the table while Cade finds mood music for dinner. Maxie. Outside, buddy."

Cade scrolled through his phone, grunting an acknowledgment, while Noah followed Brooke. She let Max into the backyard and then they gathered bowls of ingredients, plates, and soft tortillas that Brooke had wrapped in foil, and carried everything to the dining room. Soft jazz began to filter through the speakers as they took their seats.

They passed the food, building tacos, and talked about work and life and Alice.

"I called another nanny agency today. They don't have anyone available," Noah said, shoving a fork into the rice on his plate.

"I asked Grace if she had any recommendations, but she doesn't. She and Garrett have a nanny, but she's been with them for a while. The agency she came from is also short-handed at the moment."

"Jeez, was there a baby boom among rich people or something?" Noah grumbled. Not that he was rich, but he was single and he had combat pay, so he could afford to pay someone to help him until he figured things out. He also had a three-bedroom house—his own, because he'd thought investing in a house was a good idea at the time—and he could offer accommodations, which had to count for something.

"Probably," Saint said, taking a bite of his taco. "Mmm, honey, I don't know what you do with the spices, but it's always so good."

Brooke just smiled. "I'm not telling. If you ever want to leave me, then you'll be leaving my spice blend too."

"Not leaving, honey. And not because of your spice blend."

Brooke grinned, and Noah felt like he was intruding on something private. He kept his head down, eating until the conversation moved on.

"Will you be able to make Alice your dependent?" Brooke asked.

"I've started the paperwork, but it takes time."

As Alice's legal guardian, he could make her a

dependent without adopting her, which certainly made things a little easier. He hadn't given up on the idea of finding her a family, but at least he could provide for her until then. He could get her into childcare on the post. Still didn't solve the issue of what to do with her when he deployed, but for now the plan was that his team-mates and their women would help. He couldn't rely on them forever, though, so he had to figure something out.

As far as finding Alice a family, he wasn't sure how to go about it, but he knew he wasn't letting her go into the foster care system. His biggest hope was that someone in his inner circle—a teammate, or someone assigned to HOT—would be the right fit. Someone stable, like Brooke and Saint. Not someone like him, who had trouble showing emotion and wasn't sure he'd ever get married or want kids.

Sally knew those things about him, and she'd still named him as Alice's guardian. He wanted to ask her what the hell she'd been thinking. A knot formed in his gut. He wished he could. So badly. Because that would mean she was still alive.

"I'm sure you'll find a nanny for her," Brooke said. "I know it's tough right now, but the right person is out there, and she'll show up when she's supposed to."

Noah didn't agree with Brooke's optimism, or her belief in woo-woo stuff, but a part of him hoped she was right. He thought of Jenna—he didn't even know her last name—and his impulsive offer.

He didn't know anything about her, but he'd been going to the diner long enough that he knew she was conscientious and kind. He'd once watched her pull money from her own pocket to pay for a slice of cake that an elderly man ordered and then couldn't pay for. Didn't make her a saint, but he was pretty sure she wasn't a psychopath either.

And then there was that moment when she'd reached over to touch his hand. His skin had sparked, awareness prickling through him in a way that told him it'd been too long since he'd gotten laid.

"I'll keep looking," he said. "It's only been a few days."

By the time they finished eating, Alice was awake. Brooke gathered up her things, stuffed them into the diaper bag, and handed it to Noah. "We worked on potty training a little today, but I think she's probably going to be in diapers a bit longer," Brooke whispered. "She's a smart girl, but I believe all the changes in her life are holding her back at the moment."

A wave of anxiety washed over him. He'd had to learn how to change diapers, and he'd had to learn all about nighttime diapers versus daytime ones. He had a potty chair now, and he'd had to get a crib that would eventually convert to a toddler bed. If he thought about the changes in his life in one week, the overwhelm threatened to crush him. He was ill-equipped for taking care of a kid.

"Thanks, Brooke. I don't know how I can ever repay you, but if you think of anything, I'll do my best to get it done."

Brooke shook her head with a little smile. "You were part of the team that rescued me and little Amy in Colombia. You don't owe me anything."

Saint stood behind her, hand on her back, that haunted look he got when he was reminded about her abduction marring his features. Noah met his gaze and they exchanged a look that said everything about their job and how important it was for those who needed them.

"Still," Noah said softly. "If you think of something."

Brooke stood on tiptoe and tugged him down so she could give him a sisterly kiss on the cheek. "You're sweet, Easy."

Noah bent to swing Alice into his arms, said goodbye to his friends, and went to buckle her into the car seat so they could go home. It hit him as he worked on the straps and buckles that he should go back to the diner and thank Jenna again for her help.

And maybe ask her one more time if she'd consider letting him hire her to take care of Alice. The little girl looked at him with wide blue eyes, but she didn't say anything. She rarely said a word in fact. She could talk, but she just didn't.

Trauma.

"I understand, baby girl," he said as he snapped the last buckle into place. A thought occurred to him. "You want to go get some ice cream?"

She nodded.

"Okay. Let's do it."

He climbed into the driver's seat and started the Jeep. He didn't know if Jenna No-Last-Name was working tonight, but he'd soon find out.

"YOU WERE LATE AGAIN, JENNA."

Jenna had just finished cleaning the trap beneath the sink because the damned thing had clogged yet again, and she'd managed to splash stinky water all over her apron, along with some unidentified slime, and she was in no mood for Allison's OCD tendencies.

Still, she swallowed her retort and made herself respond calmly. "I know, and I'm sorry I was ten minutes late. I was talking to Mrs. Warner in the parking lot about her new roof. She wanted to tell me."

Allison popped her hands on her hips, frowning. "I don't pay you to talk to the customers in the parking lot, Jenna. I pay you to wait tables and *serve* them."

Jenna didn't bother pointing out that being kind and friendly to the diner patrons whenever you saw them *was* serving them. It was letting them know they mattered, and that made them feel good. It would also bring them back for more meals in this very place.

Allison eyed her with disdain. "And now you need to change. That's disgusting."

"It's your sink, Allison. I was fixing it because no one else ever seems to want to clean the trap."

Allison's eyes narrowed. "You know, I'm beginning to think you aren't the right fit for this restaurant. Perhaps you should collect your paycheck and find another job."

Jenna's heart throbbed. It wasn't that she liked working in the diner, but she had few options right now and needed the money. She had to buy a new battery for

Lola, for one, and she had to pay the rent. The *entire* rent since Tami claimed to be short again. She was still waiting on Tami to pay her half from last month, but she feared that Tami had rolled it up in paper and smoked it.

She wanted to find another place to stay, but how was she going to do that with no money for a deposit? Then again, maybe it was time. Maybe she needed to cut her losses, grab her belongings, pack them into Lola, and move on.

Not that she'd get all that far with a sketchy battery and no savings, but it wouldn't be the first time she'd lived in Lola. She could drive south, find a roadside motel somewhere, and clean rooms. She knew from experience that it wasn't the best job in the world, but if she lived in the car, she could save enough to get the battery and move on again.

"If it's about the ten minutes, I'll make them up," Jenna said, because though her mind always went into disaster planning mode, it wasn't a done deal yet. Allison had said similar things before. The only difference was that she'd hired a new waitress today. One with experience, which meant she wasn't going to hold up the operation while she trained.

Allison studied her. "You've been disrespectful almost from the start. I've ignored the sarcasm about it being only a few minutes each time you're late, the innuendo that you're too good to do things like clean sink traps—so I should be extra grateful when you do—but I think I'm done with that. I don't need your attitude, Jenna. You're a decent server, but you aren't the only one in the world. You can finish your shift. I'll have your check ready tomorrow morning."

She turned on her heel and strode away, leaving Jenna staring after her with a sinking heart. Jenna wanted to rip off the apron, toss it on the floor in a dramatic fashion, stomp on it for good measure, and then stalk out of the diner with her head held high.

But she needed the money tonight would get her, and she needed a plan. She could ask the other servers if they knew anyone looking for help. No job was too menial. So long as there was money in it, she'd do whatever it took. There was also a chance that Allison would change her mind by the end of the shift if Jenna did the best she could and made a lot of tips. That would indicate the customers valued her, wouldn't it?

Jenna removed the apron and went into the bathroom to clean herself up. She sniffled at her reflection, her eyes reddening. *Damn it.*

Jenna left the bathroom and tied on a fresh apron, then grabbed her order pad, determined to do well enough tonight that Allison would change her mind. Jenna wasn't good at memorizing orders, which so many of the servers did, because she found that her mind wandered when she was trying to remember things like *bald man in yellow shirt wants a cow so fresh it moos on his plate, a side of tiny green trees, and a mashed potato mountain with a river of gravy flowing down it. Bring a tiny hot pillow on the side and plenty of butter.*

There were other methods to memorizing orders, but she'd gone with the most ridiculous—and her mind still found it boring.

Maybe she wasn't cut out for waitressing after all. Maybe swishing bleach around motel toilets was more her speed.

Tami burst into the kitchen from the dining room. Jenna swallowed the resentment that flared at the sight of her roommate. Tami wasn't high right now, but she would be as soon as she got off work for the night. Maybe Jenna needed to join in and take her mind off all the shit in her life. Such as why Allison chose her to dislike when Tami was the flaky one.

"Noah's here," Tami said excitedly, hefting her boobs a little higher and fluffing her hair. "He's got a kid with him, though. Could be a tiny problem."

"Why's that?" Jenna asked.

Tami shot her a look as if it was obvious. "I was planning to let him take me home tonight."

Jenna rolled her eyes. "You say that every time he comes in."

Tami shrugged. "A girl can hope. He's in your section, but if you'd like to trade…"

"Nope, sorry." Jenna pushed through the doors to the dining area and pasted on a smile before heading to Noah's table. "Hey, welcome back," she said brightly. "What can I get for you two?"

Alice sat in a high chair, coloring on the placemat. Her hair was in those two little pigtails again, and she wore a pair of pink overalls with a cute butterfly shirt. She didn't look up from her coloring. Jenna didn't quite know what to think about that, but it had been a week since she'd held the little girl and given her a cookie.

"I said I'd bring her for ice cream, so how about a small scoop of vanilla?"

"Anything for you?"

His eyes sparked but he shook his head. "Just had dinner with friends, so I'm good... How you doing, Jenna?"

She shrugged. "Okay. Just working and sleeping, mostly."

"No play?"

Her heart thumped at the hint of teasing in his voice. "No, not really. How about you?"

He glanced at Alice. "Not lately, no."

Sympathy flooded her. "How's she been doing? You two getting settled?"

"It's been an experience," he said. "But I've got good friends and I'm figuring it out. You were right about Google."

She grinned. "Told ya."

"Still haven't found a nanny, though. They appear to be a hot commodity these days." He arched an eyebrow. "I don't suppose you'd reconsider? I'm kinda desperate here."

Jenna's heart stuttered to a halt before racing forward again. She told herself it didn't matter if Allison fired her tonight, she still shouldn't take a job with Noah Cross. She couldn't risk bringing her brand of chaos into his life. Or into little Alice's life. She should pull up stakes and go. She'd been in town for two months now, and it was risky to stay much longer.

She didn't know if the Flanagans were trying to track her down, but she also didn't know they weren't.

That was the scary part and the reason she had to keep moving. She was a loose end, and they were the kind of people who didn't like loose ends.

"What are you offering?"

He didn't hesitate. "A room in my house with your own bathroom, groceries, and some cash. We'd have to negotiate that, but I'd want you to feel like it was fair."

"Free rent, food, and spending money. Any personal time?"

"We could talk about that, too." He toyed with the end of the fork lying on the table. "I travel for work sometimes, and I can be gone anywhere from a week to a month or more. Obviously, that would mean round the clock care then. But I have friends who could help out if you needed some free time while I'm gone."

It sounded like heaven, and yet… Could she stay that long?

"It's tempting, but I have to think about it. It's a big responsibility."

He nodded. "I can appreciate that."

"Jenna," Allison said smoothly, sliding in next to her like an oily glop of sludge coming to a stop on the beach. "Can you check on table two? They've been seated for five minutes without being greeted."

"I was just going," Jenna said. "One scoop of ice cream coming up, sir."

Noah frowned at Allison. "Better give me a scoop too. And add some hot fudge to mine, please. I don't know how you talked me into it, but it sounds great."

Jenna smiled gratefully. "You got it, sir."

Then she turned and headed for table two, taking

drink orders and rattling off the daily specials. She delivered the drinks, took their order and clipped it into the ticket holder for the kitchen, then scooped ice cream for Noah and Alice.

She was thinking the entire time about Noah's offer. Living in his house would get her out of the trailer. She'd probably never get her money back from Tami, but moving out now would save her from having to cough up even more rent that she'd never get back.

Another plus was that she'd be less traceable if she wasn't working in a public-facing business. She could hide better in Noah's house than she could working in a motel or another restaurant.

The negatives were that she'd still be in town, and if the Flanagans *did* trace her somehow, she'd be dragging Noah and Alice into her problems. That wouldn't be good for them.

But it'd been over five months since she'd left Vegas, and she'd never had any indication anyone was looking for her. Maybe it was because she didn't stay in one place too long, or maybe it was simply that she was too inconsequential to attract their notice. She hadn't been involved in Sam's scheme with the Flanagans. She hadn't known anything about it until their hired killer turned up that night and shot Sam point blank through the heart.

She'd never told anyone what she'd seen and heard. The police thought she'd found Sam after the fact, not that she'd been there the whole time. She'd said she'd gone to pick up dinner, which was true, but she'd told them she arrived after the shooting, not before.

It was the only thing that had kept her alive long enough to disappear. She'd lived almost a month looking over her shoulder before she'd had everything in place so she could leave. In all that time, no one came for her, which made her second guess herself a lot now.

But in those days after Sam's death, she'd gotten the oddest sensation sometimes that she was being watched. That someone was following her. She could never pinpoint anything specific, but at least twice she'd seen the same black sedan at her apartment building and then again across town when she'd been running an errand.

It'd spooked her enough to take that final leap and run while she still could. She'd bought Lola and stowed her a couple of streets away in a parking garage. Every so often, she'd go for a short drive in her SUV and when she was sure no one was behind her, she'd stop and stuff Lola with a few more of her belongings.

The night she'd left, she'd mailed the keys to the SUV back to the dealer and snuck through side streets and a few yards until she reached Lola. She'd half expected to be gunned down before she ever made it out of the city limits, but it hadn't happened and she was still alive.

Jenna carried the ice cream to Noah's table. Alice waved her arms up and down, clearly excited. Jenna didn't ask about the wisdom of giving her sugar before bedtime.

"Thanks," Noah said as he dipped his spoon into the fudge topping.

"No, thank you for ordering something else and

saying nice things. I'm not sure my boss appreciates it, but I do."

He eyed her. "I've been coming here for a while. I remember the old man, her father, who had this place before she did. He was a lot nicer."

"That's what they tell me."

"Maybe you need a change." He winked.

"Maybe so," she laughed.

He pushed a piece of paper at her and she realized he'd torn off a section of the placemat and written down his number. "Call me if you decide you'd rather take care of Alice than put up with that woman's shit."

Jenna took the paper and stuffed it into the pocket of her apron. "Thanks." She could feel heat flaring in her cheeks. She wasn't sure why since he wasn't actually hitting on her. "I, um, better make my rounds. I'll be back to check on you both in a little bit."

"We'll be here," he said, his deep voice hitting places she'd nearly forgotten existed as she hurried away.

Chapter Four

"WHAT DID HE GIVE YOU?" TAMI ASKED AS SHE PREPPED a salad behind the counter. "Was that his phone number?"

Jenna was busy brewing fresh coffee, her mind racing through the possibilities of saying yes to Noah. She jerked and looked at her roommate. She thought about lying, but why bother?

"Yep."

"Oooh, girl," Tami practically squealed. "I hope you plan on riding that thang like a cowgirl at a rodeo!"

Jenna plunked coffee cups and saucers onto a tray along with little plastic containers of cream and sugar packets. "One thing at a time, Tami."

"Mmm, yeah, if it was me, I'd show him what I could do with my tongue"—she waggled her tongue *very* fast—"and he'd be fucking me good and hard in no time. Don't waste your opportunity, Jen."

Jenna didn't correct Tami's assumptions. "Thanks, Tam, but I plan to take it a little bit slower than that."

Tami shrugged as she plopped a tomato onto the salad. "Your call, I guess. But damn, I knew I should have waited on him tonight."

Jenna's annoyance flared. "I don't think it has anything to do with who waited on him."

Tami rolled her eyes. "Yeah, he's horny like all of them, and you're convenient. Anyhoo, who's the kid? Is he married or something? Married guys are so desperate in the sack, you know."

Jenna could only stare at the other woman. *Not asking.* And not responding to the insult either. "It's his niece. He's, uh, taking care of her now."

She didn't think it was her place to say that his sister had died, so she didn't.

"Well, a little liquid Benadryl slipped into her juicy cup, and she'll be out all night." Tami winked as she picked up her tray. "Trust me."

Jenna watched her roommate go, a shudder rolling over her. How the hell had she lived with that girl for almost two months? She'd been better off hanging out at the YMCA and sleeping in Lola. But then Tami had said she had a room in her trailer since her previous roommate had left and that Jenna could have it if she'd split the rent. Since the rent had been cheap, and her half even cheaper, she'd said yes.

Now she was pretty sure she knew why the previous roommate had taken off.

Allison emerged from the kitchen, eyes flinty. "How's everything going?"

"Fine," Jenna said, shoving away thoughts of Tami screaming like a wounded chicken in her room while the headboard banged the walls and reverberated through the entire structure at least three times a week. "Making fresh coffee for table two, and table four raved over the crab cakes and fried chicken."

"Mm-hmm. Good. You need to get the soldier and his kid out so we can put someone else at that table."

Jenna frowned. There was no one waiting to be seated at the moment, and Noah bent toward Alice, saying something. The little girl held out her hand with a crayon in it, and Noah took it and started to color his own placemat. Her heart squeezed tight.

"Doing my best," she said tightly.

"See that you do."

She disappeared as Jenna muttered under her breath about cold hearts and loose morals. She delivered the coffee to the people waiting, then returned to check on Noah and Alice again.

"Need anything else?"

Noah shook his head. "I think we're good."

She placed the check on the table. "Whenever you're ready," she told him, despite what Allison had said.

He pulled cash from his wallet and laid it down without looking. It was a twenty. "Keep the change, Jenna."

She swallowed. "That's too much."

"No, it isn't. You look like you need a break tonight." He shrugged. "I don't know if that helps or not, but thanks for everything."

"I brought you ice cream."

"And gave me a reality check last week." He put his hand on top of hers when she reached for the bill. His skin was warm, his hand big. His palm was callused, but not in the way of a man who did construction work. Not as thick or hard.

Oh lord, did she really just think thick *and* hard *in relation to this man?*

"You were the first person to show me any sympathy or understanding. I appreciate it."

"I was just the first person who happened to be there. It was nothing."

His thumb rubbed a path across the back of her hand, and lightning shot all the way down into her core.

"It wasn't nothing to me." He drew in a breath. "I want you to take care of Alice for me. I won't treat you like shit the way your boss does. I'll listen to you, and I'll make sure you don't have to hustle for tips or worry about assholes giving you a hard time. In short, I need you, Jenna."

She sucked in a breath. He was short-circuiting all her synapses. But did she care? Really? Was this decision that hard to make?

Noah Cross was offering her a lifeline. A way out of the diner and out of Tami's trailer. She should be thanking her lucky stars, not questioning if it was a good idea or not. She could take the job and keep doing what she'd always done.

Watch her back. And if she needed to go, she could at least make sure that Noah was set up to better antici-pate and understand a child's needs. Not that she was an expert, but working day care had definitely taught her a few things. If she imparted her knowledge and made him more comfortable with his sister's child, then that was enough, right?

"Don't you want to know more about me?" a stubborn part of her asked.

"What's your last name?"

She made a decision. She'd been using her mother's last name for employment, but she felt like giving it to Noah instead of her legal name was too much of a lie. "Lane."

"Okay, Jenna Lane, is there anything else I need to know? Criminal record? Warrants? Drug habit?"

"None of those things. But what if I'm flaky?"

"I don't think you are. You're still here, even though that Allison woman seems determined to be a bitch to you."

"I might be desperate for cash."

"If you are, then you'll take my offer."

Jenna's heart thumped. Her stomach twisted. "You don't know me, Noah. I could be anyone."

He didn't look worried. "And you don't know me." He leaned toward her. "I'll tell you this much, though. The job I do means I see real scumbags more often than I care to. I'm so jaded I'm not worried about—beg your pardon—one small woman with a potentially sketchy past. It's not nearly as sketchy as what I deal with on a regular basis. I'm the kind of guy you don't want to see coming for you if you're doing something that hurts others. I'm not worried about you. I've watched you work, and I know you're soft inside. You talk to the people who want to talk, and you listen to those who need an ear. You move slower than your boss wants, but that's because you're focused on helping your customers with more than taking impersonal orders."

He sat back and looked at her almost smugly. "No, I'm not worried about you at all, Jenna Lane. I want to hire you because I know you're a good person, and that's what Alice needs right now. Someone good to look after her."

She knew he was military. She'd seen him in uniform a few times. She didn't understand Army ranks or patches, but she'd been an Air Force kid—and she was pretty sure he was either military police or special forces based on what he'd just said.

That could be a good thing or a bad thing for her, depending. Good because it was like having her own built-in protector, and bad because if he figured out she was running from something, he wouldn't stop until he knew what it was.

"Are you an operator?" she asked, using the term she knew meant someone was part of an elite unit.

His eyes widened a second, and then she saw respect flare in them. He nodded. "Yes. Does that make a difference?"

"Green Beret?"

"Something like that."

"Like that, or that?"

"Like. I can't talk about it. If you know what a special operator is, then you'll understand."

She nodded. "My parents were Air Force. Mom was an officer and dad was enlisted. They died in a small plane crash six years ago."

He frowned. "I'm sorry, Jenna. That had to be very hard for you."

She shrugged. She didn't usually talk about it, but something about him made her willing to say the words. "It was, and thank you."

Tami appeared at her side, bending to look Alice in the eye. "Hey, sweetie! Aren't you a cute little honey-bear? I just want to pinch those cheeks." She shot Noah an innocent look. "I just love toddlers. So adorable."

Jenna rolled her eyes at the blatant attempt to steal Noah's attention. "They're adorable until they bite you," Jenna said matter-of-factly.

Tami was so startled she whipped her head around to stare wide-eyed at Jenna. She recovered quickly though. "You're such a tease, Jenna." She straightened and eyed Noah. "I just love kids. I'm free to babysit if you need anyone. Here's my number. Call anytime!"

She handed him a folded piece of paper, smiled a fake smile, and sashayed away in a manner designed to shake her ass.

"What the hell was that?" Noah asked, keeping his voice low.

"Surely you've met Tami before. She's been here for a year, I think."

"Oh, I've met her. She's always trying to get me or one of my friends to ask her out."

Jenna leaned toward him, hand on table, as if to impart knowledge. His gaze strayed to her chest, and she realized that he could probably see her bra. She straightened quickly, clearing her throat to hide her embarrassment.

"Best to avoid that if you can. She's my roommate, and trust me when I tell you that you'd better enjoy farm animal noises during sex. She'll put out at the drop of a hat, but you're going to need earplugs. Or a gag."

Noah sputtered. "Thanks for the visual."

Jenna shrugged. "Just doing my part."

He dropped Tami's number onto her tray. "Throw that away for me, would you?"

"Yes, sir. Anything else, sir?" she asked as Allison emerged from the back to make her rounds.

"Yes. Call me. Unless you'd like to take the job now?"

Allison was getting closer, and Jenna had already been standing with Noah for too long. "I have to go. I'll let you know."

———

IT'D BEEN a long day at work when Noah emerged at five and headed for his Jeep. He'd left Alice with his neighbor, Mrs. Barlow, who also watched her grandkids for her son and daughter-in-law. It wasn't ideal, and he felt like he was imposing, but she'd offered and he'd accepted because he still couldn't get Alice into day care on the post yet.

Soon, he hoped. His phone dinged with a message, and he took it out to look. The number was unknown, but he'd soon rectify that by making a new contact.

Hi, Noah. This is Jenna. If you haven't changed your mind, I'll take the job.

Noah leaned against the side of the Jeep and sighed.

He'd been hoping to hear from her since he'd left the diner last night. He wanted to whoop, but he didn't. Jax "Gem" Stone walked up a few moments later.

"You looking at cat videos again?"

Noah snorted. "Nope. Got a nanny."

"Really? That's fucking awesome, man!"

"Tell me about it." He tapped out a message to Jenna. *I haven't changed my mind. Thank you! When do you want to start?*

He prayed like hell it was right damn now, but for all he knew, she'd had to give two weeks' notice. He'd make it through two weeks. Somehow. So long as he knew there was a light at the end of the tunnel, he'd make it.

"When does she start?"

He lifted the phone. "Asking now."

Gem flipped his keys in his hand. "Yeah, it can't be much longer before we head downrange again. It'd be nice to have that taken care of before we gotta bug out."

"Fuck yeah it would." Because he didn't want to imagine the hell of trying to arrange around-the-clock care for little Alice—and then the hell of worrying about it while he was supposed to be doing his job.

"See you tomorrow, Easy," Gem said, unlocking his Corvette and climbing inside. It wasn't a new Vette, but the way Gem babied it, you'd never know. The car was a pristine C6 model, and Gem spent a lot of time in the garage, polishing it to a shine. It was a wonder he ever drove the thing since Noah knew he was going to go home, stick it in the garage, and wipe it down with a rag.

Noah's phone dinged again.

Jenna: I can start today. If that's not convenient, whenever you like.

Noah's thumbs practically tripped over themselves. *Today's good. Want the address, or want me to come get you?*

Jenna: Address is fine.

Noah frowned. He thought about asking her how much help she needed getting her things, but decided that was something they could discuss when he saw her. He sent her the address with an approximate time he'd be home and jumped into the Jeep a lot happier than he'd been just a few moments ago. He drove the thirty miles to Mystic Cove, relief a palpable thing within him. Having a nanny would give him *breathing* room.

He could figure out what to do with Alice once he had regular help. Someone she could rely on instead of bouncing her among caregivers. She'd been bounced around since Sally's death, which was part of what had made her quiet and observant instead of curious and outgoing. He didn't know a lot about kids, but he knew enough to know that two-year-olds tended to be dynamos.

Alice wasn't a dynamo. She was hesitant and fearful of abandonment. The way she clung to him some days when he dropped her off with a babysitter nearly broke his heart. Today had been the first time with Mrs. Barlow. She'd seemed to like the woman well enough, but the instant he'd started toward the door, she'd begun to whimper. He'd gotten out of there before she turned on the waterworks, but he knew she'd likely had a meltdown. He felt guilty about that, but there was nothing he could do.

He gripped the wheel hard. *Dammit, Sally.*

He still couldn't figure out why she hadn't gotten in touch after Alice was born. Why hadn't she at least sent a message? He got that she hadn't expected to die, but she'd had enough foresight to draft a will and name him Alice's legal guardian, so it must have crossed her mind at least once.

And she'd done nothing to prepare him just in case. His throat was tight as his eyes blurred for a moment. He shook it away, unwilling to let himself cry. There was no one he could talk to about Sally. His team knew his sister had died, but they didn't know much of anything about his life before the military.

He'd said they were estranged. He hadn't said that Sally was his first comrade in the fight for his life. Because that's how it had felt in the Parker home. Like their lives were at stake and they had to have each other's backs. Through thick or thin.

He was pissed at himself for not taking leave and going down to North Carolina. For not forcing Sally to talk to him. If he had, he'd have known about Alice. He'd have done what he could to help if Sally had needed it. But three years had passed quickly, and he hadn't done what he should have done. He hadn't been there for her.

When Noah turned into his drive, there was a beat-up blue Toyota Corolla on the street in front of his house. He got out of the Jeep, grabbed his duffel with the workout gear that needed washed and the weapons stashed inside, and slung it over his shoulder.

Someone emerged from the Toyota. He wasn't

surprised when the blond head appeared or when Jenna strolled across the lawn toward him. She wasn't carrying anything, but she had her hands shoved into her jeans pockets. She wore jeans that were torn above each knee and a white T-shirt that molded to her breasts before falling a little more loosely to her waist. Her blond hair was scraped back and piled on her head in a messy bun. Strands of hair fell from it to frame her face.

"Hi," she said, smiling a little shyly.

"Hey. Thanks for coming."

She straightened a bit as if determined to say something. "I should tell you that I got fired. Allison let me go, so it was either find another job waiting tables, clean motel rooms, or accept your offer."

He could only stare at her. He'd never seen her outside in the sunlight before. She was prettier than she'd been in the diner with its overhead lighting that made everyone look kind of sallow.

"Then I guess I'm glad Alice and I were the first choice."

She tilted her head as she studied him. "Nothing I've said makes you want to change your mind?"

"You mean that Allison fired you, or that you were thinking of cleaning motel rooms or waiting tables instead of taking my offer?"

"I sound a bit like a deadbeat, don't I? I should have a career, not be cleaning motel rooms for a living."

"You aren't cleaning rooms. You're a nanny to a two-year-old."

She shook her head. "It sounds crazy though, doesn't it? From the diner to responsible for a child."

"You sound like you want me to change my mind."

"No, I really don't. But I also don't want you to feel like you hired me under false pretenses. I've made mistakes in life."

"Haven't we all?"

He wasn't the guy to question anyone's choices. He knew what it was like to have things in your life that drove your course down one road or another, often against your will.

"Yes. Definitely." She dragged in a breath, and he sensed more confessions coming. "I left the day care center because I got a better job, and then I left that job because my boss died. After that, I wandered. I wanted to see the country, and I wanted a change. It didn't quite work out the way I thought it would."

"I can understand that."

"If you want to check those things out, I wouldn't blame you."

He could have Sky "Hacker" Kelley check into her background without her ever knowing about it. Maybe he would. But he had the kind of gut instincts that told him when someone was dangerous, and he didn't get that from her. She was reluctant to share, probably because she was ashamed of where life had taken her, but she wasn't a menace.

"I might."

She nodded. "Okay, then. I suppose I should also tell you that my roommate smokes a lot of pot, but I don't. Other than her secondhand smoke, I've never tried it."

He almost laughed, but he didn't because she

seemed so serious. "You don't leave anything out, do you?"

She dropped her gaze. He thought her cheeks might be red, and he cursed himself for teasing her. But then she looked up again. "It's relevant. You live in Mystic Cove, and you frequent the diner. You're bound to find out that Tami's a pothead—and she's bound to get arrested for possession one of these days. I just thought you should know that I wasn't a part of that. I should have left sooner, but the rent was cheap and I didn't have a better place to go."

"Noted. Did you eat yet?"

She blinked. "Not since lunch."

"How's pizza?"

"Uh, pizza's great."

"Okay. Let me get this inside and order, then I have to go next door and get Alice. She's with the neighbor."

She moved toward him, stopping when she stood on the sidewalk beside him. Her head tilted back, and he thought about how the curve of her neck would taste. And the noises she'd make as he did so.

"I'd like to come with you. I think it's probably a good idea if I'm there when you get Alice instead of being inside when you get back. It's not much, but she might be a little more comfortable with my presence if we're together from the beginning."

He dragged his mind from a place it shouldn't be. If he wanted to keep the nanny he'd just hired instead of sending her running when things didn't work out between them, he needed to keep his hands off. He knew enough about himself to know he wasn't looking for a long-term relationship, and that didn't always work so well with women.

"If you think it's a good idea," he said before going over to the door to unlock it and step inside. She was still standing on the sidewalk when he turned back to her. "Do you want to see where you'll be sleeping before we go next door?"

She hesitated. And then she walked up the steps. "Sure," she said. "I'd love to."

Chapter Five

JENNA STILL COULDN'T BELIEVE SHE WAS HERE. IN Noah's house, getting ready to eat pizza and become the primary caregiver to a toddler. She looked at her reflection in the mirror over the dresser in the room he'd given her and shook her head slightly.

"What have you done?" she whispered to herself.

She should have left town. Last night, after her shift, Allison had called her into the office and held out a check. She hadn't even waited until morning. Jenna had known it was coming, even though she'd tried to prove her worth and change Allison's mind.

But the new girl had been working last night, and she'd basically run circles around everyone. She'd been so efficient, and she was friendly and funny. The customers liked her. They liked Jenna too, but Brenda had the ability to make them feel as if they'd been friends for ages while also not getting caught up in the stories and chit chat. Jenna had never mastered that. If someone wanted to show her pictures of their grandson in his first baseball game, she'd look at them all.

Not that being friendly was the problem, really. It was her. Allison had never warmed up to her because she wasn't a local and because she often pointed out the unreasonableness of Allison's thinking. She'd known the woman held grudges. She should have quit saying anything while she was ahead.

On the other hand, did she really want to be at the Early Bird, tiptoeing around Allison and hating the fact the woman was always watching her and waiting for a screwup?

No, she didn't. And while she probably should have climbed into Lola and moved on, she'd taken the lifeline that Noah offered. She could still leave if she had to. She didn't want to, though. Not yet. She didn't want to live in Lola and scrounge for work and feel like her life was shit anymore.

She left the room and went to join Noah and Alice. The house wasn't huge, but it was nice with an eat-in kitchen, a dining room, a living room, a den and half bath, and an upstairs with three bedrooms and two full baths.

There were pizza boxes on the kitchen counter, and Alice was in her high chair, banging a plastic dinosaur on the tray. Noah turned as she walked in, smiling at her. She felt the power of that smile all the way to her toes.

He was hot, and while she'd always been just a little enamored of him at the diner, being in a room with him now was like turning up the volume to the highest setting. He overwhelmed her, but she wasn't about to let him know it.

"Hey. You ready to eat?" he asked.

"Definitely."

"Cheese or supreme?"

"Cheese."

He put a couple of slices on a plate and handed it to her. "I'm cutting up a small slice of the cheese for Alice," he said. "I googled and it said she could have pizza. I blew on it to cool it first." He touched the top of the pizza and nodded. "Yep, not too hot."

He set the small paper plate onto the high chair. Alice picked up a piece and put it in her mouth as he watched.

"Did I cut it small enough?" he asked.

"I believe you did," Jenna said. "She's not having trouble. How many months old is she? I know you said two years, but months matter a lot at this stage."

"She's not quite twenty-four months. Twenty-three and a few days, actually."

"Okay, that's good to know. There are developmental milestones that are tied to months, so it's helpful to know where she lands."

"Her medical records indicate she's on target—or was," he said. He grabbed a plate for himself and put a couple of large slices of supreme on it before taking a seat at the table. "I've googled a lot about how to take care of her this past week. It's pretty exhausting to be responsible for a child, especially a small one."

"You've done an admirable job," Jenna said, taking a bite of cheese pizza.

"You don't know that. I might have screwed it all up."

She laughed. "She's alive, Noah. Healthy. You didn't screw up."

He grinned. "Yeah, I guess that's true. Thanks for the perspective."

"You're welcome."

"Is that room going to be good for you, or would you rather trade with Alice?"

She shook her head. "It's fine. Even if it wasn't, I wouldn't uproot her like that. She's had enough change in her life recently."

"Yeah," he said, a touch of sadness tinging his voice. "Do you need help going back to get your things?"

Jenna blinked. "Going back?"

"To the place you shared with your roommate. For your furniture and stuff."

Heat flooded her. "Everything's in Lola. I don't have furniture."

"Lola?"

"My car. Lola the Corolla. It's stupid, I know."

His face cracked in a smile. "No, it's cute. I like it."

She still felt warm. "Thanks. I don't have a lot of stuff. When I decided to travel, I got rid of everything."

That was one way of putting it. The other was that she'd walked away from everything and left it for the landlord to deal with. She'd taken the important stuff—pictures of her parents and old photo albums—and left everything else. Stuff was unimportant. You could replace stuff. You couldn't come back to life if the Flanagans decided to take you out, too.

"I can get it out of the car for you when we're finished eating. You can do whatever you want to that room. Paint, wallpaper—anything you like."

She must have looked at him quizzically because he said, "It's my house. We don't need permission from anyone else."

"That's really nice of you. I think it's fine, though."

He shrugged. "If you ever want to personalize it, I don't mind."

She didn't tell him that she wasn't sure how long she'd be in it. That wasn't what he wanted to hear. "Thank you."

"Look, I really don't know how this is supposed to work," he said after he polished off a slice of pizza. "I'm just grateful you're here to help. I think Alice needs the stability, and I'll feel better knowing she can be with the same person and stay in one place instead of being shuffled among sitters."

"Stability is probably a good thing after what she's been through." She hesitated. "Do you know anything else about what happened? Was Alice with your sister?"

He shook his head. "Ms. Calvert—that's the lawyer you saw in the diner—said that Alice was in day care when it happened. Sally got a real estate license and she had some showings that day. It was raining pretty hard when she hydroplaned and went off the road. Her car rolled down a steep incline and landed upside down in a drainage ditch."

Jenna's stomach twisted. "Oh no."

"The postmortem said she died from a head injury. There was no water in her lungs, but if she hadn't been killed from the impact, she would have drowned in that ditch."

"Oh my God. I'm really so sorry."

He glanced at Alice, who was still eating pizza. She didn't understand a lot of what they said at her age, which was good. She was singing a song to herself, nonsensical words, and seemed preoccupied with her food. All good.

He pulled in a breath. "I got a highchair, a potty chair, and a crib that can transition to a toddler bed because people told me to, but I don't know what else she needs. If she needs other stuff, we can get it. I just didn't know what to buy, quite honestly. I went with the most immediate stuff."

"What about toys?"

"She had some things in the suitcase, but she could probably use some of those educational toys and shit."

Jenna couldn't help but raise an eyebrow at him, but she did it in a way that she hoped indicated amusement. "I'm sorry to tell you this, but you're going to have to clean up the language if you don't want her repeating certain words."

"Oh damn—I mean crap." He shook his head. "All right, I suck at this. Maybe neither of those is good."

"Just depends on what you want to hear repeated in a high-pitched kid voice when you're out in public."

"Point taken. Fine, she needs some more toys. And probably more clothes. She's not potty trained yet, either."

"I would imagine that's going to take time at this point."

"That's what Brooke said."

She didn't ask who Brooke was, but the pinprick of jealousy was unwelcome. "I'm not an expert in child psychology or anything. I think you should know that. I've never had kids, either. I worked in a day care center for three years, and I thought about getting a degree in early childhood education, but I didn't. I decided that while I like kids, I don't like parents very much, and I wasn't willing to put up with some of the stuff that parents do and say to their children's caregivers."

"You know a lot more than I do."

She nodded. "I had to take CPR and first aid classes while working with children as well, so I won't be helpless if something happens. Though, believe me, I don't intend to let it."

"I'm glad to hear it. I'm sure there's a lot we're going to have to talk about over the next few days. I'll get a key made for you, and I'll give you my schedule. It's subject to upheaval, as I said before."

"When you go on a mission."

He nodded. "Right. It can happen pretty much at the drop of a hat. I may not have much time to communicate, but I'll make sure you're aware. And when I'm gone, I won't be in touch at all." His eyes widened. "I need to give you a credit card so you can buy things while I'm gone, don't I?"

"I'd say I could take care of it and you pay me when you return, but since I don't know how long you'll be gone, that might be a good idea. What about your house? Utilities and stuff?"

"Automatic payments. You won't have to worry about that."

"That's good."

"Right. I can't afford to get behind on my house payment or have the utilities turned off if I'm not here to take care of it." He raked a hand through his hair. "I'm beginning to realize there's a lot more to this than I thought. If I don't come back, I need to make sure things are set for her."

If I don't come back.

She didn't like the sound of that, but she understood where he was coming from. Her dad had been in civil engineering, and he'd deployed to conflict zones to help build things when necessary, but he'd never been in active combat. Neither had her mother, who'd been in Intelligence. Noah's entire profession was active combat.

"That's a good idea," she replied. Calmly, she thought. Like they weren't discussing his death. Then again, she knew how quickly and unexpectedly death could find you. Her parents' plane crash. Sam sitting at his desk, waiting for her to bring dinner to him. If she hadn't stopped to pee first...

She shivered. If she hadn't stopped to pee, she'd have been in his office when Owen Fisher, the Flanagans' hitman, walked in. He'd have shot her without a second thought.

Noah ate another bite of pizza, frowning. "This is not anything I wanted to think about, you know? I don't have dependents, or family, and it doesn't matter what happens after I die. At least it didn't."

Jenna looked at Alice picking up another piece of

pizza and putting it in her mouth. She'd stopped singing now. Her blue eyes were big and maybe a little wary as she looked from one adult to the next. She still hadn't settled, and Jenna's heart went out to her. She'd felt lost and alone when she'd lost her mother too, but at least she'd been a grown woman who could take care of herself.

"It matters to her. Your plans don't have to be elaborate. Pick friends with kids, people who you like and trust, and name them her guardians if they agree. Make sure her situation is secure at the least."

"Like Sally did. She didn't have much money. What she had paid off her debts, according to Ms. Calvert. But the one thing she did was make sure Alice wasn't going into foster care."

The emotion in the way he said *foster care* prickled her senses, but she didn't ask any questions. It wasn't her business, but it was something she thought about for the rest of the evening. The twist to his mouth, the flash of anger in his gaze. The way his entire body seemed to tighten for a moment before the moment moved on again.

Noah Cross had a personal connection to the foster care system, of that she was certain. He'd said he had no family. She hadn't asked what had happened to them, but it seemed that whatever it was, he and his sister had very likely been on their own for a long time.

They'd been estranged, but at least they'd known the other was out there. Now, he was alone. Alone and responsible for a toddler he hadn't known existed.

Jenna gave herself a mental shake. She didn't need

to dwell on Noah's history, didn't need to imagine it, and didn't need to ask him about it. She was there for a job, nothing more. She would learn what she needed to know to take care of Alice, but that was it.

She couldn't get close to Noah. Or Alice. Because one day—maybe soon—she would have to run.

And she didn't need it to hurt more than it already would.

Chapter Six

As the days passed, Noah could breathe again. Having a toddler in his house for days on end without any help, other than his ability to search the internet or call the friends who'd said he could ask questions day or night, had been more nerve-wracking than he cared to admit.

But now he had Jenna, and Jenna didn't seem to suffer any doubts about what to do with Alice.

He'd be lying if he said he hadn't been at least a little concerned that he didn't really know anything about her. He trusted his instincts though. Sure, he'd had a moment the first day he'd left her in his home with Alice when he'd wondered if he might return that afternoon to find she'd taken everything of value and left Alice high and dry in her crib.

Or, worse, had taken Alice with her.

But of course that hadn't happened. He'd come home that afternoon to find Alice playing happily on the floor of the living room and something that smelled good coming from the kitchen. He'd had to stand inside the door for a full minute while he processed the domesticity of the scene.

Since that day, Jenna had done everything he'd hoped she would do for Alice. The little girl actually laughed now, though not often. She was less clingy, though she was still clingy whenever she thought Jenna was leaving her.

She'd quickly transferred her feelings of safety and security to Jenna. It didn't bother him at all. In fact, he was grateful for it. He could leave in the mornings and not have a knot in his stomach because the child clung to him while he tried to leave her with a caretaker.

It was almost as if his life had returned to what it was before, except now he had two roommates who mostly functioned without him but were there whenever he was. It wasn't unpleasant, though there were still toddler meltdowns that mystified him at times. He wasn't entirely off the hook, either. He had to help Jenna when the child wanted to cling while she cooked or went to the bathroom. And sometimes Alice sobbed while he did that, which wasn't the most pleasant thing in the world.

Still, he found himself looking forward to heading home at the end of the day and finding out what Jenna had made for dinner. Then he'd listen to her talk about her day and he'd hold Alice, who often wanted to be held when he walked in the door. That part was nice.

Jenna was a good cook, too. He was a decent cook himself, because he'd had to learn, but she seemed to actually enjoy it. Everything she made was done with

Alice in mind, but it wasn't kid food necessarily. She didn't heat up chicken nuggets and fries and call it a day.

She cooked good food that everyone could eat, but cut it into bite-sized pieces for Alice. When he'd asked her once why she did it, she'd looked at him with her soft brown eyes and said that Alice would learn to eat what you fed her. If you constantly gave her hotdogs and chicken nuggets, then that's what her palate would be. If you challenged her with a wide variety of foods, she'd likely grow up eating what adults ate without complaining that she wanted a kid's meal in a nice restaurant. It wasn't foolproof, because some kids were stubborn, but so far Alice was not.

Made sense to him. Not that he expected to raise Alice to adulthood. He hadn't given up on the idea of finding a proper family for her, but one thing at a time. The first thing was to make her happy and comfortable now. He didn't let himself dwell too much on what it would mean for her to change homes yet again. He couldn't.

And, really, the next time would be for the best. It would be because he'd found a forever family for her where she'd have the life she deserved. He wouldn't let her go into foster care, but he also wasn't blind enough to think he could provide what she needed as she grew older.

"Hey, Eaze," Gem said when they finished at the range for the day. "You want to come to Buddy's with us for beers and darts?"

Gem jerked his head toward the opposite end of the

range when he asked the question, and Noah followed his gaze. Ryder "Muffin" Hanson and Zane "Zany" Scott were the other two unattached operators on the team, besides Gem and Noah. They were packing up their gear and preparing to leave like everyone else. But whereas the other guys were headed home, Gem, Muffin, and Zany were going to Buddy's Bar & Grill.

The entire Strike Team went from time to time, along with the fiancées and wives, but today wasn't one of those days. Noah had often gone with the guys for a meal, because he hadn't had anyone at home cooking for him, but it hit him that while he could go if he wanted, he had people to go home to. Hell, if he was lucky, Jenna had made something yummy.

He'd told her she didn't have to cook for him, but she'd said that since she was cooking anyway, it wasn't difficult to make sure she had enough for him. He secretly loved that she did it. When he'd learned she could cook, he'd kicked himself that he hadn't made that one of the duties of her employment. It turned out he needn't have worried. She cooked for him anyway.

"Nah, sorry. I can't go today."

Gem arched an eyebrow. "Want to get home to the nanny, huh?"

Noah forced himself not to react. "Actually, I do. I promised her that I'd watch Alice this evening while she has some personal time."

He hadn't, actually, but he'd promised her time to herself so it wasn't unheard of that he'd have to babysit while she took him up on it.

Gem nodded. "Next time, huh?"

"Next time."

They left the range and went to stow their gear. "She's pretty," Gem said. "Is she single?"

Noah gave his teammate a look. "She lives with me and takes care of a two-year-old. I don't think a husband or boyfriend would appreciate that too much."

"Yeah, probably right. But that could be good for you, huh?" He waggled his eyebrows.

Noah's belly tightened. "Not even looking at her that way, Gem."

The other man looked surprised. "Really? She's under your roof, in your face—how can you not?"

"I didn't say that I haven't noticed her. I said I'm not looking at her that way." He sighed as he tossed his range bag into his locker. He had another with his personal weapons, but this one contained work weapons. "I can't afford to. If I start looking at her and she starts looking back, next thing you know we're getting friendly. And if we get friendly, then there are expectations because she's under my roof. And if I fail to meet the expectations because it's just a hookup, then she might get mad enough to quit. Which means I'm back to square one, which means no nanny. So, no, I'm not looking at Jenna as anything but Alice's nanny. She's off limits—and that goes for everyone here," he said, raising his voice so Muffin and Zany heard, too. "Just because she's single, and just because you're going to be seeing her more often at work events or if you come to my house, does *not* mean that I want you trying to hook up with her. You chase my nanny away, and I'm going to put a boot up your ass."

Gem held up both hands in surrender. "Got it, dude. No flirting with the nanny. No hooking up. Friendly but distant."

Muffin and Zany nodded in acknowledgement. Noah nodded once, firmly, the knot in his gut easing. "I appreciate it. I don't mean to be a hard ass about it, but I tried for a solid week to find a nanny, and there were none available. Getting Jenna to take the job wasn't a simple feat, and I'd rather not lose her now that I have her."

"Understood. I guess she's working out, then?"

"Alice seems happy with her. She doesn't cry when I leave anymore. She plays, and she laughs a little more often. Still not talking much, but I think it'll happen."

"Man, I'm really sorry about your sister. I wasn't trying to be an asshole about Jenna. I just thought maybe you were interested in her."

Noah took a deep breath and clapped his teammate on the shoulder. "It's okay. You're right; she's pretty. And I've noticed. But I won't do more than that because I can't lose her. It's been a week of heaven with her around, and Alice needs her a lot more than I do."

He thought of Jenna playing on the floor with Alice, and something inside him ached. Didn't make a bit of sense, but that's what happened. "I can gratify any itches elsewhere," he said, though the idea of hooking up with a stranger for sex wasn't all that appealing at the moment.

He'd never been one of those guys who cultivated fuck buddies. He didn't think the concept actually worked. Someone was always more emotionally invested than they ought to be, and people got hurt. Or that'd been his experience when he'd tried it with a woman he'd thought could handle the arrangement.

She'd only been pretending, hoping that his feelings would grow to match hers. Meanwhile, he'd met her for sex a handful of times, thinking they were both getting what they wanted.

Until she'd had a meltdown in Buddy's because she'd seen him talking to another woman. A woman who happened to be engaged to a friend, in fact. That was his one and only experiment with a-friends-with-benefits situation.

"You can, but that means you actually need to go out with us," Gem said with a grin. "Unless you've found an app where you can order in?"

Noah snorted. "No app. At least not one where you don't have to wade through a lot of bullshit first—and most of those women are looking for relationships anyway."

"Truth," Muffin said. "My cousin met his wife through a dating app."

"Aw, that's cool," Zany said.

"Not really. They're getting divorced, and it's pretty ugly."

"And on that uplifting note," Noah said. "I'm outta here. See you losers on Monday."

———

IT WAS A WARM SPRING DAY, and Jenna was wearing a pair of short shorts and a tank top as she danced around the kitchen to Tom Petty. Not that Tom Petty was dance music, but she didn't care. He was one of her all-time favorites. Probably because he'd been her dad's favorite, and she'd grown up with Petty blasting on the speakers whenever her dad had to do something like wash the cars or clean the house.

Dad would queue up the playlist, turn up the music, and sing "Don't come 'round here no more!" at the top of his lungs. It made her heart hurt to remember, but it also made her smile because she'd loved her dad and he'd loved her.

Mom loved Tom too, so it was all good. She'd come home, walk into the garage or the house, wherever Dad was blasting it, and they'd start duetting "Stop Dragging My Heart Around" like nobody's business.

God, she missed those days. She wished her dad had never decided to learn how to fly. He'd wanted to be a pilot in the Air Force, but he hadn't had the college necessary at the time. He'd ended up in civil engineering instead. When he'd decided to take flying lessons, he'd been older and wiser and had the money to do it. It wasn't the same as flying a fighter jet, but he'd loved it all the same.

Jenna swallowed the lump in her throat and took Alice's hands as she looked up from her toys. Alice got up and Jenna started dancing her around too, bent in half while she helped the little girl move. Alice laughed like she was having the best time, and Jenna laughed with her.

"It's never too early to learn to appreciate the

musical stylings of Mr. Tom Petty," she said very seriously to the toddler.

"Pey-ey!" Alice yelled back.

"That's right. Petty."

"Pey-ey!"

Jenna laughed and swung Alice up into her arms, dancing them both around as she grabbed things from the refrigerator for dinner. Today, it was chicken sandwiches with homemade pasta salad. Simple, but good. She'd wouldn't fix a sandwich for Alice, of course. She'd cut up grilled chicken and feed it to her with the pasta salad, which she'd made with veggie noodles so that Alice would get all her vegetables. Not that she refused to eat any, because so far she hadn't, but Jenna wanted to mix it up a bit.

Taking care of a single toddler wasn't a bad job at all, at least not with this one. When she'd been at the day care center managing a classroom filled with them, it'd been a different story. One small child was a piece of cake in comparison. Or at least this one was.

Not that it was without challenges. Trying to get time to pee or shower was always interesting, but that was why she tried to be awake before Alice. At least she could get dressed that way.

There were also nap times, which gave her a breather. Alice was good about naps, probably because she'd had structure in day care before, and Jenna used the time to catch up on sleep or plan dinner or read, or any number of things that allowed her to enjoy the quiet.

She wasn't quiet now. Neither of them were. Jenna

sang about living like a refugee, and Alice yelled along with her. It was fun, and probably a little funny too. They danced around the kitchen, gathering spices. Jenna was oblivious to the opening door and to the man who was suddenly there when she turned.

Her heart shot into outer space, and a scream erupted from her throat as she turned with Alice tight in her arms. All she could think was to run. If she made it outside, she could scream for the neighbors. He wouldn't shoot her with witnesses.

"Jenna!"

A hand closed around her arm, halting her progress at the same time she realized who it was. *Noah.*

Oh Jesus. Oh dear Jesus.

Jenna sank to the floor with a bewildered Alice in her arms, adrenaline still crashing through her system and making her shudder. Alice didn't cry, thank God.

"Pey-ey?" she asked, patting Jenna's face.

The music still thumped, a bit louder than she probably should have had it. If she'd kept it lower, she'd have heard his key in the lock.

Noah's face was there beside her, looking concerned and contrite. "I'm sorry, Jenna. I didn't mean to scare you. I should have made more noise or something. I'm really, really sorry."

She set Alice down and the toddler lurched her little body toward the toys she'd been playing with before. Unaffected, thankfully.

"It's my fault," Jenna said, feeling along the top of the counter for her phone. She found it and put an end to Tom's voice coming through the Bluetooth speaker that Noah had in the kitchen. It seemed unnaturally quiet after that.

Noah was still hunkered down beside her. "No, it's mine. You didn't have to turn that off. I love Petty."

She turned her gaze on him, her belly flipping as their eyes met. His were so blue. His jaw was chiseled from granite, and she had the meltiest feeling in her deepest recesses that if she pressed her mouth to his, her world would never be the same.

"You do?"

"He was always a bucket list favorite, you know? One of the rock stars I wanted to see if he ever came to town when I could go. But then he died, and that's it. No more Petty."

Sadness twisted inside her. "Same."

"Maybe you should turn him back on then. So we can enjoy him this way since we won't get to see him."

She lifted her phone in shaking hands, but couldn't quite manage the task. She gripped it tight and sat with her head bowed, breathing deeply.

For a moment, she'd thought they'd found her. As ridiculous as it was, as unrealistic, she'd thought the Flanagans had found her. That a cold-blooded killer had come to end her life—and Alice's too—without remorse. She should have known better. Noah was wearing camouflage, which meant a uniform. A hitman probably wasn't going to wear military camo.

"I'm sorry," she said to the floor, knowing that Noah had to be wondering what was going on. Her reaction was out of proportion, and he wasn't stupid. "I, um, don't like surprises."

Surprises? Really?

He rose and held out a hand to her. "Think you can get up? Maybe sit in a chair for a little while?"

She nodded as she put her hand into his. And it was there, that same spark she'd felt before. Zinging and zipping, crashing through her body like she was starved for affection.

Maybe she was.

Once she was standing, the terror faded fairly quickly. She was in Noah's sunny kitchen, there was food on the counter, and Alice played with blocks, stacking and restacking them as if it was the greatest thing in the world.

Jenna put a hand on her stomach. "I know that was over the top. I just wasn't expecting you."

He raked a hand through his dark hair. "Yeah, sorry. We got out of work a little early today. I should have texted."

Everything was returning to normal now, the shadowy men of her imagination fading away. "I was getting ready to fix chicken sandwiches for dinner and teaching Alice the benefits of Tom."

Noah's mouth crooked in a grin. "There are definite benefits to Tom. And I'm not gonna lie; part of the reason I didn't say anything was how much I was enjoying watching you two dance and sing. I should have though. I'm sorry."

"It's okay. I'll be fine. I'm already fine." She pulled in a breath and reached for the chicken. She had to do something, or the adrenaline was going to make her shake even harder as it faded. "I need to grill this..."

He put his hands on hers, gently, and took the chicken. "Why don't we go out to dinner? I'm buying."

She hesitated. But why not? It wasn't like she hadn't been on display at the diner every day, working in the public view. At least now she was in Noah's home most of the time, and it would be a lot harder for anyone to find her. They certainly weren't going to do it while she was out to dinner with Noah and Alice.

Besides, she could really stand to get out now that she'd nearly had a heart attack in the kitchen. Some fresh air would do her good.

"Okay. That sounds great."

"Good. Any requests?"

"Only one, if you don't mind. Can we *not* go to the Early Bird this time?"

He laughed. "That's an easy one. Wasn't planning on it anyway."

Relief washed over her. "Thanks. I'll need to change before we go."

"Me too. You go first and I'll watch Alice."

Jenna nodded then went upstairs to her room and opened the closet. She had one flowery summer dress hanging there, nothing at all like when she used to work for Sam and bought designer clothes. She shut the door again and grabbed her jeans. It wasn't a date, and she didn't need to look like a million dollars.

Even if a part of her wanted to prove to Noah that she could.

Chapter Seven

NOAH'S ATTENTION WAS DIVIDED. THEY WERE AT A TABLE outside and his back was to the Chesapeake as he enjoyed the warm weather. He could turn his head and see the view easily enough if he wanted, but his focus wasn't on the view.

It was on Jenna. And Alice. And what'd happened earlier.

Jenna sat across from him with Alice between them. She'd changed into jeans and a lacy tank top that was a little dressier than the one she'd had on earlier, and she'd taken the hair that'd been in a ponytail and piled it onto her head in a messy bun. He'd noticed that seemed to be one of her favorite hairstyles at the diner.

She had a strand that kept dropping into her face as she ate, and she kept pushing it behind her ear, seemingly more annoyed each time it happened. Not that she said so. It was the tightening of her jaw and the flash of her eyes that told him. Not to mention the viciousness with which she'd shoved the hair back the last time.

He almost told her to go fix it if it was bugging her so badly, but he figured that was one of those spaces where he needed to stay silent. They weren't dating, and even if they were, her hair wasn't his business.

He kept thinking of the way she'd come unglued when she'd seen him watching her earlier. Once he'd considered it, he'd realized he'd been in silhouette before he'd fully stepped into the kitchen. Her fright wasn't unwarranted.

And yet her reaction, and the inability to come down from it at first, concerned him. It was almost as if she half expected someone to appear suddenly—but it wasn't anyone she wanted to see.

He thought of his teammate Malcolm "Mal" McCoy and his fiancée, Scarlett. Scarlett had been hiding from a stalker ex when Mal met her at physical therapy. It'd been so bad that she'd had help getting a new job under an assumed name, and she'd done a lot to hide herself. But not quite enough, because the ex found her.

And when he'd found her, they almost hadn't gotten to her in time.

Noah shuddered when he remembered bursting into the motel room where Joshua Wright had tied Scarlett up and started carving words and symbols into her body with a knife. The blood had dripped down her naked form, and Mal had nearly lost his shit and killed Josh right there.

Not that Noah blamed him. He'd wanted to kill the fucker too.

Scarlett was doing okay these days, or seemed to be.

Noah didn't really know what she went through in private, or how Mal helped her navigate her emotions, but whatever he did worked. Scarlett and Mal were in love and seemed very happy.

Noah took a sip of his iced tea and studied Jenna as she cut up a few bites of her shrimp and put it on Alice's tray. Was Jenna running from someone who'd hurt her? Or who wanted to hurt her? An ex-boyfriend? Ex-husband?

It was logical, and it was possible. Not that he could ask her outright. He suspected that wouldn't go over very well.

"How's the fried shrimp?" he asked as she returned to her meal.

"Delicious, thanks." She took in the view, waving her fork. "I can't believe I haven't been here before. It's lovely."

"It's a little out of the way. It's the kind of place the locals try to keep local so it's not overrun, but of course there are tourists sometimes."

"Are you a local?" she asked.

His gut tightened a little at the question. Most people belonged somewhere. Not him. He'd never felt like he belonged anywhere after his mother died.

"No. Just here with the military."

She nodded. "Have you been in the area long?"

"A couple of years. The unit I work for is headquartered nearby."

"Do you move often?"

"I did."

"My mother was an officer and my dad was enlisted," she said. "We moved a lot for her career."

"Anywhere you call home?"

She shrugged. "Not really. You?"

"Nope."

"Were you a military brat, too?"

There was an ache in the pit of his stomach. He should have realized the conversation could go this way. It was inevitable, really, the longer they spent in the same house. Best to answer it and get it out of the way now.

"No. I was a foster kid. My mom was a single mom, and she died when I was ten. I had some anger and abandonment issues, so I wasn't a good fit with some of the families who wanted to adopt me. I got shuffled around a lot."

She looked a little shocked and a lot sad. "I'm sorry, Noah."

"Thanks." He looked at Alice happily eating shrimp. "Sally was my foster sister. We spent five years with the same foster family before aging out. We had the same birthday, so we used to joke that we were twins." He pulled in a breath and toyed with his straw. "I don't talk about this stuff usually, but you're caring for Alice, so I think you should know a little of it. Sally and I were tight for a long time, but stuff happened that affected her. She used alcohol and drugs to cope, and we fought over it. She got clean for a long time, but a few years ago she started taking pills again. That's when we had our big falling out, and that's when she stopped speaking to me."

"She must have gotten clean again," Jenna said. "For Alice."

He nodded. "I think so too. I also think she would have called me, but I know her well enough to know she was waiting for the right time. She wanted to surprise me with how well she was doing. It was always her way."

Sally had lived to please people. When she wasn't dealing with the fallout of her life with the Parker family, she had an almost imperative need to please. As if by pleasing people, she could prove she was a good person worthy of love.

But it was never enough. She stopped believing she was good, and she slid into the muck again. Over and over.

Noah wanted to shout his anger at the unfairness of it, but he bottled it up and buried it deep. There was nothing he could do for Sally anymore. Nothing except take care of her baby girl and find the best home possible for her. He *would* do that. He wasn't going to shuffle Alice out of his life just to get rid of her. He was going to find a forever family who would love and cherish her, and if it took time, then it took time.

"I know it must be difficult for you to talk about this," Jenna said. "I appreciate that you told me a little more about Alice's mother, though. I won't share it with anyone."

"Thanks." He nabbed a fry from his plate. Time to shift this conversation to something else. "Where was your parents' last duty station?"

She studiously divided the coleslaw on her plate. As

if she were thinking about what to say. *That* was interesting.

"Nellis."

"I've been to Vegas a couple of times," he said, trying to keep it light. Nellis was home to some of the Air Force's top secret projects. It was also where they piloted the drones that dropped bombs half a world away. "I'm not much for gambling or casinos, but some of them are amazing."

"I've always loved the Venetian. The square in the center where it feels like you're dining beneath an Italian sunset? Incredible."

He nodded. "It really is. Did you ride the gondolas?"

"Once. It was fun, but not the same as doing it in Venice."

"So you've been to Venice?"

"My parents were stationed at Aviano Air Base when I was in fifth and sixth grade. Venice was an easy train ride away. For the record, gondolas in Venice do *not* have trolling motors."

He snorted. "Yeah, that's kinda funny, but to be fair it's easier with the motors than without."

"True. And the gondoliers at the hotel haven't spent their lives plying the canals of Venice, so I guess you have to make allowances."

"No doubt. Sounds like you've been a lot of places, then."

"A few."

"Have a favorite?"

She seemed to think about it. "I loved Italy, but I was young then. Germany is also pretty terrific. We were in

Hawaii, too. That's spectacular—but there are bugs. Nobody thinks about the bugs when they're thinking they'd love to live in Hawaii. Centipedes the size of your arm, and flying roaches that could carry your car away. Oh, and then there were the rats that lived in the palm trees and came out at night. I didn't like any of those things, but the rest of it was great."

"Did you learn to surf?"

"Nah. Too scared of sharks."

He wasn't fond of them himself, but being a Special Operator meant you had to be a combat swimmer. He'd spent a lot of time bobbing in the ocean, waiting on a pickup. You got used to it. "Seems like a reasonable objection."

"I thought so at the time. I still think so, quite honestly. Did you know there's a website where you can look up shark attacks in Hawaii? It's sobering."

"Is it a hobby to look up shark attacks in your spare time?" he asked a little disbelievingly.

"Not really." She shrugged. "I'm an information junkie. And the internet is tailor-made for finding out stuff, right? If I start thinking about when we lived in Hawaii and regretting I didn't learn to surf, I go look at the shark attacks and change my mind. I mean they aren't frequent, but frequent enough. And some of them are fatal. No thanks."

He ate another fry. "So what about aliens?"

She blinked. "Aliens?"

"You were at Nellis Air Force Base. Did you research aliens?"

She shook her head, but she was grinning. "Of course I did."

"And?"

"And what? Are you asking me to confirm the existence of aliens? I'm afraid my skills involve Google, not government servers."

She reached over and took one of his fries. He'd offered earlier, but she hadn't taken him up on it. Apparently, she was getting more comfortable with him as they talked. He liked that. "No sightings on the base, huh?"

"Nope." She popped the P, and he laughed.

"Well, dang," he said, proud of himself for not swearing. "And here I was hoping you'd tell me something fun."

"Sorry to disappoint. Never saw an alien, but I saw plenty of people who thought there were aliens in Nevada. They'd hang out at the base gates with signs sometimes. Crazy."

"I don't think there are any aliens either. Despite the History Channel—what a ridiculous name for a channel that shows stuff that's definitely *not* history, right?" He shook his head before continuing. "Despite the alien crap they show, I don't buy any of it. Why would aliens with superior technology come here and *not* take over our primitive asses? And how the hell did they get here? If it takes light from the nearest star over four years to arrive, how in the hell do aliens travel across the universe without it taking thousands of years? Nope, don't buy it at all."

Jenna laughed, which was what he'd hoped she would do. "You seem to have thought about this a lot."

"When I first joined the Army, one of the guys at bootcamp was a conspiracy theorist. He had all these crazy ideas about alien technology and the military. He didn't make it through bootcamp, which is no surprise, right? He also thought Bigfoot was a thing, but I digress. Anyway, I've always been a science geek, and I'd binged a lot of Neil DeGrasse-Tyson stuff at that point, so I asked him those questions. He never had an answer for the science of traveling beyond light speed other than it had to be possible and they knew how to do it."

She was still laughing. "I mean, they *are* aliens. It could happen that way."

"Yeah, and if it did, are they going to waste time crossing the universe to abduct us from cornfields in the middle of the night and shit so they can stick probes up our asses? I think not. It'd be more like *Independence Day* when they show up and blast us out of existence for some reason."

It occurred to him that he'd said *ass* twice and *shit* once, but Alice was eating her shrimp and not paying attention, thankfully.

"I love that movie," Jenna said a touch wistfully. "I used to watch it with my dad every July. It was a tradition."

She'd said her parents had died in a small plane crash six years ago. He'd been orphaned as a child, but losing a parent—and in her case both parents at once—had to be hard, even as an adult. It made him wonder if she was completely alone or if she had other family out there. "I didn't ask if you had any brothers or sisters."

"Just me. Mom couldn't get pregnant again. In fact,

the doctors said she would never get pregnant in the first place. But it happened. They called me their miracle baby."

Ouch.

"I'm really sorry, Jenna. I know what it's like to lose your family, though it was a long time ago for me."

"Thank you." She sniffled, but it didn't turn into tears. She was working so fucking hard to stay strong. He could see it, and he admired it. "It was hard. Still is because I want to call them up sometimes. Can't do it, though." She closed her eyes then. "Dang it, no crying. No crying. I was doing *so* well, too."

She kept repeating *no crying* as a whisper, and he wanted to reach over and tug her into his arms. Just hold her and comfort her until the feeling passed. But he didn't have that right. "You can if you want to," he said, his throat tight. "I won't tell."

She shook her head and opened her eyes to look brightly at him. "I'm okay, really. Sometimes it still socks me in the gut and leaves me breathless, but mostly I'm fine. I was an adult when it happened, so I wasn't dependent on them for food or shelter."

"Still hard to deal with."

"Yes. Anyway, they're gone. They hadn't owned their house long because of all the moves, so there was no equity. And they didn't have a big 401k because, hello, military retirement now and then social security and TSP withdrawals someday. Which means I didn't inherit much of anything, in case you're wondering."

"I wasn't, but I understand."

"I sold the house, sold most of their things except for

some of the more sentimental stuff that I put in storage because I couldn't fit it into my apartment at the time, plus I kept thinking I'd buy my own place. I'll get it out someday. I hope."

"But then you decided to travel the US and work different jobs."

He thought she looked a little panicky for a second. But then she shrugged. "I was tired of living in the desert. I wanted to try some new places—green places— and figure out where I want to settle. I might go back, but at least then I'll know."

She dropped her gaze to her lap, and he felt kind of bad for asking questions. But it bugged him how freaked she'd been earlier, and he kept thinking he needed to know more about her. About what drove her.

She'd told him in the diner that she had nothing to hide. But that extreme reaction to his sudden appearance had him wondering if maybe she wasn't telling him everything.

He should have sent her a text or made a noise. Something.

And maybe it wasn't an overreaction for her. Maybe he'd just scared the utter shit out of her and she'd intended to protect Alice. That was possible too, he supposed. *He* could be the one reading more into it. Probably was. His profession made him pay attention to anything that seemed out of the ordinary, but it could be ordinary for her.

For anyone, since he didn't often go around scaring people just to get their reaction.

"I joined the military so I could go places. Makes

perfect sense to me. For the record, I don't know that I've found the place I want to settle yet."

She smiled at him. "That's the thing about the military. You go so many places, and a lot of them are really great. Makes it hard to choose."

She leaned back on her seat and turned her head to watch a sailboat making its way across the channel. He studied her profile, thinking that she was prettier than he'd thought when he'd first seen her at the diner. He'd been going there for a long time, and then one day a new server had waited on him. A petite woman with a messy blond bun and a nervous energy that seemed to radiate through everything she did. She'd been pretty in a plain way but not stunning, and he hadn't thought any more of her.

Until he'd gone back to the diner a couple of days later, and she'd waited on him again. Over the past month or so, they'd exchanged pleasantries many times, and she'd always brought him what he wanted exactly as he wanted it, which he considered a stellar quality in a server. She didn't flirt or giggle like a couple of the other women did, and he'd always appreciated that. He'd started asking for her section specifically because he liked talking to her, and he knew she'd be efficient and dependable.

Now they were at dinner in a romantic setting—though not a romantic situation—and something about her pulled at him, made him want to reach over and take her hand so she'd look at him. And then what?

Shit. This could get complicated really quick if he let it.

He wasn't going to let it.

"You about ready to head back home?" he asked. "I need to mow the lawn and take some yard waste to the dump."

She turned and blinked at him. "Yeah, sure. Alice is done anyway. She's just playing now."

Noah signaled for the check. The sooner they were home, the sooner he could do something that made him sweat and took his mind off Jenna's vulnerabilities—and her pretty profile.

Chapter Eight

JENNA TRIED NOT TO LOOK OUT THE WINDOW VERY often. If she did, she got a full view of Noah Cross in cargo shorts, hiking boots, and no shirt, pushing a lawn-mower across his backyard.

It was very disconcerting.

He was, of course, utter perfection beneath his shirt. Not that she'd doubted it since he was a Special Opera-tor. She still hadn't figured out what, though. He'd said *like* a Green Beret, but not, so that was out. Delta Force? Something else?

Not that it mattered, really. He was highly trained and probably lethal, and that was a good thing for her.

And just how is that, missy? It's not like you've told him you kinda sorta witnessed a mob hit and now you have to keep running.

Jenna frowned as she bit the inside of her lip. No, she hadn't told him. She wasn't *going* to tell him. There was no reason to do so. It'd been five months since she'd left Las Vegas. Six months since Sam was executed in the next room while she crouched on top of the toilet in the bathroom stall, praying they wouldn't come looking for her.

She was careful. She didn't use credit cards or a bank account, opted to be paid in cash or checks she could cash at the local bank they were drawn from, and only took jobs where she either didn't have to fill out tax forms or where she could get away with using her mother's social security number for a while.

If Allison had tried to verify her SSN right away, then Jenna would have known because Allison would've told her there was an error and she needed to correct it. Allison never had, which meant she wasn't verifying anything, just filing forms away until tax time. Jenna would have moved on by then anyway.

But now she was living with Noah, taking room, board, and some cash in exchange for her time. There was no paperwork. No IRS forms to file. No way anyone would find her. She had a Tracfone that she added minutes to when needed, and she had her laptop that she used to log onto other people's Wi-Fi and check the news and other things.

She called Aunt Maggie once a month and told lies about where she was and what she was doing. She still had social media, but she rarely posted on it. When she did, she had geo-locating turned off and lied about where she was. It was enough to keep her few friends happy.

Jenna sighed. She didn't know what the end game was. Not really. Would there ever be a moment where she could start over and not worry? Or would she always be looking over her shoulder? When would she know she was safe?

People disappeared all the time, and some of them started new lives, sometimes within spitting distance of the old life. They lived that way for decades, and then somebody figured out they were wanted for insurance fraud in the next county and it was all over the news about how they'd lived this other life.

She wanted that to be her, but without getting caught.

When Noah finally came inside, Alice was down for the night. Jenna walked into the kitchen for a refill of her water and stopped short at the sight of him standing in the hall that came in from the garage, sweat dripping down his muscled torso as he rubbed his head with his balled-up shirt before tossing it into the washer.

His shorts were sweat streaked, and he was barefoot. Bits of grass clung to him in places, too. He looked up and their eyes met. His hair was plastered to his head, though parts of it stuck up, and his blue eyes were piercing. There was sweat on his throat, glistening...

Oh crap. Jenna closed her eyes and gave herself a mental shake before opening them again and smiling at him. "Want some water? I can get you a bottle."

"Yeah, that'd be great," he said after a moment's hesitation. "I finished what I had already."

"Cold or room temp?"

"Room."

He sauntered into the kitchen as she reached into the pantry and grabbed a bottle. When she turned, he was right behind her, all glistening masculinity in her face.

Rock-hard abs, shorts that sat low enough on his hips to showcase that ridge-and-crease thing on either side of his abdomen. Her mind went blank, though she knew what the damned thing was called.

Those ridges tended to drive heterosexual women wild and probably gay men, too. And then it hit her —*inguinal crease.*

Yes, that crease that went down both sides of his abdomen, tapering toward the magic kingdom area. He had a line of hair—a happy trail—that pointed the way down, and a smattering of chest hair that she wanted to slide her fingers into.

"Uh, Jenna?"

She jerked her gaze upward to find him watching her.

"Water?"

"What? Oh, yes!" She shoved the bottle at him and he took it with a knowing look. "Sorry. I thought I might have heard Alice."

She'd thought no such thing. Alice was a sound little sleeper for a toddler. Thank God. Really, the kid was so easy to care for that it was borderline ridiculous.

"But you didn't?" he asked, twisting off the top and upending the bottle.

She watched his throat move as he swallowed. She told herself to drag her gaze away, but it was physically impossible. Parts of her she hadn't used in a long time were coming out of hibernation at the sight.

Living with Tami, listening to her animal sounds and

the men grunting along with her, hadn't exactly been arousing. Far from it.

But this? Whoa. Serious whoa.

"No," she blurted, remembering he'd asked a question. "I didn't. False alarm."

He finished the water and crushed the bottle. "Good."

She breathed in and out, unable to think or move— and then he took a step away and it was like he'd taken a force field with him as thought flooded back to her head. *Good grief.*

"Did you get everything done that you wanted?" she asked politely.

"Most of it. Cut the grass, bagged the clippings and put them at the curb. I need to trim some bushes, but I'll get that tomorrow."

"Nobody likes a messy bush."

He shot her a look, eyebrow arched, and the aching pit in her stomach hollowed a little more. Why had she said that?

"Why Jenna Lane, you have a dirty mind. Who knew?"

Heat flared in her core. "No," she said primly. "You do. I didn't say anything wrong."

He snorted a laugh. "Nothing wrong, but definitely leaning toward naughty."

"Only if you have a dirty mind."

He ran a hand over his sweaty chest as if absently scratching himself, and her pulse kicked up. "I'm a man. Of course I do."

"See? It's you, not me. I was making an observation."

His eyes sparked. "Uh-huh. But you're right. Messy bushes look so much better with a little trimming."

Oh dear heaven. Why was her skin on fire?

"Which is why you're doing it tomorrow. No one will make fun of your bushes for being out of control again."

He barked a laugh and she felt the glow inside. A different glow than before. A happy glow.

"No, no more teasing about my bush…*es.*"

Jenna leaned back against the counter, elbows behind her. He flustered her, but she liked being around him. He made her laugh, and he definitely made her pulse pound. "What a relief," she replied.

His gaze darkened as he studied her, and she realized that her breasts were thrust upward against her tank top because she was leaning on her elbows. She started to shift, but that would be too obvious. So she stayed as she was and counted the seconds in her head until she could move.

"Relief is always important." His voice was a little low, a little tight, maybe. "We all need relief sometimes, don't we?"

"I… um, yes. Definitely."

His gaze dropped a little, and she knew he was looking at her breasts. There were times in her life where it irritated the shit out of her when a man couldn't keep his attention on her face.

And then there were times like this when all her nerve endings blazed to life and her body practically screamed for his touch. Her skin felt sensitive where her clothing scraped against it, and her nipples—good heavens, her nipples—tightened into hard little knots inside her shirt.

He couldn't fail to notice. Heat washed over her. It was both embarrassment and arousal. Embarrassment because she couldn't believe the way her body responded to a look and arousal because she also wanted him to act on it.

It simultaneously wasn't a good idea and also the greatest idea ever.

He lifted his head, his eyes blazing into hers again before the heat banked abruptly. It was like he'd flipped a switch or doused himself in ice water. One moment he was looking at her like he wanted to eat her alive and the next he wasn't interested in anything about her.

"I need to shower," he said as he turned away. "And then I'm going to watch TV in bed. I'll see you in the morning."

He left, taking all the heat and light with him. Jenna straightened, frowning to no one in particular. What the hell had just happened? And why did she feel like she wanted to go outside and scream?

She didn't though. Instead, she went and got a cold bottle of water from the fridge then traipsed upstairs to peek in on Alice before retreating to her room. She could hear the hum of Noah's television through the wall. She imagined him in there lying on his bed, freshly showered, his body naked on the sheets.

Heat bloomed between her legs, no matter how hard she tried to shift her thoughts away from Noah's naked body. She'd seen enough of him that she could imagine the rest, and she spent a lot of time imagining before she finally shut off the lights and tried to sleep.

It didn't work, though. There was only one way she was getting over this itchy feeling beneath her skin. She slipped her hand beneath the sheets, skimming downward until she encountered wet heat.

And then she made herself come—three times— before the ache subsided enough to sleep.

———

JENNA HAD GREAT TITS. Noah already knew that, but seeing her nipples poking against the fabric of her tank top last night had riveted his attention in a way he'd managed to avoid thus far.

Now he couldn't stop seeing it. Her leaning against the counter, back arched just enough to thrust her tits forward—and then those nipples tightening as he'd stared at her.

He'd worked his ass off in the yard to get his thoughts off Jenna. And then he'd gone inside and she'd been there in the kitchen, watching him. He should have taken the water bottle and gone up to shower immediately.

Instead, he'd joked with her about trimming bushes and stared at her tits. When his balls began to tingle, that was the alarm he'd needed to get the hell out of there before he started something he couldn't afford to start.

He didn't one hundred percent know she'd have

been receptive, but he wasn't going to take the chance. Not last night, and not today either. Even if he was still thinking about her nipples and wondering if they'd be dark or light and how they'd feel under his tongue.

He was totally a tits man. He loved breasts, loved sucking a woman's nipples while she moaned. But he loved the rest of the package too. He loved exploring, finding a woman's erogenous zones, and exploiting them until she was boneless.

Fucking hell, he needed to get laid. But how was he going to do that now that he had a woman and child under his roof? He could leave them for a night or two, but that didn't feel quite right. Not for getting laid, anyway.

The smell of coffee floated through the air. He lay there for a few more minutes, then swore softly as he got out of bed. He couldn't avoid her. She lived in his house because he'd asked her to, and he needed her to stick around and take care of Alice so he could work.

He tugged on a T-shirt and athletic shorts and then went to brush his teeth. He stared at his reflection while he did it, frowning hard at the face in the mirror.

"You're a fucking elite soldier, dude," he muttered when he was done brushing. "You're used to deprivation and hardship. You can manage to coexist with an attractive woman without spending all your time thinking about seeing her naked. And even if you *do* think about her naked all the fucking time, you'll live through the boners."

With that bit of advice to himself, Noah went downstairs to get coffee. The sun was shining through the kitchen window, and Jenna was at the table looking at her laptop while Alice sat in the high chair and ate cereal.

The morning light streamed across the room, highlighting the domesticity of the scene and the golden hair of both the woman and girl. It hit him that in another world, Noah might be walking into the kitchen to kiss his wife and child. It was disconcerting enough that he halted, staring.

Jenna looked up. "Hey," she said. "There's coffee."

"Thanks," he replied, his voice a croak as he moved to the cabinet and took out a mug. He poured a steaming cup, intending to retreat to another room, but Alice looked up at him and grinned, and his heart tugged. It was the first time she'd smiled at him without him doing something silly since he'd brought her home.

"Morning, Alice," he said. "How's the baby girl today?"

"Eeeeee!" she replied. "No!"

Noah looked at Jenna. "I don't understand."

Jenna was grinning. "Well, she's happy to see you. And I believe that's her attempt at your name. No-*uh*," she said to Alice.

"No-no!"

"Oh boy, that's going to be fun, isn't it?" He put his coffee down and went to pick Alice up out of the high chair. She wrapped her chubby little arms around him and his heart melted.

Jesus, Sally. Why did you do this to me?

"You mean your name and the word that means stop doing that thing?" Jenna asked. "Yep, lots of fun. I suggest we tack *uncle* on there or something. Up to you."

"Uncle is fine." He looked at Alice, amazed at how much she was smiling. She'd been a lot more wary when he'd first brought her home. And a lot quieter. Not that he blamed her. He hadn't had a clue what to do. He was still learning, but at least he could change a diaper, bathe her, feed her, and try to potty train her. Not that she'd done great on that score so far.

"What's Uncle Noah doing with Alice?" he asked in a higher-pitched voice than usual. He swooped her down and around, making zooming noises, and she laughed.

"No-no!"

"Uncle Noah." He sounded it out. She studied his face so he said it again, slowly.

"Unk No-wuh," she repeated.

"Good job, kiddo." He zoomed her over to the high chair, but she didn't want in it. She clung to him, so he got his coffee and went over to the table. He told himself it was because of Alice that he sat down next to Jenna, but he knew he could have carried her to the living room.

Alice sat on his lap and reached for the coffee. "I don't think so," he said, moving it farther away.

She turned her little blue eyes up to him and frowned. "Want dink."

"It's too hot. And it's yucky." He made a face. Alice watched him intently. Then she gave up the notion as fast as she'd started it and reached for the floor. "Is she done with breakfast?" he asked Jenna.

"Yes. You got here toward the end."

Noah set her down and she toddled off to the basket of toys Jenna had created for her. She dragged out blocks and puzzles and scattered them everywhere.

"She's talking more," he said.

"Mm-hmm. She's opening up because she feels more secure, I think."

"Because of you," he said, studying her face. She had her hair up again, and she wore minimal makeup. She had on a pair of black leggings that went to about mid-calf and a loose tank top.

Her lashes dropped over her eyes, shielding them, and he realized he'd been looking at her pretty intently. When she looked up again, she gave him a tiny smile. "I don't think it's just me, but thank you."

"Okay, maybe not just you. But as much as she liked Brooke or Mrs. Barlow, it was too much upheaval for her. Staying here every day with you is perfect."

"It's certainly contributed to her feeling like her world isn't going to turn upside down any moment."

Noah wanted to lean forward and kiss her. It was the strongest urge, and the oddest one at the same time. Why? Why Jenna and why now? She was pretty, but he'd been near pretty women plenty and hadn't thought about how desperately he wanted to kiss them. Hadn't imagined sliding his hand into their hair and tugging it loose so it spilled over their shoulders in a silky cloud.

He sipped his coffee and didn't lean anywhere near her. "That's what she needed after losing her mother and getting hauled from one place to another while they sorted everything."

"Poor little girl," Jenna said softly. "What an upheaval."

He blew out a breath. "I need to find a family for her. I want her settled before she gets too attached to me."

Jenna's mouth dropped. "Wait—you want to give her up for adoption?" she whispered. "She's not a puppy, Noah. You can't just get rid of her."

His jaw tightened. "I can't keep her either. My life isn't the kind of life that's good for stability. She needs a mom and a dad who can be there for her."

Jenna had reared back in her seat to stare at him like he'd grown another head. And, he had to admit, he felt like squirming beneath that gaze. What he wanted wasn't unreasonable. Hell, it was better for Alice. But it sounded cold. He got that.

"I just… I can't believe what I'm hearing."

They were hissing at each other now, speaking low to keep Alice from understanding what they were saying, especially when she got up to bring them each a block. Once she walked away again, he said, "Why not? You aren't staying forever. We aren't her parents, and that's what she needs."

"But you're the person your sister chose. She must have done that for a reason."

"Because she knew if anything happened to her, I'd never let Alice go into foster care. But I *can* find a family for her. People I know who want a child. That's the only way I'd do it."

He hated explaining himself, and yet he felt like he had to. He needed to temper the judgment in her gaze. And yet he felt like an asshole. She did that to him, and she wasn't really trying.

Finally, she blew out a breath and shook her head, breaking their eye contact. When she looked at him again, it wasn't as intense or emotional as before. "You know what? I'm sorry. It's not my business, and you're right that I can't stay forever. You're active duty military, and you can't go in and quit tomorrow or ask for a less dangerous job than what you already do. I know that better than most since my parents were in. I also know that kids can handle the military life better than you think. But, yes, she's lost her mother, and I understand why you want stability for her. If you know the people who adopt her, that's a good thing."

He ought to feel vindicated in his thinking, and yet he still felt that knot of guilt tightening inside. "It's the only way I'll do it. I have to know who they are."

She nodded once, briskly, and snapped her computer closed. "I fed Alice, but I didn't eat yet. Do you want eggs and toast? Or something else?"

His belly rumbled. "Whatever you want to make. I can help."

"Grab the eggs then, and the butter. I'll get a pan and the bread."

He did as she asked then worked on the toast while she started the eggs. Alice played happily on the floor and the sun continued to shine. It felt right to be here with Alice and Jenna, in his kitchen making breakfast, but he knew what the feeling really was.

It was the longing of a little boy for the family he'd never had. It wasn't real, and it wasn't going to be. He'd learned a long time ago what he was meant to do and meant to be. He couldn't change it—and he didn't want to, no matter what the drumbeat in his brain was trying to say.

Chapter Nine

Jenna had said she understood what Noah wanted to do with Alice, and she did, but part of her was angry with him over it. Which was insane because she had no right to be. Alice was a sweet little girl, an easy child to take care of, and she deserved the family Noah wanted for her.

But the fact he stubbornly believed *he* couldn't be that family bothered her. Both her parents had been highly successful, career-oriented people. Her mother especially. But they'd managed to have a child, and they'd juggled deployments and new assignments and given her the best life they could give her. She'd been everywhere, and she'd had experiences that a lot of kids never got.

She missed them every day, terribly, and she'd give anything to have them back again. And maybe she was mixing up her own feelings of abandonment and loss with Noah's plans for Alice, and that wasn't fair to him.

It wasn't a *bad* plan for a single soldier in a

dangerous job. But she couldn't help thinking it was a short-sighted one. Especially as Alice grew closer to him. She was close to Jenna too after only a couple of weeks, and it would be hard enough when Jenna had to leave them—but Noah should be a constant in her life. He might not be her blood relation, but he *was* her uncle. Her only link to the mother she would never know. The only one who could share memories and stories of the woman who'd given birth to her.

He didn't want to be the foundation in Alice's life, though. Didn't think he could be. It was sad to Jenna, but it wasn't her place to tell him what to do. Or to pass judgment. God knew she had her own mess to take care of.

She lifted the lid of her laptop and returned to the tab where she read the local news in Las Vegas. Noah had taken Alice outside with him while he walked around the yard and looked at the bushes he wanted to trim. He'd promised to watch her closely, and Jenna was happy to have a few minutes alone to scroll the computer.

She was always on the lookout for something about the Flanagans. She didn't know why. It wasn't like they would announce any criminal activities in the media, or debate about whether or not she was a person of interest to them.

But she had to do it anyway. It was almost a ritual for her. Like throwing salt over your shoulder to keep away the bad luck, looking for the Flanagans—seeing the Flanagan name in the media—was her talisman. If they were *there* then they weren't *here*.

She knew it didn't make a bit of sense, but it made her feel better. For a little while, anyway. She moved her finger up and down the trackpad, scrolling, and there they were. Charlie and Billy Flanagan, up to their eyeballs in real estate and construction projects throughout the city, especially the epically expensive Venus Casino and Resort currently being built on the strip.

Sam had done contract work on the Venus, and on several of the other projects the Flanagans had going. She'd met Charlie and Billy once when she'd accompanied Sam to their office. She'd prepared paperwork for their people to pick up, delivered contracts to their office a couple of times, and thought nothing about any of it other than wondering how the hell people got so rich in the first place.

Jenna shivered as she snapped her laptop closed. She stood and walked over to the windows that looked out over the backyard. Noah was inspecting his handiwork with Alice, but they weren't getting very far. The little girl kept pointing at things and looking up at Noah.

Noah was talking back, so he must be explaining what things were. Or acknowledging the kinds of basic things one did with a toddler.

"*Bird?*"

"*Yes, bird! Very good.*"

"*Buwehfy?*"

"*Yes, butterfly! You're so smart!*"

Jenna smiled. He wasn't a bad guy at all. He might be a bit overwhelmed at the thought of keeping Alice, being a parent to her, but he could do it. He'd adapted to the situation quickly. He was still adapting, but he didn't try to avoid it.

He'd even taken Alice to the potty chair after breakfast. She'd used it, but she was pretty good at that if you caught her in time. She hadn't made the connection between the chair and every urge she had yet, so the diapers were still necessary.

Some kids took longer than others, and Alice had plenty of reasons to take her time. Her entire world had been turned upside down in a matter of days. It was still being righted, and that's what broke Jenna's heart about Noah's plan, even if he was doing it for the best of reasons.

She sighed as she watched them, then took out her phone and dialed. Aunt Maggie answered on the fourth ring. "Jennie?" she said, using the name that Jenna's parents had so frequently called her when she was growing up. "Is that you?"

"Hey, Aunt Mags. Yes, it's me. How are you?"

"Oh, you know, my arthritis has been kicking up with the rainy weather we've had, but I'm good. I've been out digging up the potatoes. Got a good crop this year."

Aunt Maggie was really her great-aunt, her father's aunt on his mother's side, and she'd be eighty-two in the fall. But that didn't mean she was stagnant. Nope, Maggie was always busy in her garden or at church. "That's great. You giving a bunch away to the church again?"

"Going to have to. I can't eat all this stuff myself."

Jenna laughed. "You could can it, right? I remember

Dad's stories about Great-grandma making everyone can a bunch of stuff one summer. He remembered specifically that a jar exploded and there were tomatoes everywhere."

Aunt Maggie laughed. "That's true. Mama insisted we can the garden every summer when she was still alive. Poor Luke must have been about ten that year. He'd have rather been riding bikes with his friends, and maybe playing that Atari game, but nope, Mama said it was all hands on deck."

Jenna leaned against the windowsill as she watched Noah and Alice making their way around the yard. It wasn't a huge yard, but it was big enough for a small plot of vegetables. Not that she knew how to garden, but she could watch YouTube for that.

Except she wasn't going to dig a garden into Noah's yard because, A, it was a lot of work. And, B, she wasn't going to be here forever. She couldn't saddle him with something he couldn't manage.

Still, the idea was appealing just because it felt like a connection to her father.

Someday.

"Where are you calling me from this time, Jennie? Anywhere near Delaware yet?"

Jenna's face heated. "No, sorry, Aunt Maggie. I'm still in Washington state. Working at a winery now," she lied. "Not in the vineyards or anything. Working in the tasting room."

"It sounds wonderful, honey. Though I do wish you'd come for a visit during your travels."

"I'm going to get over to the east coast, I promise.

Next year. I'm just banking up material for my travel blog at the moment." Her eyes prickled with unshed tears as she made up so many lies, but she didn't want her aunt to worry. It would have probably been better not to contact her at all, but Jenna hadn't seen how she could cut off ties with her only family. Aunt Maggie had never married, never had kids. She was beloved in her town, and her church family was there for her, but Jenna was the only family who'd stayed in touch. If Jenna ghosted her, she'd be no better than the ones who'd left town and stopped calling years ago.

They talked a bit longer, thankfully about other things like Aunt Maggie upgrading her cable and the reverend's Sunday sermon, before Jenna said, "I need to get back to work, Aunt Mags. I'll call you next month, okay?"

"Of course, honey. Oh, wait. I just remembered. A man called last week and said he was looking for you."

Jenna's heart tripped and fell before stumbling into high gear. "Oh? Did he say what he wanted?"

"Not really. He was looking for an address or phone number. I told him I didn't know where you were, and that you only called me once in a while and I didn't know the number. He asked me to let him know if I heard from you—but I'm not going to do it. He didn't have any manners, Jennie. He was very abrupt. What's wrong with people these days?"

Jenna thought her throat would close up. She put a hand to her forehead and forced herself to breathe. *In. Out. In. Out.*

"There's a lot wrong with people, Aunt Maggie."

She tried to think. "If he calls again, don't tell him you talked to me. And don't talk to him, either."

Aunt Maggie laughed. "Oh, I won't. There are advantages to being an old lady, my dear. I'll act like I've never spoken to him before and he'll think I'm batty."

Jenna didn't like that she wasn't there to watch over her aunt, but she also didn't think that going to Delaware was the answer. If someone was watching Maggie's house, they'd see her arrive. That couldn't be a good thing for either of them.

"You don't know where I am, okay?"

"I really don't, honey. You said you're in Washington state at a winery, but you didn't say which one. Why didn't you? I've been wondering why you never share details."

Jenna's heart thumped. "I just… I don't know how long I'm staying so it doesn't make sense to say. If you tried to call me here next week, I could be gone."

Aunt Maggie sighed. "All right, Jennie. I'm an old woman, but I'm not a dumb one, you know. I wouldn't call the winery anyway. I'd call your phone. But I can read between the lines, honey. You don't want to be found. I don't know why, but if you're in trouble I want to help you."

"It's okay. I'm not in trouble."

Outside, Noah swooped Alice into his arms and started walking toward the back door.

"I have to go now. I'll call you next week, okay? I won't wait a month this time."

"That's fine. I love you, Jellybean."

"I love you too, Aunt Maggie."

The call ended and Jenna sucked in a breath, willing her heartbeat to slow again. She couldn't get worked up. She couldn't go tearing off to Delaware because she was worried about her aunt. A man had called looking for *her,* but that didn't mean it was the Flanagans, or any of their people. It could be simple. It could be her old landlord, or the car dealer, or any number of people.

Aunt Maggie was her next of kin, and though it'd been a long time since she'd filled out paperwork asking for a next of kin, she would have used her aunt back in the days before Sam was killed and she'd decided to run.

Noah came inside with Alice. He was looking at her instead of Jenna, and that gave her a moment to smooth her expression into something she hoped looked normal.

"We found a bird's nest, didn't we?" he asked the little girl.

Alice nodded. "Bird. Ness."

Jenna pasted on a smile. "Really? That's wonderful."

Noah's gaze narrowed as he looked at her. "Is something wrong?"

"What? Me? No, not at all. Why do you ask?"

Oh shit, she was babbling. And Noah wasn't stupid. His gaze stayed narrow as he put Alice on the floor. She immediately went over and seized her blocks then brought them back to hold them up to Noah. He took one, praising her, and she took it and toddled away again.

"Something's wrong," he said.

Jenna squeezed her hands together, willing herself to stop giving off whatever vibe it was that had his hackles raised.

"I called my aunt. I'm worried about her. That's all."

"Is she sick? Do you need to go to her?"

She shook her head. "She's not sick. She's eighty-one, and I worry. She just sounded a little tired. That's all."

He didn't say anything for a long moment. "Okay."

Jenna spread her hands, the knot in her belly uncoiling a little. "She's the only family I have left. I get a little uptight sometimes."

Noah poured another cup of coffee then turned and leaned against the counter. "When's the last time you visited her?"

"It's been a while. She came to Vegas after my parents died."

"Six years ago."

She swallowed. "Yes. I talk to her often, though. Sometimes we video chat, but a lot of times I just give her a call."

"Where does she live?"

She thought about lying, but at some point there would be too many lies to keep up with. "Delaware. Near the Maryland border on the south. Not super close, but close enough for a quick trip. I know that's what you were thinking. And I intended to, but I haven't been here all that long and I didn't have time yet."

"You don't have to explain."

She crossed her arms. "It feels like I do."

Why had she said that? Way to make him suspicious.

"You don't, Jenna. It's not my business." He sipped the coffee. "You just looked… spooked. That's the word.

You looked like something worse than worry was bothering you, so I asked."

She squeezed her arms around herself.

"You don't have to tell me," he went on. "Unless it affects me and Alice somehow, I don't need to know."

Part of her wanted to tell him. To unburden herself and share her fears with another soul. One who had some professional expertise when it came to protection.

But she couldn't. She couldn't risk him throwing her out. Maybe she should go before he could, but it shocked her to realize that she didn't want to.

For the first time in months, she felt like she could breathe just a little bit easier. And she liked being here. With him. If she left, she'd never see him again. That thought made a fresh knot of pain pull together inside.

Jenna drew in a breath and faced him as calmly as possible. "I'm fine, Noah. I worry about my aunt, and I worry about the future. But I'm fine, and I'm happy here with Alice."

And you. That part remained unspoken.

He nodded. "Okay. Good." He set the coffee down and headed for the stairs. "I need to get my shoes and start work on the bushes."

She didn't have it in her to make a joke this time. Instead, she slumped at the table and ran her thumb back and forth over the lid of her laptop while watching Alice stack blocks.

The blocks toppled in a heap. Just like the pieces of her life.

Chapter Ten

Monday morning, Noah strolled into work and dropped his bag at his desk. Then he strolled over to Sky "Hacker" Kelley's desk and braced his hands on the flat surface. Hacker kept typing.

"What do you want, Easy?"

"Information."

"I take payment in gold coins and dragon's eggs."

Noah rolled his eyes. "I'll owe you, buddy."

Hacker sat back, one finger beneath his chin, and waited.

"It's my nanny. She had a phone call on Saturday that seemed to spook her. She said she was talking to an elderly aunt, but she seemed pale and out of sorts for a while afterward."

"And you want to know who she was really talking to."

Noah nodded. "That'd be a good start."

Hacker reached out and crooked his fingers. "Okay, gimme."

Noah took the piece of paper he'd written Jenna's number on from his pocket and handed it over.

Mal wandered over with a donut in his hand. "Checking out the nanny, huh?"

Noah eyed him. "Don't judge. You dug into Scarlett's background."

He took a big bite of the donut and nodded. "Yep. That was the night she saw a guy in Buddy's who recognized her. Then she told me about her ex stalking her. I had to dig then."

"Definitely." Noah raked a hand through his hair. "I don't know if I should be doing this, quite honestly, but what do I really know about Jenna? I hired her to watch Alice, for God's sake. What if my instincts are wrong and she's a fucking loon?"

Hacker shrugged as he typed. "If you're wrong, then it's time to retire."

"I'm not old enough to retire."

Hacker didn't say it, but Noah thought it—if his instincts were that off, how could his teammates trust him in the field with their lives?

"She's not a loon," Mal said. "She's good with Alice."

"News flash, people can be crazy and good with kids at the same time," Noah replied.

"She has too much empathy to be crazy," Mal said.

"How would you know?"

"I went to the Early Bird often enough. I saw her pay for food out of her own pocket for people who didn't have the money. She's empathetic as hell. I mean I guess she could have taken one look at your handsome face and lost her marbles, but if she's not boiling bunnies, then I wouldn't worry about it."

Noah sputtered. "Boiling bunnies? What the fuck?"

Mal waved a hand. "Some old movie I watched with Scarlett. *Fatal Attraction*. The woman was obsessed with the guy, and she boiled his rabbit."

Hacker was laughing. "Man, you're a sick fuck, you know that?"

Mal spread his arms wide, scattering powdered sugar on the floor. "Me?" he practically screeched. "*I* didn't boil a rabbit. The woman in the movie did!"

"Yeah, but your mind went there. Telling Easy that he's okay so long as Jenna doesn't boil a rabbit." Hacker was laughing though, which meant he was yanking Mal's chain. Easy enough to do sometimes. And fun, too.

"She's not boiling rabbits," Noah said. "But she does make a delicious pot roast."

"You *suuure* it was pot roast?" Mal asked.

"Yeah, I'm sure. With carrots and potatoes. So good."

"Gravy?"

"And gravy. I brought some for lunch today."

Gem had walked into the office at some point during the conversation and now he whistled. "Man, Easy, you're getting all domestic and shit. Leftovers for lunch? Did she pack it in a cute little lunch box for you?"

Noah punched him in the shoulder. "She didn't pack it. I did. It's a fucking paper bag and a plastic container."

She'd offered, though. Noah wasn't telling his teammates that. He would have let her except that she'd had her hands full with Alice at the time and he'd thought, shit, he could do it himself. Save her the trouble.

After she'd gotten over whatever it was that had bothered her Saturday morning, the weekend had gone well. They took Alice to the park to play on the slide that afternoon, then he'd grilled steaks for dinner while Jenna made corn on the cob and sliced tomatoes with feta, Greek olives, and onion. She'd topped it with a drizzle of olive oil, and he'd found himself eating sliced tomatoes like they were the best thing he'd ever put in his mouth.

They'd gone their separate ways after Alice went to bed, but Sunday morning was a repeat of the day before with coffee and breakfast. Noah had watched Jenna closely for any signs of worry or fear, but she'd seemed fine. They sat on the back deck in the afternoon, drinking beer and watching Alice play—though Jenna had nursed exactly one beer—and then the pot roast she'd put in the oven to slow cook all day was done and they'd eaten dinner.

Once more, as soon as Alice was down for the night, they went their separate ways. And now here he was, handing over her phone number and wondering if she'd really been talking to her aunt or if the whole thing was a lie.

"I'm not going to have this for a while," Hacker said, looking up at the three of them standing around his desk. "So get lost."

Noah didn't know how Hack found some of the stuff he did, but the dude was good. It wasn't until the end of the day, after they'd sat in on mission briefings and trained on the obstacle course, that Hacker caught his eye and motioned him over.

Noah was apprehensive but he needed the answer. When he was in front of Hacker's desk, the man handed him a print out with phone numbers.

"She has a Tracfone."

Didn't surprise him, really. A Tracfone was a burner, but it could still be traced. He looked at the list of calls and texts. They were sparse. He recognized his number among them.

"I circled the one on Saturday morning. It goes to a Margaret Anne Miller in Dunkirk, Delaware. She's lived at that address for better than fifty years, she's eighty-one years old, and Jenna Lane is her great-niece. Jenna's father was her nephew."

Relief rolled through him, sharp and hot. "Okay then. She called her aunt."

"Like she said," Hacker replied.

"Like she said," Noah repeated.

"But you still think something was wrong?"

Noah frowned. "Remember when we busted into that jungle compound in Colombia and found Brooke Sullivan and that little girl with a bomb strapped to them?"

"I wasn't actually on the breaching team, but yeah."

"Well, Brooke had a look on her face when we got there. Fear and an awful resignation that her fate was locked in. That's what Jenna looked like Saturday. Like it's locked in and waiting."

"Not everything is a puzzle, Easy. Not everything is

complicated. Maybe she really is just worried about her aunt. The woman is older—and who knows, maybe she's frail. Or maybe she has a disease. Jenna could be processing something her aunt told her, you know."

Noah nodded. "Yeah, you're right. Shit."

Hacker stood and squeezed his shoulder. "You just lost your sister and inherited her kid. It's a lot to handle. And then to have to worry about the person you've hired to care for the child? You were right to check. But it doesn't look like anything you have to worry about."

He was glad for that, and yet as he drove the miles to his house, he couldn't help but think he didn't know nearly as much about Jenna as he wanted.

Maybe it was time to start asking questions.

———

ACID FLARED in Jenna's belly as she stared at the headline. Panic tried to crawl out of the box she'd put it in, but she didn't let it.

Still, though. *Still!*

She should have changed her name entirely and cut off all contact with Aunt Maggie. She'd made a huge mistake, thinking all it would take was using cash and a pay-by-the-minute phone to conduct her life as she took odd jobs and hoped the Flanagans would forget about her.

The headline blared its message at her.

CASE DISMISSED: POLICE ILLEGALLY OBTAINED EVIDENCE IN OWEN FISHER CASE; FISHER FREE

Owen Fisher, the man who'd shot Sam as he sat

behind his desk, was a free man. She wasn't sure how that was scarier than Charlie and Billy Flanagan having been free all this time, but it made dread pool in her body.

Fisher was the trigger man. He wasn't the only one they had, but he was the most dangerous. She closed her eyes and thought of that night when she'd carried the boxes containing hers and Sam's subs into the break room and dropped them on the counter before running to the bathroom.

She'd just finished and opened the door when she heard voices coming from Sam's office. Ordinarily, she'd have gotten the food and went back to her desk to wait for Sam's meeting—the one he'd forgotten to tell her about—to end.

But something in the tone of their voices made her curious. She could hear perfectly fine from where she stood in the bathroom door, so she'd kept listening.

"Where's the money, Baxter? The bosses know what you've been doing, and they want every cent—with interest—returned."

"I don't know what you're talking about. I don't have the Flanagans' money. All I do is shuffle the paperwork and make everything look right. I take my cut, and that's it."

"Sure you do. Got a fancy new house, didn't you? Ten thousand square feet, I heard. What's one man need with all that space, huh?"

Sam's voice sounded a little less certain when he spoke next. *"I'm planning to get married. I need the room."*

The other man snorted. "Again? Didn't learn your lesson the last two times?"

"This one's different. I'm doing it right this time."

"Not if you don't tell me where the money is."

"I told you. I don't have the money. I don't know what you're talking about."

"That's how you're going to play this? Last chance, dickhead."

There was a brief hesitation, and then Sam's voice came again. Angry this time. "You aren't going to kill me. I'm the one who keeps the Flanagans' asses out of trouble with the law. They need me. They need what I do to keep the heat off their side hustle."

"You talk too much, you know that?"

"Yeah, and I'm gonna talk louder. I know where the bodies are buried, so you'd better fucking get out of here with that shit before I slip up on the paperwork."

Jenna heard what sounded like two pops. "Yeah, yeah, asshole," the man said. "Nobody's that special."

Sam didn't speak again, and Jenna slipped into the restroom, hurrying into a stall and perching on top of the toilet, her heart hammering as her ears pounded with blood. She listened hard—and then she heard footsteps in the hall. The bathroom door opened. She held her breath, praying.

When it closed again, she nearly cried with relief. She perched on top of the toilet, shaking for a good twenty minutes before she felt brave enough to creep out.

The office was empty, the food still on the counter—thank God the sandwiches were cold and not hot or the killer might have known she was there from the fragrance.

Sam was at his desk where she'd last seen him, his body reclining in the chair, eyes wide open. There was a small hole in the fabric of his shirt, right over his heart, and one in his head, between the eyes.

Jenna had lost the contents of her stomach then called the police.

She shuddered as she remembered that night. The endless questions, the suspicion, the hours spent writing her statement. But she had no weapon and no powder burns, and the police finally acknowledged she wasn't a suspect.

She'd never told them what she'd heard, because she suddenly knew what the Flanagans were capable of and she'd been terrified. And Sam had been a part of it, which made it even worse.

Sam, who'd been so nice to her. Who'd plucked her from the day care center and given her a chance. She'd felt betrayed and confused by what she'd heard him saying about money and knowing where the bodies were. And she wasn't able to identify the man in his office anyway. She'd never seen him. It wasn't until the police arrested him for a different murder and she'd heard his voice on television, denying the charges, that she'd realized who he was. Her blood had gone cold at the sound, but she still hadn't talked.

It wasn't safe to speak the Flanagan name, much less admit everything she'd heard. Prison was prison, and she'd assumed Owen Fisher was going to be in it for a very long time based on what he'd allegedly done. The police had claimed to have an airtight case, and they'd held him without bail until the trial. Which had just gone sideways, apparently.

She looked at the headline again. *Free.*

Dread filled her. Was it a coincidence he was free

and someone had called Aunt Maggie? Maybe. Maybe not.

"Pee-pee," Alice shouted. "Pee-pee!"

Jenna jumped up and went to where the little girl stood with her hand clutched to her crotch, trying to hold it in. She'd been playing with her stuffed animals, bringing them to Jenna and chattering, and now she was doing the pee-pee dance. *Progress.*

"Good girl, Alice," Jenna said, taking her to the bathroom and helping her get her pants off so she could sit on the potty chair.

When she was done, Jenna helped her wipe then got her dressed again. "Such a good little girl, Alice. You did a perfect job."

"Cookie?"

Jenna shook her head. "Not yet, honey. After dinner."

She knew better than to get in the habit of giving the child treats for using the potty. Next thing you knew, she'd be using it when she didn't have to just to get a treat.

"We have our stamp kit though. You get a stamp for using the potty like a big girl." Jenna took out the stamps and washable ink. "How about a cherry this time?"

"Yes," Alice said, nodding her head enthusiastically.

Jenna stamped her hand, then blew on it so it dried. "We'll count them up at the end of the day, okay? It will be so exciting!"

When Alice was occupied with her toys again, Jenna sank into the chair and watched, her eyes tearing over.

She'd been taking care of Alice for almost three weeks, and she was getting attached. It was hard not to when she saw parallels to her own life. Losing her parents, being alone. Alice needed love and patience and a place to grow into herself, not another upheaval.

Yet, Jenna feared it was time to go. Time to run again and pray Owen Fisher didn't start looking for her. This time she'd change her name entirely. She'd look into getting fake papers, a fake ID, and she'd cut off communication with Aunt Maggie. Maybe she should have done those things in the first place, but it had seemed so final. Like she would never be Jenna again if she took that step. Her old life would be gone forever, and she'd always be in hiding.

This time, she would remake herself into someone new, and she wouldn't miss the life she'd started in Mystic Cove. She wouldn't miss Noah or Alice, wouldn't miss Vicki at the diner, or Mrs. Hanley and Mr. Pruitt. She swiped beneath her eyes, irritated with herself for getting emotional.

She'd been in town for more than three months. It wasn't a tragedy to leave now. Except she needed to give Noah time, which meant she needed to tell him she was going. She couldn't just leave him with Alice with no notice. He was trying so hard to do the right thing for the little girl.

Jenna gritted her teeth. She had a little time, but not much, and she needed a plan. She'd tell Noah she was going to go take care of Aunt Maggie and that she needed to leave soon. That way he'd have a chance to get Alice into day care on the military base and she'd be able to get that new battery for Lola.

It would take a week—maybe a little longer—for everything to fall in place. Then she'd drive away and not look back.

Chapter Eleven

IT WAS FRIDAY, AND NOAH WAS FRUSTRATED. HE'D SPENT the last few days trying to find the right way to ask Jenna questions about her past, but it never seemed to happen. Whenever he got home, she had dinner ready to go, or almost ready, and Alice was busy showing him her drawings and her toys from the day.

She was learning to use the potty more often, and she had to show him that too. And damn if his heart wasn't melting a little more each day for the kid. He could see Sally in her, and it just about broke him.

"Did you know this was going to happen, Sally?" he'd muttered more than once. "Did you know it was going to be hard for me to give her up when you made that damned will?"

She probably had. Sally hadn't been stupid. She'd just been overwhelmed by life. She'd known that giving her child to Noah was the smartest and best thing she could have done. Of course she hadn't expected it to happen, but when she'd thought of the possibilities, he'd been first.

His emotions were a tangle every time he thought about it. He put off asking Jenna any questions while he grappled with his thoughts. Now it was Friday and they'd hardly spoken about anything but Alice all week. He'd almost felt as if she was avoiding him. Maybe that was why she'd disappeared to her room every evening once Alice was down for the night.

He'd hung out in the living room, waiting for her to return so they could at least talk a bit, but she never did. He'd thought about asking her to come back, but he didn't do it. It felt too much like flirting.

She was the nanny. He was the employer. She was off limits because he didn't want there to be any misunderstandings.

Except he couldn't help but steal glances at her tits and ass, at the way her legs went on forever despite her petite size. She wore shorts and tank tops most of the time, along with some athletic wear that hugged every curve, and he imagined so many things.

Touching her. Tasting her. Kissing her until she begged him for more.

That annoyed him, too. Jenna Lane wasn't the only woman in the world, and he was the king of easy lays according to his teammates. He could walk into a joint, set his eyes on a woman, and go home with her before the night was over.

He didn't want to, though. He wanted to feel Jenna wrapped around him, not a stranger.

And she isn't a stranger?

Maybe she essentially was, but she didn't *feel* like one. They lived together. She cooked for him. Took care of his niece. She was there when he woke up and there when he went to bed, and he couldn't stop thinking about her laugh or the way she blew raspberries on Alice's skin and made her giggle.

He couldn't stop thinking about the way she'd flirted with him the night he'd been sweaty from mowing the lawn. He wondered what would have happened if he hadn't backed away. If he'd pressed into her where she leaned on the counter and let her feel all his hard edges.

He hadn't missed the way she'd been staring at him. At his body. He knew he was in the kind of shape that made people pay attention to him. All his teammates were. They worked hard and played hard and pushed their bodies to the breaking point. They were packed with lean muscle, and they looked like they could chew nails for breakfast.

If he'd made a move, she would have melted under him like snow on a warm day. Noah forced the images from his head as he pulled into the driveway after work and got out of his Jeep.

The house was empty when he walked inside, but the smell of something cooking told him she was there. He dropped his hat and backpack on a chair then continued through the house until he reached the kitchen. He could see a kiddie pool outside and Alice splashing happily. Jenna was in a lawn chair in the shade, and she'd opened the outdoor umbrella to position it over the little pool. Her laptop computer sat on a side table, and she looked at it from time to time. Mostly, she watched Alice.

His heart thumped. She was good with Alice. Not just good.

She cared.

He couldn't have chosen better if he'd tried. And he had tried. He was glad none of the places he'd called had anyone who could take the job.

He opened the door and Jenna looked up. She smiled, and his heart thumped again. *What the fuck?*

"Hey," she said. "You're early."

He glanced at his watch. "A little. How's it going?"

"Great. We're having some splash time."

He could see that she'd only put about two inches of water in the pool. She thought of things like that. He hoped he would have, but he wasn't sure.

"I see that. I didn't know we had a backyard oasis."

Her laughter was sweet. "Your neighbor a couple doors down set this little beauty on the curb. I asked if they were getting rid of it, she said yes, so I dragged it back here. There's nothing wrong with it. Their kids just got too big, and it's not worth the hassle of a yard sale. Or so she told me. Her name is Molly."

"Molly Hinds. Her husband is Dan. They have three kids. Fourteen, twelve, and eight. I guess the eight-year-old is done with splash pools, huh?"

"Yep. They're putting in a pool in the fall, she said. In-ground."

Alice splashed around happily. "Unk No-wuh! Look!"

Noah went over and looked. "My goodness, are your dinosaurs enjoying the pool too?"

"Yeah," she said. "Dyn-sar. Dey swim."

"That's good. I'm glad they swim."

She started singing and dipping her toys in and out of the water. He returned to sit beside Jenna. It was hot, even in the shade. He unbuttoned his uniform shirt with one hand and tugged it off so he could sit in his T-shirt.

"Want some iced tea? Or a beer?" Jenna asked.

He glanced over at her. "You don't have to get it for me."

"I know. I'm offering because I need to run to the, er, facilities. And I couldn't do that with Alice in the pool."

"Ah, gotcha. Yeah, a beer would be good."

"Don't take your eyes off her for a second," Jenna said. "You'd be surprised how quickly that can go bad."

"Eyes. Got it."

Noah leaned back in the chair and watched Alice. He felt surprisingly drowsy, but he wasn't going to fall asleep. He shifted in the chair, waking himself again. It was the sun and the heat, and the fact it'd been an early day today. He'd had to be at HOT HQ for a briefing at 0600.

There was some shit going on in the world, like always, and the strike teams were active. When the time came for Strike Team 2 to deploy again, he'd be leaving Jenna alone with Alice for at least two weeks, maybe more. He didn't relish it, but that was the job. Thank God he had her.

She returned with the beer and a glass of iced tea.

He clinked his bottle with her glass and took a long drink.

"Something smelled good when I walked in."

"It's a chicken enchilada casserole."

His mouth was watering just thinking about it. He could understand why Saint, Wolf, Hacker, and Mal liked this domestic thing. Not that he knew their women cooked dinners every night—or thought it was their job to do so—but just the part about going home to someone was nice. He liked walking in and having two people greet him. It wasn't as lonely as it used to be, with all the noise and chaos of three people in the house instead of one.

He'd never thought he was the kind of guy who'd want people in his house. After being in the foster system, and then spending his teen years with the Parkers and their full house, he'd relished solitude when he'd gotten his own space. It was why he bought his house, and why he didn't have a roommate anymore.

Solitude.

But now he had Jenna and Alice, and it wasn't bad at all. Made him realize just how quiet things had been. Too quiet sometimes.

Alice was singing a song to herself and splashing. Birds chirped. The sun dappled the patio through the trees. He looked at the backyard and started imagining better landscaping. Maybe a swing set. And a hammock. He could lie in a hammock right now and have a nap, softly swinging back and forth while Alice sang her little songs and Jenna spoke to her every once in a while.

"She's talking more," Noah said as the singing kept going.

"She is." Jenna's voice caught at the end and he looked at her in concern.

"You okay?"

She sipped her tea. "Fine. It's just…" She shook her head. "She's coming out of her shell, trusting her environment more. She doesn't cry as much for her mama. The meltdowns are fewer."

"I'm happy to hear it."

"Have you, um, made any progress on that family thing?"

He frowned as he watched Alice's chubby little arms move. "I haven't really had time."

"I see."

He turned to look at her. Soft brown eyes met his, and something tightened deep inside. "Now you're disappointed with me for not doing it?"

"I didn't say that. It's just——" She sighed. "She's attached to you. That's only going to get stronger."

"And to you," he pointed out. "You're the one who's with her the most."

She frowned. "Well, that's one of the dangers of being a nanny. I don't let her call me *mama*, though. She did that a few days ago, but I explained why I'm Jenna."

His heart ached. It seemed as if Sally was being forgotten already, but Alice was young and she wasn't going to remember her mother at all as time went on. The only memories she would have of Sally were the ones she was given later when she was capable of understanding. Assuming someone was there to tell her about her mother. He had pictures of Sally on his hard drive. He'd make sure they went with her.

"It's not like opening up a catalog and choosing one of the options," he said, though in fact it could work like that if he was willing to entertain the idea of strangers adopting Alice. He'd seen the websites of people begging pregnant women to consider them as parents for the baby they were planning to give up.

Always babies, though a blond two-year-old girl would have no problem finding people who wanted her. He didn't fault those people who wanted to start families and couldn't have their own for one reason or another, but why couldn't some of them want a ten-year-old boy? He'd wondered that a lot when he'd been a kid without a home.

"I know. It's just—well, I won't be here forever. I thought if you were planning to do this, you might want to get it done before too long."

"Wait a minute—you were totally against it the last time we talked about it. And now you're telling me to hurry it up?"

She dropped her chin, and her hair curtained her face before she looped it behind an ear. Jenna had long hair, thick and golden. He found himself wanting to spear his hands into it and find out if it was as soft as it looked.

"You're the one who's determined to go through with it. I just figured you might want to get on with it."

"I'd love to get on with it," he growled. "For her sake. But I'm not rushing into anything either. It has to be the right people."

She nodded but didn't say anything.

He felt suddenly restless inside. And guilty. Like he was wrong for wanting to find a loving family for an orphaned little girl. But Jenna didn't know what it was like. She couldn't. She'd had two loving parents and her childhood had been stable. She didn't know the terror of being told to grab the plastic bag with your things and go with the social worker who'd come to collect you from yet another family who was done with you.

Because you weren't the perfect little boy. Because you had anger issues and abandonment issues and nobody wanted to deal with that. They expected you to keep it inside and be grateful you were there. Grateful they were giving you a home—except they were getting paid to give you that home and as soon as they couldn't handle you, they'd send you back and get another child in your place.

It hit him that he was in essence doing the same thing to Alice. Sending her onward because he didn't want to be a parent to her. Because she was messy and chaotic along with sweet and adorable, and he wasn't sure he could handle it. He definitely couldn't handle it alone.

"There's another option," he said as a thought occurred to him. It was a crazy thought. A way-out-there thought. Maybe even a colossally bad idea. But sitting in the warm shade of the patio, watching Alice splash with her chubby little arms and feeling the pull of attraction to the woman beside him, it seemed like a decent idea. Even a logical one.

"You keep her and be her fierce, protective parent?"

He nodded. "Yeah… but I'd need help. A co-parent."

She arched an eyebrow. "A co-parent. What is that?"

He arched an eyebrow in return. "You really don't know?" She stared at him blankly. "A wife, Jenna. I'd need a wife."

"Ooookay, sure. I could see how that would work. But where are you getting a wife? Is there a significant other you've failed to mention? An ex-girlfriend you want to make another go with? Because I gotta tell you, that seems the exact opposite of stable to me. You want to give Alice a family, not a reason to seek therapy later on."

He pulled in a breath. *Crazy*, a voice whispered. *Fucking crazy to even consider it….*

Well, yeah, he was. It kinda went with the sort of personality that signed up for a job that required being willing to sacrifice one's life at any moment. Still, it was the only other plan he could think of that might work.

"I mean *you*," he said. "Marry me and help me raise Alice in a good home."

Chapter Twelve

Jenna's mouth dropped open. She blinked. Heat swirled in her belly and flared beneath her skin. Tiny beads of sweat popped up on the back of her neck, between her breasts.

"I... What did you say?"

He must be joking. Except he didn't look like he was joking. Blue eyes stared back at her. His expression was serious.

"I said marry me. Help me give Alice a stable home."

Jenna picked up her tea and took a big swig. *What the hell?* He hadn't had quite enough beer to be drunk. Unless he'd been drinking before he got home. She didn't believe that, though. She'd never seen him drink more than two in an evening. And she'd never smelled it on him when he came home at the end of the day.

Drunk was out, then. High? No, not with his job. Random pee tests were a thing, and he wouldn't risk his entire career that way.

"I can't marry you, Noah," she finally managed.

"Why not?" He seemed almost hurt by it.

She gathered her hair nervously and twisted it on top of her head. Secured it with the hair tie she had around her wrist. Stared at him. He was still watching her. Still waiting.

She'd been trying to work up the nerve for days now to tell him she had to leave, and she hadn't been able to do it yet. She'd told herself she'd do it this weekend, most definitely. And he'd just thrown her a curve ball she hadn't seen coming.

"You really can't be serious. We don't even know each other. Not really."

"We can fix that."

"Noah." She pinched the bridge of her nose even as her heart thumped like a bass drum. "Good God, it's not that easy!"

He leaned forward. Put a hand on her knee. Her bare knee. Her body took notice, desire rising to the surface like molten lava.

"I know it's not easy. I didn't mean tomorrow. We could see if there's anything between us. Any spark. If there is, that's enough to build on."

Oh, there was a spark all right. There was a shower of sparks waiting to explode if she saw his Adonis belt again—a term she'd just discovered, by the way.

Because you couldn't unsee his torso. Because you looked it up, and then looked at examples online even if they didn't quite compare to seeing it in person.

She had done that. Definitely. It'd made her skin feel

too tight to keep looking at images and knowing she had the perfect example in the same house.

"It's not a good idea," she said, pushing aside her lusty thoughts. "We've known each other not quite a month—"

"Longer than that. A couple of months at least."

"Because I waited on you at the diner. That's not knowing who I am as a person. That's me being nice in hopes you'd leave a big tip!" She shot to her feet and stared him down, that insane heat still rising inside her. "I'm not going to marry you and be your live-in maid and cook. What if we're miserable together after six months? You planning to stick it out for Alice? Because that's *not* the future I want. I want heat and passion and a man who wants me because of me, not because I'm good enough to sleep with and capable of taking care of his kid."

Noah was frowning now. "That's not what I mean, Jenna. I *like* having you here. You're good for Alice, and you're good for me." He raked a hand through his hair again, and it stood on end. He was so attractive with his mussed up hair, his tan T-shirt and tan camouflage pants with combat boots.

The T-shirt molding to the muscles beneath made her mouth water. His biceps flexed as he lifted his beer again, and she nearly moaned. If military guys did it for a girl, this was what they pictured when they thought about it.

A hot, uniformed dude with muscles that wouldn't quit. A definite fantasy. She imagined pushing his T-shirt up, feasting her eyes on his ridged abdomen again.

Touching him. The heat in her body flared to nuclear levels.

"Shit, I've fucked this all up, haven't I?" he muttered.

Jenna sucked in a breath, willing herself to calm the fuck down. Part of her wanted to straddle his lap, tug his head back, and kiss the hell out of him. See if Noah Cross kissed as hot as he looked.

The realistic part told her not to cross that line. She needed to be extracting herself from his life, not getting more tangled in it. And kissing him was definitely getting tangled. Especially when she thought about what she wanted to do after that.

"I understand where you're coming from. Really. You've been put into an impossible position. But marrying someone you don't know because your niece likes her isn't the answer."

He was quiet for a moment. And then, "I would've asked you out. When you were at the diner. I thought about it. More than once."

"Then why didn't you?"

He let his gaze drop over her. "Because I thought you were too nice for me."

"Too *nice*? How can anyone be *too* nice? That's like saying too rich or too sexy or too smart. They aren't bad things."

"No, not bad things at all."

"I would have gone out with you if you'd asked."

His gaze speared into her again. "And if I ask now?"

Oh shit, oh shit, oh shit.

"I-I don't know." *Jeez, Jenna, tell the man you have to leave.*

"Why not? Because you're living here?"

"Maybe."

"I would have agreed with you before, but I don't anymore. What if we could make something of this? What if my proposal isn't so far-fetched after all? Shouldn't we find out?"

Panic wound through her—but so did heat and happiness. He wanted to explore the possibilities. Part of her wanted it as well. But it was too late.

Yet, what if it wasn't? She'd been so focused on leaving, on changing her identity, that she hadn't stopped to think how well she was hidden in his house. And if she married him and took his name? She could be a suburban mom, not a woman who worked random jobs and worried about being too visible. She'd given up on the idea of ever being a lawyer now, so why not be a mom instead of someone who was always hustling to make a living?

Jenna gave herself a mental shake. She was grasping at straws because a man she found outrageously sexy both inside and out was suddenly expressing interest in her.

"I have to leave," she blurted.

Noah blinked. "You mean leave the conversation right now, or leave as in move out and find another job?"

Jenna's courage faltered as she fumbled for the answer. A buzzer sounded from the kitchen, saving her.

"I mean I have to get the enchiladas out of the oven and fix the salad. Can you watch Alice?"

He nodded, but he was frowning hard as he did so. "Of course."

"Thanks," she called over her shoulder as she hurried inside. She took the casserole from the oven and set it on the stove to cool. Then she sucked in a breath and leaned against the counter, her gaze going to Noah and Alice like a magnet to metal.

She didn't want to leave them. The thought of driving out of their lives and never seeing them again hurt far more than she'd thought possible. But she had to. For all their sakes.

———

NOAH CLEANED up the dinner dishes while Jenna took Alice upstairs for bath time and getting into her PJs. They didn't speak much for the next couple of hours, though Noah played with Alice for a while and then helped tuck her into bed. She wanted a story. But not just any story. A specific book about a puppy who dug a hole under a fence.

Jenna slipped away while Noah read. Alice cut her gaze toward Jenna as she left, but then her attention riveted on Noah until her eyes drooped and she slept soundly. Noah watched her for a few moments.

She looked like Sally, and his heart ached with pain. He missed his sister. He'd missed her for three years. Maybe he'd been wrong to be so hard on her about the pills and drinking, but he'd hated seeing her make the same mistakes again and again.

He hadn't known she'd stop speaking to him, but he should have realized she would. He should have also refused to let it go on for so long, but life got in the way and missions took up a lot of time, and before he knew it he was getting a call that she'd died. He knew her well enough to know that she'd stayed silent because she'd wanted to get back on track and show up again one day with her life together. She'd wanted him to be proud of her.

He'd never get to tell her that he *was* proud of her. Sally had been a survivor, and she'd done so much to keep going. He could tell Alice one day, but only if he was still in her life to do so.

Noah closed his eyes and blew out a soft breath before creeping from the room. He went downstairs, intending to sit on the patio and listen to some music for a while.

He'd made a pretty big mess of things with Jenna. He didn't know why he'd gotten the idea to marry her, but it'd popped into his head and seemed like a solid plan. And, if he had to admit it, it was an easier plan than searching for a family.

That wasn't a good reason to propose to a woman, though. He still thought the idea was sound, even if Jenna had acted like he'd popped a balloon behind her back without warning.

Noah grabbed a beer and went out to light the wood in the fire pit. He got the portable speaker and queued up some Steely Dan, then leaned back and listened as the strains of "Hey, Nineteen" began to play. He'd never managed to change out of his combat boots and uniform pants, but it didn't matter. He was more than accustomed to wearing desert camouflage around the clock.

He heard the screen door open and shut. He smelled her sweet scent as she halted nearby.

"I'm sorry I bailed on the conversation earlier," she said.

He turned his head to look up at her. "It's okay. I came on a bit strong."

"You did, but I understand why." She spread her hands, staring at them for a moment before dropping them again. "You're getting attached to her. I am, too. It'd be hard not to."

"You said that my sister chose me for a reason. You were right." He was silent. "Maybe it was to find her a forever family without letting her go through the foster system, or maybe it was because I'm the only person Sally would trust with her child. I won't ever know which one, quite honestly. She didn't leave any instructions, or I might have had a better idea what her wishes were." He snorted. "She left me a two-year-old without an instruction manual. Just what every single guy needs, right?"

Jenna laughed. "I told you where to find a basic instruction manual."

"You did, and it worked. Want to join me?"

She hesitated, and then she shrugged. "Sure, why not? But I need to get a drink."

He picked up the second beer he'd set on the ground near his chair and twisted off the top. "Here."

She took it. "Thanks."

She dragged a chair over to the pit, diagonally from him so he could see her face, and sat down. She put the baby monitor on the arm of the chair, and he thought once more how lucky he was to have found her when he did.

"I met Sally when we were both thirteen," he said when they'd been sitting in silence for a few minutes. He could tell that Jenna was listening because she slanted a gaze at him while also watching the fire. "She was scrawny, but her eyes speared daggers into anyone who looked at her. As if daring them to try it, you know? I think I must have sensed a kindred spirit…"

He stared at the flickering tongues of flame, remembering the way Sally had looked at him when he'd arrived at the Parker house. Like she'd burn it all down if she got a chance. He'd been intrigued.

"I'd been kicked out of the last foster home I'd been in, and when the Parker family wanted me, the social worker hissed that it was my last chance. I was rebellious and destructive, so that's why I got tossed out of so many homes."

He couldn't believe he was saying these things, but maybe he'd held them in so long that they had to get out. There was nobody else to tell. But it was more than that. Jenna was Alice's nanny. If he wanted her to be more, if he really wanted to keep Alice, then he needed Jenna to know who he was. She'd said she didn't know; he was going to tell her.

"The Parkers took all the tough cases. The children no one else could deal with. They had this image of being a godly, clean-cut, moral family. They were willing to sacrifice their own leisure and peace of mind to help the kids who rebelled and acted out. Saints, they were."

The words were bitter on his tongue. He could feel Jenna watching him. Waiting. Somehow, that gave him the courage to continue.

"You already know they weren't really saints. It's baked into the story, right? Saintly couple taking in orphans and turning them around? But *how* did they turn them around. That's what nobody ever asked."

"Noah," she said, her voice a choked whisper.

He met her gaze. She looked worried. He felt a wave of gratitude for that. "It's okay, Jenna. It's already happened, and it's over. Alan Parker's in prison for abusing little girls. Shirley's doing time for being an accessory. There was other stuff too. Cages, chains, beatings. Threats. They were subtle and they were good."

Jenna dragged her chair over and squeezed his hand. He didn't let go when she tried to pull away again, and she subsided, her hand relaxing in his.

"Sally was being abused when I arrived, but I didn't know it at first. And when I did know, I didn't do anything about it. I didn't know what to do. Not until I was seventeen and finally growing into my gangly body. I filled out that year, got bigger than anyone expected, and I cornered Alan. Threatened to tear him limb from limb if he touched Sally again. If he touched *any* of the girls. He stopped, believe it or not. For a while. But they punished me. Kept me chained to my bed for a week until the truant officer showed up and threatened to get a search warrant. I was back at school the next day."

She squeezed his hand again. "I'm so sorry, Noah."

"I know. Believe me, I know."

"You couldn't tell anyone?"

"Not really. Alan and Shirley were good. They hid all that stuff, and they were pillars of the community. I was a troubled teenager who'd just spent a week skipping school, right? Nobody would have believed me. They'd have thought I was trying to cause trouble for those lovely Parkers." He drew in a breath. "Sally and I shared a bond because of our birthdays at first, and then because of the continuing trauma. She was my sister in every way except genetically."

"I hope those people never get out of prison," Jenna choked. "My God."

He ran his thumb in circles on her wrist. "Thank you. It means a lot. I'm okay. I didn't keep up with the others because it was too hard. I wasn't close to any of them but Sally, and I had my hands full with my own issues and with her after we got away." He sipped his beer. "We lived together for a while, working odd jobs and sharing the bills. I tried to get her to join the Army with me, but she wouldn't. I think the idea of being told what to do, of suffering through boot camp, was too much for her. She was never going to be able to handle that kind of authoritarian control over her life after what she'd been through."

There was a knot in his throat. "She was angry that I joined. That I left her alone. That was our first break,

147

but after I got through boot camp and training and got my first assignment, we were speaking again."

Steely Dan had moved on to "Rikki Don't Lose That Number." He thought of his mother singing that song as she washed dishes. Before she found out about the cancer and stopped singing along to anything.

"I wish I had the right words," Jenna said. "But I don't. People like your foster family should be shot, and kids should *never* suffer the way you and Sally did."

He couldn't help it. He lifted her hand and pressed his mouth to the back of it. He didn't linger, though. He didn't want her to think he was angling for more.

"My only consolation about the Parkers is I'm sure Alan is somebody's bitch now. I intend to go to every parole hearing I can and tell my side of the story. Same for Shirley. She could have stopped it, but all she did was enable. And punish. She loved her goddamn chains and withholding food for transgressions."

"I think you're pretty incredible. And I think I understand how Sally was so broken now. She must have gotten herself together though, because Alice is beautiful and sweet. She's bright, too. She's wary because she lost her mother and got shuffled around, but she's coming out of her shell a lot more lately."

"She trusts you."

"She trusts you, too," Jenna said softly. "You're her Uncle Noah."

He couldn't help but grin despite the sadness that tried to grip his heart and soul. "Yeah, I am." He shook his head and swore. "It's crazy, but I think I love her. That damned fast. I mean I'll do what I have to do to make sure she has the best life, but if I could have it be with me then, yeah, I'm ready to make it happen."

"I don't think it's crazy. I think it's wonderful."

He frowned as he watched the flames flicker. "Realistically, a mom and dad would be better for her."

"Not every kid gets a mom and dad," Jenna said.

"I know. I only had a mom." He raked a hand through his hair. "This is my night for confessions, apparently, because now I have to tell you that I only had a mom and she died of cancer when I was ten. That's how I ended up in foster care. I can't let that happen to Alice."

"You won't. Sally didn't, did she?"

He shook his head. "No. Sally had her issues and her demons, but she was smart." He toyed with her fingers, trying to lighten the mood a little bit. "You sure I can't talk you into marrying me?"

"I don't think you tried to talk me into it at all if you're being honest about it." She let go of his hand and leaned back, sipping her beer. "Why Steely Dan?"

She was right that he hadn't tried very hard to talk her into marrying him. He'd proposed then didn't understand why she wasn't leaping at the opportunity to marry a guy like him with a good job and great benefits.

As if those were his most stellar qualifications. He hadn't even acquainted her with what he could do with his tongue yet.

"I should have known a Tom Petty girl would recognize Steely Dan. My mom loved them. She used to sing their songs to me. I came to Tom later on my own, but

Steely Dan was first. I don't know why, but that was her band."

"Not a bad choice. My mom was a fan too. Dad was as well, but Mom was the bigger fan. I heard plenty of their music growing up too."

"Who was *your* favorite? You must have had one."

"Maroon 5, of course. Adam Levine was so hot. Still is."

"That skinny dude? Seriously?"

Jenna laughed. "Oh come on—his torso is as ripped as yours."

"Hardly," Noah said, enjoying teasing her. "He's got a bunch of bad boy tattoos, I'll grant you. But no. Just no."

She was still laughing. "Okay, fine. He's a sissy boy compared to you. Now tell me your favorite growing up."

"3 Doors Down."

"Oh, I liked them too," she said softly. "Very angsty. "Kryptonite" was so good."

"Yep. I needed an emotional outlet back then, and they were perfect. I liked "Kryptonite" like everyone else, but "Loser" was my theme song for a long time. I eventually learned to channel all that anger and self-hate into something good… And here I am."

She stood abruptly and he thought she was going to go back inside. But then she was standing over him, gripping his face in both hands. A moment later, her lips crashed down on his.

Chapter Thirteen

She couldn't take another moment.

Literally. Could. Not.

Noah Cross was an amazing man, and yet he had this shitty past that had made him and his sister into damaged human beings who hadn't deserved what was done to them. He wasn't a loser, and the fact he'd identified with that song so strongly as a kid made her ache. She knew the lyrics, and it gutted her to think of him playing that song on repeat, identifying with it.

Maybe that was the reason why she'd felt compelled to go to him, why she forced his head back, and why she kissed him. Why she *was* kissing him.

Whatever the reason, she didn't want to stop. She wanted to sink into him and not come up for air until this humming beneath her skin had stopped.

Her tongue swept into his mouth and he groaned. He tasted a little like beer and a lot like heaven. Her heart pounded in her chest as her body sizzled. Her temperature was spiking into the danger zone.

He didn't touch her at first, as if he expected her to come to her senses and stop, but then he did. And holy hell, she'd been insane to think she was the one in control. He wrapped strong arms around her and tugged her into his lap until she straddled him. She sank down, knees on either side of him, body trembling.

His belt buckle was hard—but his cock was harder where it snugged against the most sensitive part of her. If she jerked her hips back and forth just a tiny bit, she could make herself come from the pressure.

His broad hands splayed against her back, pulling her into him as his tongue met hers. Their mouths fused hotly, lips sucking and nipping, tongues thrusting, devouring.

His hands slid around to her front, cupping her breasts. He didn't squeeze or grope or do anything that made her recoil. He gripped her firmly, his thumbs sliding across her nipples. Teasing lightly. Asking for permission to go farther.

Did she want to give it to him? She imagined herself climbing into Lola and driving away very soon—and, yes, she wanted Noah to touch her. Just once at least.

She jerked his shirt from his waistband and spread her hands on hot skin and firm muscle. He must have gotten the message because he unbuttoned her shirt with deft hands and pushed it open. Then he tugged the cups of her bra down until her breasts mounded over them, her nipples hardening into tight little peaks.

Her heart hammered as she explored his torso, tracing her fingers over all the ridges and dips of hard muscle. He broke the kiss and trailed his mouth down the column of her neck, over her collarbone, down the slope of her chest until his tongue darted over her nipple.

Her body was incandescent with heat. Arousal was an aching pain in her center as Noah sucked a nipple into his mouth and tugged lightly. Jenna gasped at the lightning streaking through her.

It'd been a long time since she'd had sex, and though a part of her brain told her she shouldn't be doing this, another part said, *What the hell?* She liked the *what the hell* part best right now.

Noah sucked both nipples until she squirmed in his lap, until she craved the part of him he hadn't given her yet. The part she could feel beneath her, insistently solid and real.

She'd given in and started moving her hips against him, riding that ridge of pleasure, when he took his mouth away. She didn't realize it at first, until the night air on her wet nipples made her eyes pop open. He gently replaced the cups of her bra, covering her, as she stared down at him in disbelief.

His gaze was troubled when his eyes met hers. "You have no idea how much I want this," he said. "How much I want you. But I feel like it's taking advantage of the situation. I didn't tell you about my past to soften you up for sex."

Jenna blinked as fresh heat flooded her. This wasn't the heat of arousal though. It was the combined heat of embarrassment and anger.

"I can make my own decisions, Noah."

"I realize that, but can you tell me honestly that you would have made the same decision if I hadn't just told you my sob story?"

She frowned as his words echoed through her head. "Maybe not at this very moment, but it's not like you magically made me want you. That was already a thing."

He leaned back to gaze up at her. Her pussy ached with the need to keep moving, but she didn't. He reached up to brush a finger against her cheek.

"Already a thing, huh?"

"Don't pretend like you didn't know. I've been attracted to you since the first time you sat at my table. I'm not the only one, by the way. Tami would be pleased to perform her farm animal impersonations for you whenever you're ready."

He chuckled. "No thanks. Not into the barnyard thing."

"You'd be surprised how many guys are," she said, feeling self-conscious and achy. And awkward since she wasn't sure what to do with herself now.

"Actually, I wouldn't. If a guy's horny, he'll put up with a lot to get some."

"You say that, but I don't think you would."

"Nope. I can afford to be picky."

She didn't know why, but that pierced her. Like maybe he was being picky now. Like she wasn't good enough for a sexy Special Operator.

"Whoa, whoa, whoa," he said, studying her. She

dropped her gaze and he tipped her chin up with his fingers. "Me putting a stop to this is not me being picky. It's me not taking advantage of your kind heart. It's me making sure you know I didn't say all that stuff to make you feel sorry for me and want to soothe me with sex."

His gaze dropped to her chest. Her shirt still hung open, though her bra was back in place now. "I'm regretting my nobility, trust me. I could have you naked in my bed right now. Believe me, that's a thing I want very much."

He reached up and started to button her shirt and she tried not to feel hurt by it. He'd said he wanted her. He just didn't want to take advantage of her. "Tomorrow," he said, his voice sounding a little hoarse. "If you still want this tomorrow, I'll be with you all the way."

Jenna started to stand, but Noah held onto her hand. "Stay with me? I wouldn't mind the company."

He confused her, but she nodded and shifted until she could sit sideways on his lap. He pulled her back against him, and she lay against his broad chest, looking up at the stars as the music softly played. It was warm and comfortable—and it felt right.

For the first time in months, she felt as if all the tension was draining right out of her. The fear wouldn't simply disappear as if it'd never happened, but it could take a backseat while she cuddled into the strong body of an alpha protector and felt like no one could harm her while he held onto her.

But like all good things, it wasn't going to last.

———

JENNA BLINKED AWAKE, feeling as if something was off. Sunlight streamed through the curtains and she jerked upright. Her stomach sank as she realized she'd overslept. Somehow.

She was late getting Alice, and the little girl was certainly ready to be fed by now if the strength of the sunlight was any indication.

Jenna groped for the baby monitor as she threw the covers back. When she was on her feet and searching for her yoga pants, she realized she still had on her shorts from yesterday.

And her shirt. The buttons were done up and the material was wrinkled as hell. She'd slept in her clothes? How much beer had she had anyway?

It took her a few moments, as she stumbled through brushing her teeth, to realize what must have happened. She hadn't gotten drunk. She'd fallen asleep on Noah when she'd been sitting in his lap. The soft strains of Steely Dan had been filling the air, and she'd been looking up at the stars with Noah's warm breath close to her ear.

"Oh jeez," she moaned. She didn't bother to change as she dashed toward Alice's room. The baby monitor wasn't on her bedside table, which meant she must have left it downstairs. She pushed the door open to Alice's room and stopped cold.

The bed was empty. Jenna stared, fear swirling to life in her belly. Had the toddler climbed out of the crib? Had she made her way downstairs?

Shit!

Jenna took the stairs two at a time and skidded into the kitchen. Noah looked up from his seat at the table. Alice swung her head around from her high chair. Both of them looked at her like she was a crazy woman.

"I, uh, I overslept."

"You seemed like you needed it," Noah said. "I gave her some yogurt and cheese. She liked it. She wore a lot of the yogurt on her face and hands, though. But at least I'm not wearing any."

He grinned, and she felt like she'd entered an alternate universe. "Good. I'm glad. Though not about the yogurt. I can clean her up."

"I already took care of it. Just needed to wipe her face and hands."

Jenna huffed a breath. "I'm sorry I wasn't up in time to get her."

He shrugged. "It's Saturday. And I'm an early riser, regardless. I was up, so I took care of it."

"I think I left the baby monitor outside." Heat bloomed across her skin at the reference to last night and what they'd been doing. Which was silly because she was a grown woman and if she wanted to let a man suck her nipples, then she was well within her rights.

She'd wanted to let him do a lot more than that but, alas, he'd had to be noble.

"I have it. I took it to bed last night, just in case."

"But that's my job."

"You get time off, Jenna. And once you fell asleep on me, I realized you really needed the rest. So I didn't wake you."

"Did you carry me to bed?"

He nodded. "Hey, sit down. Want some coffee?"

She couldn't believe he'd carried her up the stairs and she'd never known it. How had she not awakened? Was he that strong that he could carry an adult human up a staircase like they weighed nothing?

Apparently so.

"I should shower," she said, hooking her thumb over her shoulder.

He got up and poured a cup of coffee. Then he added sugar and cream like she preferred. "Here, take a cup up with you. I'll fix breakfast when you get back."

"Breakfast? You cook?"

"Well, yeah. How do you think I survived before you came along?"

"Restaurants?" she joked.

He laughed. "Those too. I can fix you a full breakfast, or maybe a bagel with cream cheese? You tell me."

"A bagel sounds great."

"Go shower. We'll talk when you get back."

She took the coffee and fled.

———

ALICE WAS on the floor playing with her toys, though she kept bringing them over to him every couple of minutes. He didn't know what to do, so he praised her. That seemed to make her happy. She kept doing it until Noah thought he'd lose his mind, but then she got engrossed with pressing the buttons of one of the educational toys they'd gotten her, and her need for immediate attention stopped.

Was this what Jenna went through every day? No wonder she'd been exhausted last night.

Noah looked up as he heard her coming down the stairs. Jenna had piled her hair on her head as usual, but this time she wore a dress. It wasn't fancy, just a sundress with tiny little flowers all over, but it was feminine and pretty. Her feet were bare, and he imagined himself tracing the line of them with his fingers before opening her legs and sinking deep inside her body.

He'd have tugged the dress from her shoulders, exposing her breasts, and he'd have the skirt up around her waist. She'd still be in the dress, but she'd be exposed to him. And he'd take full advantage, giving her so much pleasure she would end up boneless in his arms at the end of it.

His balls tightened, and he had to push the image of a tousled and thoroughly fucked Jenna Lane away. If he didn't, she'd know where his mind was pretty quickly since he still wore athletic shorts and they'd turn into a tent.

"Feel better?" he asked.

"Yes, thanks. And thank you for letting me sleep."

He took her coffee mug and motioned for her to sit while he refilled it. She hesitated, but then she did. He gave it to her and started work on the bagel. "Like I said, you seemed to need it."

"I guess so. I didn't realize."

"That's how sleep deficits work," he told her as he grabbed the cream cheese from the fridge. "You survive on less sleep than usual until you can't anymore. Then your body catches up all at once and you feel like you've been asleep for six days. Or maybe that's just me after a mission. Still, that's what happens. You sleep, and your body is refreshed."

"I didn't sleep well at Tami's place. Between the sexcapades and the pot smoke, it wasn't a restful environment."

He slathered cream cheese onto the bagel, put it on a plate, and set it in front of her. Then he sat down across from her. The sunlight brightened the kitchen and made her look almost as if she had a halo as she sat with her back partially to the window.

"Sexcapades, huh?"

She bit into the food, chewed and swallowed a small bite. "Oh yes. Tami loooooves to, er, do the nasty," she said, throwing a glance at Alice. "I mean she must, right? She was always bringing guys home, always screaming and grunting and losing her shi—mind in the other room. The things I heard her say." Jenna shook her head. "There's nothing wrong with a woman who loves to get it on a regular basis, and more power to her, but I swear she'd ride anything with a, uh, stiff one."

Noah laughed. He couldn't help it. Hearing her talk about her roommate, while trying to keep it sanitized for the little ears that didn't seem to be paying the least bit of attention but would probably start shouting *fuck* or *dick* at the top of her lungs the next time they were in public, was fricking hilarious.

"What kind of things?" he asked.

Jenna's eyes widened a bit for emphasis. "Can't say it. Little ears."

Noah leaned forward. "So whisper it to me."

"You can't be serious."

"I'm serious. I want to know what Barnyard Tami says in the throes."

"A lot of stuff," Jenna said, lowering her voice, leaning in. "But things like 'Fuck my cunt til it squeals, big daddy,' and 'bring it home to mama, you big-dicked motherfucker,' along with 'pound that pussy like you stole it,' are some of her better ones."

Noah snort-laughed. He couldn't help it. "Pound that pussy like you stole it? Til it squeals?"

"Meanwhile, she's squealing so loud it's a wonder the dude has any eardrums left. Sometimes, they squeal with her. I am *so* glad to be out of there."

Noah leaned back, watching her eat, feeling a bit aroused at those words—no matter how ridiculous—coming out of her mouth. "And I had to talk you into taking the job I offered. How is that possible? You really wanted to stay?"

She shook her head. "No, of course not. I just felt obligated, you know? Like I didn't want to leave her in the lurch. But then she needed me to cover her portion of the rent again, and I thought I was looking at a trend rather than a temporary setback since it'd happened last month too. With Allison firing me, I figured it was time."

"Lucky for me and Alice then."

She gave him a shy smile, and somewhere deep inside him a light flared to life. He *liked* being around her. And not just because she had fabulous nipples he wanted to suck again as soon as possible.

Noah shifted in his chair. *No nipples. No tongues. No sex thoughts.*

Easier said than done, but he managed it. He had incredible self-discipline, honed through years of foster care and then the military. He could wait as long as it took for the time to be right when he wanted something.

His phone pinged and he picked it up to glance casually. It could be a message from his team leader, telling him to get ready because they were about to be deployed. Except it wasn't. It was Mal. He read the text then read it again.

"You want to go to a party at Mal's place today?"

"Mal… The one who got injured in the leg, right?"

"That's him. He's engaged to Scarlett. You may have met her at the diner. I think they came out a time or two together. Anyway, they're having a spur of the moment cookout and we're invited. It starts at four. We can be out of there by seven so we can get Alice to bed."

She swallowed her bite of bagel. "I could bring her home if you wanted to stay."

"I won't want to stay. I want to be with you and Alice. We can sit by the fire again after she's in bed, or watch a movie."

He felt like maybe he was trying too hard. But then she dropped her gaze before slanting that shy smile at him again. "Okay. It sounds like fun."

"Which part?"

She pretended to consider it. "All of it, really. But sitting by the fire with you, listening to some Petty and talking about whatever—well, I think that sounds like a perfect end to the day."

He could think of an even more perfect end than that. One thing at a time, though.

One thing at a time.

Chapter Fourteen

NOAH'S FRIENDS MADE HER FEEL RIGHT AT HOME. JENNA had gotten out of his Jeep, unbuckled Alice from her car seat, and perched her on a hip. She'd intended to walk into the backyard at Mal and Scarlett's place holding Alice, but Noah took Alice and led the way, which didn't give Jenna anything to fill her hands with.

She needn't have worried about her reception. She'd met some of the guys at the diner when Noah brought them over there a couple of times. Gem, Muffin, Zany, and Mal. The others she had not.

There was Wolf, who was with a woman named Haylee, a gorgeous woman with curly black hair and a baby bump, who worked as a reporter. There was Saint, who was with Brooke. She turned out to be the Brooke that Noah had mentioned that time Jenna told herself not to get jealous. A man named Hacker was with a gorgeous, expensive-looking woman named Bliss. Mal and Scarlett were hosting.

They all talked and laughed and joked with the ease

of people who had known each other for a long time, and they somehow managed to include her in their conversations without making it awkward. The men inevitably split off to play a game of volleyball while the women sat around a table in the backyard and monitored the grill. Alice was the only child, but she was passed around and treated like a visiting princess by everyone there. Bliss was the only one who didn't seem all that comfortable with a child, but she tried to show enthusiasm when Alice handed her a rock.

"Oh my goodness, what's this?" she asked, her expensively manicured nails a sharp contrast to the ordinary piece of gravel.

"Wock!" Alice said.

"It's a nice rock. What are you going to do with it?"

Alice didn't say anything as she took the rock out of Bliss's open palm. She went over and put it in a pile with some others she'd found. Bliss shrugged as she caught Jenna's eye. "Kids don't like me all that much."

Jenna smiled. "She likes you fine. She brought you the rock, right?"

"That's true, I guess. I think I was just convenient."

Haylee curved her hand over her small bump. "I don't have a clue what I'm doing, but Wolf and I will figure it out together. Our kid will either be well-adjusted or a hot mess. I'm not sure which yet."

Brooke laughed. "Seriously, with you and Wolf as parents, I think your kid will be just fine. You're both smart and beautiful, plus he's athletic, so there you go."

"Hey, I'm athletic too. Just not right now."

Bliss arched a brow. "Really? I've never seen you

break into a jog, much less any other feats of athleticism."

Haylee stuck out her tongue. "I trekked across the jungle the night I met Wolf. We also swam a piranha-infested river."

"Were there really piranhas?" Brooke asked, wide-eyed.

Haylee laughed. "I don't know, but it sounds good. We were in South America, after all."

Jenna wanted to know more, but Scarlett let out a low whistle. "Oh my, speaking of athletic." Scarlett's gaze had moved to where the men congregated.

"Whoa," Bliss said, turning her head. "I never tire of that."

"No red-blooded heterosexual woman does," Haylee laughed.

Jenna was inclined to agree. The men had taken off their shirts as they played a rousing game, slapping the ball, spiking it, calling insults to each other. Noah, aka Easy, played with Gem, Muffin, and Zany. They were playing against Saint, Wolf, Mal, and Hacker.

Tattoos rippled across lean muscle. Abs were tight enough to bounce a quarter off. Shoulders and biceps screamed, *I can carry you across a battlefield and not break a sweat, darlin'.*

"Where are Jake and Eva?" Bliss asked Scarlett.

"They went up to Jake's cabin in Virginia for the weekend. I think there might be a proposal or something."

"Ooooooh," the women said in unison.

Haylee leaned over. "Jake is the only Strike Team 2

member not here. Eva is his girlfriend. She's an absolutely amazing tattoo artist, if you're looking. She's done some of the ink for the guys."

"Oh, wow. Thanks." Jenna smiled, though her brain had latched on to the Strike Team 2 designation. What did that mean? "You know, I've never really considered a tattoo. Too scared of needles."

Haylee laughed. "You and me both, girlfriend. Wolf has a few, as you can see. And don't get me wrong, they are gorgeous and I love exploring them. But it's not my thang."

"Food's almost ready," Scarlett said, checking the grill again.

Jenna saw hamburgers on one side and chicken on the other when Scarlett lifted the lid. It smelled heavenly. It also made her think of her parents. Her dad had loved to grill, and her mom would fix all the sides—with Jenna's help—before they converged on the patio to eat. Didn't matter if it was Germany or Italy or Hawaii or the desert, they spent time outside with a fresh breeze and a full belly.

A wave of homesickness rolled over her, but for what? For a memory. A dream. Something that was gone and would never happen again.

"Maybe we should tell them to wind it down," Bliss said.

Brooke was busy staring at Saint. "Don't you dare."

Haylee laughed. "You're horny, aren't you?"

Brooke giggled. "Always when I've got Cade to go home to. Plus I think I'm ovulating, which shouldn't matter a damned bit except for you, Haylee. Making a woman think about kids with your cute little baby bump."

"Puh-lease, girlfriend. Your bestie has a baby, and that's what's got you thinking. Not me."

"Maybe so," Brooke admitted. "I also babysat Alice before Jenna was here, so it's no wonder I'm thinking of little girls with pigtails."

Scarlett closed the lid with a snap. "Ladies, I don't care how hot you are for your men, I will not burn the food. I've been entrusted with the sacred grill, as Mal calls it, and I will not fail my quest. Get your minds back on task and off your men's hot bodies. Only consider babies when sober and unaffected by the most amazing male torsos known to humankind."

Brooke laughed again. "Right, right, right. Must focus."

Jenna loved how easy these women were with each other. "Sorry, Brooke," she said. "I didn't know Noah had a babysitter when I took the job."

Brooke reached out and grasped her hand. "Oh, honey, no. Alice needed a nanny, and you're perfect. She's clearly attached to you."

Jenna felt a little spear of guilt. "She needed a constant in her life, poor thing. But I'm not her mother, nor do I pretend to be."

"Of course not," Brooke said. "Still, she needed stability, as you say. Hopefully Easy will get married someday and she'll have a mommy."

Jenna didn't say a word about Noah's plan—former plan?—to adopt Alice out. She just nodded, murmuring, "Yes. That would be so nice."

She could feel the women's speculative gazes on her, but she pretended not to notice them. If they only knew he'd asked her to marry him last night, they'd probably lose their minds. Of course it wasn't for love or anything, which made it a lot less romantic, but still. He'd asked, and that would be enough to give them plenty to discuss.

"Easy said your parents were military," Brooke said, smiling. Digging, more like. But she was so sweet and disarming that Jenna wasn't bothered.

"They were in the Air Force. Dad was a Senior Master Sergeant and Mom was a Lieutenant Colonel. They're gone now. Plane crash."

Brooke squeezed her hand. She was an effusive woman, but Jenna didn't mind. "I'm so sorry."

Jenna's cheeks ached from smiling as if it didn't still steal just a bit of her soul when she talked about her parents being gone. "Thank you. I'm sorry, I didn't mean to bring the mood down. I just always feel like I need to explain."

"No explanations necessary," Scarlett said. "My parents are gone too. I think I understand just a little how you feel."

"I'm sorry for your loss," Jenna replied automatically.

"Thank you. I didn't mean to shift the conversation to me—I just wanted you to know that I understand." She came over and gave Jenna a quick hug. "You're with friends here. You'll be in Alice and Easy's lives for a while and we want you to know you can count on us, especially when the team is gone."

"Does it happen often?" Jenna asked, feeling brave enough to voice that much.

Bliss's expression was solemn. "It depends. More often than you probably expect, but not so often you forget what he looks like. It's lonely, I won't lie—but what am I saying?" She waved a hand as if waving away a fly, and Jenna knew it was also to wave away tears. "You aren't a couple. It won't be the same."

Jenna's belly twisted. "No, we aren't a couple."

"If you need help with Alice while Noah's gone, call me," Brooke said. "I don't mind helping so you can have some personal time."

"Thank you. I will."

"I'll tell Noah to give you my number."

"Okay, y'all," Scarlett interrupted, looking at the food on the grill. "I've timed this perfectly. The meat is done. Strike Team 2," she yelled over her shoulder. "Get your shirts back on and let's eat!"

————

IT WAS after eight when they climbed into Noah's Jeep to head home. Alice was sound asleep in her car seat, and Jenna was quiet as they drove toward Mystic Cove. The sun had set a little while before, but pink still tinged the sky in the west. It was a typically beautiful Maryland summer's night, and Noah was feeling pensive and restless.

"I'm sorry we're later than I thought we'd be," he said. "I thought we'd be home in time to bathe her and put her to bed."

Jenna turned toward him. "It's okay. It was a fun evening. She's sound asleep, so I'll just put her to bed and give her a bath in the morning."

"Did you like hanging out with everyone? Or should I put an X beside this activity for the future?"

He wanted her to like his friends. His brothers-in-arms and their women. It mattered more than he'd thought it would. He also wanted them to like her, but he thought he was good on that score.

"Your friends are great, Noah. The women—they made me feel like one of them. I think they were careful not to say too much, but I gleaned a little from the conversation. About what you do, I mean."

"Oh." He'd expected that might happen. Jenna wasn't dumb.

"Haylee mentioned a jungle adventure the night she met Wolf, and a swim in a piranha-infested river. Not your typical meet cute."

"Meet cute?"

"It's the scene where a couple meets for the first time in a movie or novel. It's not always cute, but it's called that. I don't know why."

"Okay. Something I did not know."

"Maybe read a romance novel or two. Or watch just about any Sandra Bullock film."

"You mean it's a meet cute when she meets Keanu on a bus that can't stop or it'll blow up?"

"Yep, you got it. Great movie, by the way."

"Hell yes, it is. Set my expectations for the kind of girl I wanted to meet someday."

She was laughing now. He loved hearing her laugh.

"Oh, you wanted to meet the kind of girl who could jump a bus over a giant gap in a bridge and successfully land it?"

He aimed a finger gun at her. "Got it in one."

"You're hilarious, Noah Cross. But you didn't distract me a bit. Haylee and Wolf met when your team rescued her from a jungle in South America."

No use denying it. Jenna knew better because she knew more about the military than the average person. It'd be hard to fool her. "Yeah, that's about right."

"Not a Green Beret. Delta Force?"

"No."

"What then? I'm at a loss."

"Saint said this might happen." He sighed. Saint had told him to tell her what he had to in order to make her understand. And to keep it quiet. "I can't tell you much, but I work for the Hostile Operations Team. It's a Black Ops organization that works directly for the president—much like Delta. You go around talking about it though, and you're going to find yourself in a window-less room with a light shining in your face and some angry people interrogating you about your loyalties."

"Wow. Okay. Don't want that experience, *thankyouverymuch*."

"Nobody does."

"I won't talk, Noah. Dad was in civil engineering, but Mom was an Intel officer. I understand better than most what to say and what not to say. OPSEC is a word I grew up with," she said, using the military abbreviation for operational security, "so you don't have to worry about me."

"That's good. We used to be so deep nobody knew our name. But congressional budgets and all that crap—well, we're known like Delta is known. But who's in, where we go, the things we do—top secret. Haylee should have known better, probably, but that kind of thing is an open secret among the women who love a HOT operator. She wasn't thinking about how you differ."

"Right."

She dropped her gaze to her lap and didn't say anything else. He began to wonder if he'd said something wrong, but then they were in Mystic Cove and he didn't know how to get her to talk again. A few minutes later, he pulled into the driveway and shut off the engine.

He unbuckled Alice and carried her upstairs while Jenna brought up the rear with the gear. They undressed her and tucked her in bed, and his heart twisted at the feelings swirling inside him at the sight of a sleeping toddler. Alice was work, but she was also innocent, adorable, and she didn't deserve anything less than everything he could give her.

The idea of finding a family for her died a quiet death as a shaft of moonlight crept across the bed and onto her sleeping form. The baby powder and diaper smells of her room invaded his senses as confusion and a tentative happiness blossomed in his heart.

He didn't have a single fucking clue how to make this work. Not one. But he knew he had to. Somehow.

Jenna touched his shoulder, and warmth flooded him. "You okay?"

"Yeah. Fine."

He stood, towering over her, but she didn't back away. She gazed up at him with concern and—maybe? —anticipation.

"This is the moment when I tell you that you should go to your room," he said in a deep, growly voice. "Because if you stay, I plan to kiss you. And if I kiss you, I plan to get inside you and make you come as many times as I can. I can't deny it's what I want any longer. If you don't want it too, then walk away now and I won't mention it again. Because I need you, Jenna. Alice needs you. But right now, I need you in ways that aren't a part of what I asked you to come here for. Walk away if it's not what you want too."

He thought she was trembling, but he wasn't sure. Another moment, and she stepped into him, wrapping her arms around his waist and tilting her head back to meet his gaze. "Kiss me, Noah. Kiss me and make me forget everything but you."

Chapter Fifteen

His mouth met hers, and Jenna sighed. She wasn't the kind of woman who hopped into bed with a man, never had been, but she knew herself well enough to know she'd regret it if she didn't go there with Noah.

Probably didn't help that she'd watched him playing volleyball, sweat glistening against his rippling muscles as he jumped into the air. He and the other guys had hosed off when they were done, and he'd come to the table with wet hair and sparkling eyes as he'd laughed with his friends.

They'd eaten good food, shared stories, and laughed until Alice cuddled up in Jenna's lap and fell asleep. Noah had announced it was time for them to go, and everyone got up to hug them and walk them to the Jeep.

Jenna liked it more than she had thought she would. It felt like being a part of a family. Like the kind of good memories she had of being at bases with her parents, them hosting get togethers or attending them, hanging out with people who understood each other because they were in the same boat.

Maybe that was why she'd told Noah to kiss her, or maybe it was simply the desire to be close to someone for a little while before she had to be alone again. The idea of walking away from this place—from Noah and Alice—was like a dagger twisting in her soul. The more time she spent with them, the worse it was.

Noah kissed her gently. More gently than she would have thought based on what he'd said to her before she'd asked him to do so. His tongue slid into her mouth, teased hers, made her seek him out.

His palms skimmed her sides, glided around to her ass, and squeezed softly. Her body reacted with a flood of heat and wetness. She wrapped her arms around his neck and arched into him, pressing against all the hard angles of his body.

And then he bent and swept her up with no effort at all. He kept kissing her as he carried her from Alice's room. She reached for the doorknob and shut the door gently, then he was moving again, knocking his bedroom door open with a foot and carrying her to his bed. There was a light that burned in the hall and spilled into his room, illuminating the bed.

He fell onto the mattress with her, cushioning her fall with his arms and making sure he didn't land hard on top of her.

Jenna's heart pounded and her head swam dizzily at the speed this was happening. He'd told her that if they kissed, they'd end up in bed together. Still, she hadn't expected it to happen quite so suddenly. Then again, was it sudden if they'd been heading this direction for the past few weeks?

She'd burned with hot need just thinking about him. Had he been thinking about her too?

Noah broke the kiss and moved downward, licking a trail of fire across her skin. His fingers found the buttons of her sundress, flicking them open one by one before he pushed it off her shoulders. Her bra went with it until her breasts were exposed. Noah lifted up on an elbow to grin down at her.

"That's what I wanted to see again." He traced a finger around one nipple, and it beaded beneath his touch. "Pink. I wondered for the longest time. Would they be pink or darker? I found out last night, and I've been imagining since."

He pinched her nipple softly between his fingers, and Jenna gasped. She was exposed and vulnerable while he remained clothed.

And yet she felt safe. She didn't feel as if she was in danger, or that he was taking monstrous advantage of her. She was curious, needy. She reached for the hem of his T-shirt and he helped her tug it up and off. And then he bent down to suck a nipple into his mouth and Jenna gasped.

"Noah. Oh…"

He cupped her other breast, tweaking her nipple while he sucked. She curled her fingers into his arms, holding on while he sent her sailing toward paradise.

A moment later he captured her mouth again, kissing her harder this time. Deeper and more insistent.

He slid her dress up her thighs before hooking his fingers into her panties and tugging them down.

"I want to lick you," he whispered in her ear. "You cool with that?"

He had to ask? Jenna swallowed and nodded before managing to find her voice. "Yes."

She'd have to ask later if he'd encountered anyone who'd said no. Then again, did she really want to know about his experience with other women?

Probably not.

Noah slipped down the bed until he was between her legs. Her dress was bunched at her waist, but she hardly cared as he pushed her legs open. He traced a finger along the wet seam of her body and her back bowed off the bed.

"So wet," he purred. "I fucking love it."

Then his mouth dropped to place a kiss on her mound before his tongue glided down the path his finger had taken.

"Oh my God," Jenna moaned. And then she had to hold on—literally hold on to the blanket beneath her— as Noah showed her what was possible when a man knew exactly when and where and how to use his tongue.

She had no time to prepare for it. She came in a gasping, moaning rush, body shaking as she rode the edge of the wave, as Noah drove her into an orgasm so perfect she saw stars. She closed her eyes tight, letting herself feel everything. Letting herself go.

When she opened her eyes again, he was looking up

at her, grinning like he'd just won the lottery or something.

"Feel good?"

Part of her thought she should be embarrassed. She wasn't though. She was thrilled. She grinned back, and she knew her whole heart was in it.

"Oh hell, yes."

"Want another?"

She couldn't help but laugh at the question. "Um, *yes*." She reached down and ran her fingers through his hair. She'd wanted to touch him, but she'd been too focused on what he was doing to her.

"I aim to please, Ms. Lane," he said before licking her clit again.

Jenna's entire body jerked, and he reached out to hold her in place before she could close her legs. She wanted to protest, and she didn't at the same time. But it soon didn't matter because she was moaning again, lifting her hips to ride his amazing mouth, moving herself to get the most pleasure from what he did to her.

It didn't take long to explode. She stiffened and jerked as wave after wave of pleasure rolled over her. This time when he finished, Noah crawled up her body, kissing his way along her skin. He sucked her nipples in turn, then stood and stripped out of his cargo shorts and briefs.

Jenna sat up before he could join her again. His cock was hard, of course. Big. She reached for him, wrapped a hand around his hot flesh, and squeezed. He groaned, biting down on his lower lip, and though it should have been impossible, she grew even wetter.

He didn't stop her as she licked the tip and tasted the drop of precum that resided there. She took him in her mouth, and he stiffened as he let her play.

It didn't last long, though, because he gently pushed her back onto the bed again before reaching into the nightstand and pulling out a condom packet. She didn't let herself be disappointed or stupidly jealous or anything.

It was Noah's house, he was a responsible man, and of course he'd had women in his bedroom before. Women he'd fucked the way he was about to fuck her.

Don't care, she told herself. So long as he gave all his attention to her right now, that's what mattered. And tomorrow?

Well, tomorrow would be interesting. She might very well pack up and go, or she might stay in his bed if he asked her to. She simply didn't know what the emotional fallout would be, or how she was going to react.

She started to pull her dress the rest of the way off as he rolled on the condom. "Don't," he said. "Please. I've fantasized all day about this. About you in that dress, how sexy you'd look with it bunched around your waist while I made you come."

She let her hands fall away. "Okay."

He knelt between her legs, his gaze slowly moving from her face to her pussy and back again, his fingers following the path. "There's something about you, Jenna. Something I wasn't expecting, but that I can't stop thinking about."

Her heart hitched. "I'm sorry."

His body dropped down over hers, and he hooked

her leg and spread it wide to wrap around his hip. "Don't be. I'm not."

And then his mouth sank onto hers. He kissed her sweetly as his cock nudged her entrance before he shifted his hips and entered her. He took his time, which she was grateful for, but her body didn't offer much resistance. When he was inside her fully, she could feel his heart against her chest, beating strong and hard. Hers beat harder, but she didn't think he knew it.

He lifted up on an elbow to look down at her. "You okay?"

"I am. You?"

"No, not really. I want to fuck you until the bed shakes and your moans fill the room, but I don't want to wake Alice."

Something inside her melted at that. He was a man buried inside a woman, but he was thinking about the toddler in the next room. "I'm sure we can manage something. I'll moan quietly. But no bed shaking."

He laughed. "This is a first. Don't think I've ever joked with a woman when I was balls deep inside her before."

Jenna ran her palms over his shoulders and down his thick biceps. *So sexy.*

"There's a first time for everything, right? Let's see how far we can go before the headboard bangs the wall."

He started to move, and Jenna bit her lip to keep from moaning too loudly at the feeling of his cock dragging against the bundle of nerves behind her clit. He increased his pace and she gripped his biceps hard, holding on for the ride. The first time the headboard hit the wall, he swore and slowed again. Jenna could have cried because the feeling had been so perfect—

But it was still perfect. He found the right rhythm, the right pace. They moved together, bodies rising and falling, breaths mingling as their mouths met, sucking and nipping and playing. Time seemed to slow, or maybe it disappeared entirely. All she knew was that she loved every moment of this. It'd been a long time since she'd been with a man, but it hadn't been this good.

Had it ever been this good? She doubted it. Noah seemed to know, instinctively, how to move to make her feel the most pleasure. The sensations inside her grew stronger, the pressure winding tighter as he angled his hips and drove into her just hard enough to make it happen.

"Noah," she cried out as the pressure shattered inside her. "Please… like that… oh God…"

Jenna squeezed her eyes shut as her orgasm slammed into her. She had to put her mouth on his shoulder to keep from making too much noise. He didn't let her come down from the high, though. He kept rocking into her as she shuddered—and then he stiffened, his cock pulsing inside her.

"Oh shit, I'm coming," he groaned. "I didn't want it yet, wanted to make you come again…"

She held onto him while he came, framing his face with her hands and capturing his mouth. He kissed her hard, feeding her the moans in his throat until the tremors subsided.

He propped himself on his elbows to gaze down at

her, still hard and still deep inside her, and she shimmied just a bit in order to send another lightning bolt streaking through her.

Noah gasped as she did so, then moaned. "Oh goddamn, that's good. And almost too much."

She stopped moving. "I know, right?"

"I'd ask if you're okay, but I think you're just fine based on that little move."

"Very fine, thanks." She grinned.

He grinned back. "I was worried it might be awkward after."

"Oh, I'm sure there will be moments of awkwardness. Like in the morning when we see each other at breakfast."

"See each other at breakfast? Do you plan to leave me here and go back to your room? I feel so used."

She couldn't help but laugh at his mock offended tone. "I thought that's what you'd want."

His gaze dropped to her naked breasts. "What I want is more you. More of this. Can you handle that, or do you prefer to sleep in your own bed?"

She skimmed a finger over his mouth. Such a masculine mouth, and so good at licking her just right. "I'm not sure what the rules are," she told him honestly. "I don't want it to be weird. I don't want you thinking I expect a relationship because we've had sex, but I also want more sex. Lots of sex, actually. It's been a while."

He shifted his hips, and she had an intense desire to push him over and ride him hard. Tami would be so proud.

"I'm prepared to give you all the sex you can handle.

But don't plant the thought of you with another man in my head because I don't want to think about it."

She liked how possessive he sounded, but she also had to say something. Maybe this was where it all fell apart and Noah Cross turned into a jerk. "You think women should be virginal while men should have all the experience?"

"What? No." He shook his head for emphasis. "I like an experienced lover. I just don't want to think about how you got that experience *right now*. I might start wondering how I compare. That's never good for a man's ego."

She skimmed her palm down his arm, enjoying the hard feel of it. "I'm pretty sure you're in the top five, but I'll need another demonstration to be sure."

"Only the top five? Damn. Guess I'd better work harder."

"Mmm, definitely. Harder is good."

"I have to go take care of this condom," he said, kissing her. "Then I'm coming back here and fucking you so good that I move up to number one."

Jenna watched his ass as he strolled into the bathroom. It was tight and perfect—and she couldn't wait to wrap her hands around it while he drove into her again.

Chapter Sixteen

NOAH WOKE A LITTLE LATER THAN USUAL AT SIX A.M., momentarily confused at the warm body beside him. Then he remembered the night's activities, and his cock started to grow. Jenna was turned away from him, curled on her side, and he reached over to caress her bare hip, shifting until his cock was nestled against her ass.

He'd never intended to fuck the nanny, but damn if it hadn't been spectacular. Jenna was soft and sweet and she made him laugh. Then she made him come apart. Twice.

He wanted more of that. A lot more.

He kissed her shoulder and she shifted slightly. Then she turned into him, and he put his arms around her, kind of surprised at how that made him feel.

Content. Happy.

"Mmm," she said against his chest. "Someone's ready for action this morning."

He laughed. "I'm always ready, babe."

"What time is it?"

"A little after six," he said, tonguing her shoulder. She tasted sweet. He thought about the leisurely trip he'd get to make down her body, sucking her nipples until she squirmed before making his way to her pussy. He planned to take his time there, licking and sucking her into a frenzy. Then, when she was boneless, he'd roll on a condom and fuck her doggy style while she gripped the headboard...

She stiffened and pushed away from him. "Alice will be waking soon if she isn't already. I need to get dressed."

"The monitor's on the table. I didn't hear anything."

"She's quiet at first. She'll sit there for a good ten minutes or so before she starts to fuss."

He reluctantly let her go. "You hit the shower, and I'll go peek at her."

"Thank you, Noah." She grinned at him as she grabbed her clothes from the floor and rushed out of the room.

Noah lay back on the bed for a moment, wallowing in disappointment. His dick stared up at him accusingly. "Sorry," he muttered as he sat up and reached for his pants. "I tried, buddy. Better luck next time."

He went to brush his teeth, dragged on a shirt, and then checked on Alice. Sure enough, she was sitting up in her crib. She tugged herself up when she saw him, a big smile breaking over her sweet little face. "Unk No-wuh!"

His heart did that melty thing all over again as he went to pick her up. "Morning, kiddo. How'd you sleep?"

"Pee-pee," she replied.

Shit, her potty chair was in the bathroom where Jenna was currently showering. "Okay, honey," he said as he carried her to the hall bath. The shower was running, but he knocked anyway.

"Yes?" Jenna called.

"Alice has to pee. Can I bring her in? Or can you take her?"

"It's okay, you can come in. I'm already in the shower."

Noah pushed open the door and helped Alice to the potty. Jenna peeked around the edge of the shower curtain.

"Pee-pee, Denna," Alice said from the potty.

"Good girl. You get a stamp. Uncle Noah can put it on for you."

"Yay!"

Jenna smiled at him and he smiled back. It felt like a goofy grin, but what the hell. He was stupid happy inside for some reason. Even though he was helping a toddler pee and had to stamp her hand when it was over. Not how he'd envisioned his life, but it wasn't awful. It was kind of like rescuing people in a way because he was protecting a young life and helping her learn necessary skills. The effect in the end was that he'd made a difference to someone. He liked that.

"Thanks for helping me out," Jenna said.

"No problem. I'll want payment though."

"Oh, really?"

Steam wreathed around her head, and drops of moisture ran down her face. Her hair was darker when it was wet and plastered to her head. He wanted to see the rest of her with water dripping down her skin, but that wasn't going to happen right now.

"Definitely. I'll think of something." He waggled his eyebrows at her and she giggled before slipping behind the curtain again.

"I won't be long," she told him.

"Take your time. Alice and I will fix coffee and breakfast, won't we, sweetie?"

"Yuh-huh," Alice said. "I finiss now."

"Make sure she wipes," Jenna called.

"On it," Noah said. He helped Alice take care of business, got her nightie on and hands washed—and stamp applied—then took her down to the kitchen to start the coffee. He didn't know what Jenna wanted Alice to wear, so he didn't attempt to dress her first. He figured there was plenty of time for that anyway.

"What do you want for breakfast? Eggs? Oatmeal? Cereal? Toast?"

A few short weeks ago, he wouldn't have known what to feed her, but now he knew she could eat whatever the adults ate. Yesterday he'd given her the yogurt and cheese, but today he let her decide. She seemed to consider it before she said oatmeal. He knew she meant she wanted it with sugar and cinnamon so he got to work. Jenna sliced bananas and strawberries to make faces in the oatmeal. She also used blueberries for eyes. He'd watched her do it enough times that he knew what to do.

By the time Jenna entered the kitchen, Alice was eating her oatmeal and Noah had finished his first cup of coffee. The moment he saw her, every protective instinct he had flared.

"What's wrong?"

She blinked at him. "I... um, nothing. Nothing's wrong."

Noah poured coffee, fixed it the way she liked, and handed it to her. "I don't know why you're lying to me, but you are," he said softly. "You don't have to. Let me help."

She took the coffee in shaky hands, then lifted it so she could take a sip. "I wish you could," she whispered. "I'm so sorry, Noah, but..." Her eyes filled with tears. "I have to go."

Alarm snaked through him. "Go where?"

"Just go." She flung an arm out. "Leave."

He could only stare at her in disbelief. After everything that'd happened last night in his bed. And, hell, the past few weeks where he'd gotten used to having her around. *Liked* having her around. He couldn't imagine her walking out on him now. On Alice.

Then again, he was used to people leaving him. Or sending him away. It shouldn't hurt anymore, but it did. More than he'd expected it to. He started to tell her to go ahead and leave. Get out and let him and Alice figure things out. They didn't need her. It's what he would have done with anyone else. What'd he'd done so many times in his head when he'd been sent away. *I don't need you anyway.*

But he couldn't say the words because it wasn't what he felt. He opted for the truth, no matter how hard it was to admit.

"I don't want you to go," he said quietly. "Alice doesn't want you to go either. If this is about what happened last night, it doesn't have to happen again. I'll respect your boundaries. I won't touch you."

"It's not that. I just… I can't stay." She set the cup on the counter and turned to walk away.

He knew he should let her go, but he reacted instead, grabbing her arm, stopping her. She stiffened as he wrapped his arms around her from behind. "Jenna," he said in her ear, his mouth so close to her soft skin. "Please. Tell me what's wrong so I can help."

He liked this life they were leading. He wanted to keep it going. He was in uncharted territory, but he was a fighter and a survivor. He didn't quit, and he wasn't quitting now. Not so easily.

She stood stiffly, and he almost let her go. Then she surrendered in a rush, her body relaxing into his. "No one can help me. It's too late for that."

"Try me, Jen. Just try."

———

JENNA STOOD IN HIS ARMS, trembling as he held her to his strong body. Her head was bowed and her heart ached. She wanted to believe, but Noah was one man. Even with his team, they were no match for the Flanagans. Those men were rich and ruthless, and they were looking for her.

The phone call she'd just gotten proved it. She didn't get too many calls, but she did get them, so when her phone rang, she'd been distracted and she'd answered it.

A man's voice spoke. What he'd said chilled her to the bone.

"You're a hard lady to find, Jenna Lane."

"I—who is this?"

"Charlie and Billy send their regards. And a message. They want their money. If you give it back, nobody has to get hurt."

Her heart was in her throat, pounding out of control. "I don't have their money. I don't know what you're talking about."

"Funny, but that idiot boss of yours said the same thing. You've got three days. Return the money, or your sweet little Aunt Maggie will be getting a visit from me. You don't want that to happen. Trust me."

Noah turned her in his arms. Set her down at the table and put her coffee cup in front of her. Then he got his. Alice was humming a song to herself as she spooned oatmeal in her mouth. She got a lot of it on the tray and her bib, but she was doing it herself and that was good.

Jenna's eyes filled with tears. She didn't want to leave sweet little Alice. And she definitely didn't want to leave the tiny girl's big, strong, sexy uncle.

She could still feel the ache between her legs from all they'd done, and she'd thought until just a few minutes ago that she'd be doing more of that with him. She'd been daydreaming about it, remembering the way he'd touched her. The things she'd felt.

Noah sat and put his fingers beneath her chin, tipping her head up gently. Forcing her to look at him. Blue eyes studied her very seriously. "Tell me what the problem is, Jenna. Is your aunt sick? Do you need to go to her?"

She swallowed, still torn. "It's not Aunt Maggie... I shouldn't drag you into it. It's not your responsibility."

But Aunt Maggie *was* in trouble if Jenna didn't return the Flanagans' money. She didn't have a single clue what Owen Fisher had been talking about, but she remembered he'd had a similar exchange with Sam. Only now she believed that Sam had the money and he'd been brazening his way through the conversation.

What money, Sam? What did you do?

And how was she going to convince the hitman that she didn't have it or know where it was? How was she going to move the focus from Aunt Maggie to her and make sure her aunt stayed safe?

"It is now," Noah said, drawing her attention back to him. "You live here. With us. You're part of the family."

Part of the family. Considering he was a man who hadn't really had a family, she understood how incredible it was for him to feel that way about their little threesome now.

"I don't mean just you, me, and Alice," he continued, as if sensing the direction of her thoughts. "Though I do mean that. But I also mean you're a part of my HOT family, too. Those men you hung out with yesterday would do anything to help you. So would the women."

She thought of everyone at the barbecue and how welcoming they were, and her gut twisted. Did she want to bring them into it? Put them in danger?

"I should go, Noah. You should let me leave. You don't want to be a part of this, believe me. I... I think it's the Mafia. And they aren't playing."

His beautiful eyes hardened. "Honey, I'm not afraid of the fuc—fricking Mafia. None of us are. They want to go up against elite operators? They won't win. Trust me."

"I don't want anyone getting hurt because of me."

"It's not because of you. It's because of them. The kind of people they are. They aren't worth the brass it takes to make the bullet that puts an end to their shit."

"Sit!" Alice yelled.

"Crap," Noah muttered. "You can't go, Jenna. She'll be cussing like a new recruit in no time."

He was making a joke, but her shoulders slumped anyway. Every instinct she had told her to run—but she was beginning to believe those instincts were wrong. She'd been running for months, and it hadn't helped a bit. They'd found her anyway. Or found how to get to her. She could have cut off all contact with Aunt Maggie, but she didn't think that would have stopped the Flanagans or Fisher.

They'd have gone after her aunt anyway, and when Aunt Maggie couldn't produce a number or address, they'd have eliminated her out of sheer evil.

"My aunt's in danger," she blurted. "And I don't know how to protect her."

He put his hands on either side of her face. Held her. "I've got this, Jenna. I won't let anyone hurt your aunt. My team will go get her, and we'll keep her safe until it's over. But if you want me to help put an end to the danger, you have to tell me everything. Who's after her and why? What do you have to do with it? I need to know it all."

Jenna took a sip of coffee. Her hands shook. What choice did she have? It was time to trust someone with her secrets. If it ruined everything, it was the least she deserved for hiding it from him. "Okay. Yes."

She took a deep breath and started to talk. She told him everything, from her job with Sam to hearing him get murdered to feeling like she was being followed to leaving town and using her mother's last name and social security number for jobs when she needed a social. She told him about living in Lola sometimes, about how she'd planned to leave again before he'd offered her the job, and how she shouldn't have taken it because she'd been afraid of putting him and Alice in danger.

It was a lot to tell, and when she was done, her stomach was in knots. Because surely he'd tell her to get out now. She'd stayed in his house for weeks and never mentioned that dangerous people were looking for her.

He took her hand and wrapped her fingers in his. The move shocked her because she'd thought for sure he wouldn't want anything to do with her. Maybe he still didn't, but he was too kind to literally put his foot against her behind as he threw her out the door.

"I'm sorry, Jenna. For everything you've been through."

Her eyes felt scratchy and achy. She hadn't cried, but she wanted to. "You aren't pissed off at me for bringing my junk to your door?"

"Did you bring it to my door? Seems to me like you were trying to leave."

"I shouldn't have accepted the job. I should have left."

He shook his head and kissed her knuckles. The thrill of desire that shot through her was no surprise. "I wish you'd trusted me sooner, no doubt. But if you hadn't taken the job, where would Alice and I be right now? She'd still be moving among sitters, and I'd be certain I was screwing her life up by being so bad at taking care of her."

"You aren't bad at taking care of her. You're good with her."

"Because you taught me what to do. Hell, I might have figured out that I needed to google things, but I was so overwhelmed that it didn't occur to me until you said it. So, yeah, you got me and Alice onto the right track. *You* did that, Jenna. And then you moved in with us and made it all work. I'm not mad at you."

He squeezed her hand gently. "Strike that. I'm a little mad at you for not trusting me. You know what I do. I told you before that I wasn't the kind of guy you wanted to see coming if you were doing something wrong. Did you think that didn't extend to these Flanagan people? Or Owen Fisher?"

"You're Army, Noah. They're civilians. No, I didn't think it applied."

He grabbed his phone from the table. "It applies, babe. I need to call a team meeting so we can make a plan. First we have to get your aunt out of Dunkirk."

Jenna reared back to gape at him. "You know the town?" And then it hit her. "You checked me out."

He didn't look apologetic in the least. "Not

completely, but I wanted to know if you were really talking to an aunt that day. Hacker confirmed it. That was all I asked and all he did."

She wasn't sure how she felt about that, but then she realized it was hypocritical as hell to be even the remotest bit offended that he'd looked up her aunt. In his position, she'd have done the same. More, actually, since she hadn't given him a lot to go on when he'd taken her into his home and trusted her with his niece.

"I understand. If you looked her up, then you know she lives alone and she's almost eighty-two. Aunt Maggie isn't a wilting flower by any stretch, but she's not going to be able to stop a man like Owen Fisher. She wouldn't even think to. He'll approach her with some kind of lie, and she'll be polite even if she doesn't like him."

"He gave you three days, right? We'll have her out of there by tonight."

Jenna's heart began to beat with hope instead of dread. It wasn't going to fix the problem of the money, but she'd have more time to think if Aunt Maggie was out of harm's way.

"She won't want to come. She has her garden, and her church and friends. She'll want to stay home."

"She'll come, Jenna. She won't have a choice." She must have looked alarmed or something because he gave her a smile. "Don't worry, honey, my guys know how to coax women into doing what they want. She'll come along willingly."

"Maybe I should go get her—"

"No. It's not a good idea. Trust me when I tell you

that I have experience in this stuff, and you don't need to be anywhere near your aunt's house."

"How can you be so sure?"

"Because Fisher isn't giving you three days, Jenna. He's baiting a trap, and he expects you to walk right into it."

Chapter Seventeen

Noah called Saint and explained the situation. Saint whistled, but he didn't hesitate.

"I'll call Hacker, Wolf, and Muffin. You call Zany and Gem. Harley and Eva aren't returning until tonight. We can get him up to speed later."

"Thanks, Saint."

"No problem, man. All those who can be there should converge at your place at 1400. Hopefully Hacker and Bliss will have some information for us by then, assuming they're around today."

Noah hoped they were, but of course everyone had private lives. Not that the guys wouldn't drop everything to help each other out, because they would, but it wasn't going to take all of them to go to Delaware. "Copy that. See you then."

He ended the call and phoned the other two men. Jenna had taken Alice upstairs to wash her off and get her dressed. She hadn't seemed as pale as earlier, but she wasn't completely at ease either. He wasn't entirely sure she wasn't half thinking about slipping away anyway. If she was, he wasn't letting that happen. Besides, she didn't have a new battery and she wouldn't get all that far if she tried.

Noah blew out a breath and shoved a hand through his hair before getting up to pour more coffee. Last night, he'd gotten Jenna naked and had a hell of a good time. He'd planned to do it again today. What he hadn't planned on was landing in the middle of a Mafia operation and finding out his nanny was involved up to her eyeballs.

She'd heard a murder, for fuck's sake. He got why she didn't come forward about it. It was the kind of thing where she'd have needed witness protection if she had. And with Fisher being arrested for another murder, it hadn't seemed necessary to her.

He got it. He really did. She hadn't seen anything. All she'd done was hear it, and a good lawyer would tear her statement apart. Unless there was another piece of evidence tying Fisher to her boss's office at that time, then it was her word against his.

The money was the key. Noah believed her when she said she had no idea what Fisher was talking about. She hadn't known her boss was part of anything illegal, and she didn't know about any money. Considering the way she lived like a nomad—sleeping in her car, taking low-paying jobs, moving on before too long—he didn't think she was hiding a fortune from the Mafia.

But they thought she was, and that was enough.

Jenna returned with Alice and set her down to play with her toys. Alice was wearing a pink sundress with little pink sandals and pink bows in her pigtails. He watched her pick up a stuffed animal, and his heart squeezed tight. She carried it over to him and he took it, oohing and aahing before he handed it back. She returned to the pile, dropping the animal and selecting another, and he knew she'd do the same again.

He glanced at Jenna. She shrugged. Sometimes you just had to play the game and hope the toddler gave up.

Jenna had left her hair down for a change, and it cascaded over her shoulders and almost to her ass. He loved long hair on a woman. He could wrap it around his hands and tug her head back so he could kiss her long and hard.

She was wearing a loose T-shirt and denim shorts that she'd half tucked the shirt into. She looked casual and at ease, but he knew it wasn't real. Inside, she was a mess of fear and nerves.

"You okay?" he asked.

She'd shoved her hands into her pockets as she came over to stand by the table. "I'm trying to be."

He realized that she'd never eaten. He hadn't either. He'd been waiting for her, and then she'd walked in and looked like Death was nipping at her heels. Everything went sideways after that. He pushed the chair out with his foot and stood. "Sit. I'll fix breakfast."

He thought she might protest, but she did as he said, playing the toy game with Alice. Noah scrambled eggs and made toast with butter and set a plate in front of Jenna. It wasn't impressive, but it was hot and filling. She toyed with the eggs, pushing them around her plate as she acknowledged all of Alice's toys one by one.

"Eat, Jenna. You can't defeat the bad guys on an empty stomach."

She looked at him. "You're taking this remarkably well for a guy who just found out his nanny is wanted by the Mafia."

He forked eggs into his mouth. Swallowed. "You think that's the worst of what I've dealt with? Au contraire, Miss Lane."

She sighed and touched his arm. "Noah. I'm not an idiot. I know the military doesn't go after civilians, and especially not within the borders of the US. It's not legal. The last thing I want is for you to get in trouble because of me. For *any* of you to get in trouble."

"You're right," he said. "We don't operate within the borders, and not against civilians. But we have resources. Friends, you might say." He thought of Ian Black and his Bandits. They were mercenaries, and though it would gall Noah up one side and down the other to hand this over to those fuckers at Black Defense International, he'd do it in a heartbeat if it meant Jenna and her aunt would be safe. BDI could do things Strike Team 2 could not.

But they weren't helpless, and this wasn't an official mission. They were skilled, and they could make plans of their own. If they needed more resources, they'd call BDI in.

"Are you sure your guys don't mind helping? I feel guilty that they're giving up their Sunday for this."

"It's what we do, Jenna. It's fine." She sounded like the guys were coming over to move furniture, or something equally mundane, when it was far more serious. He found it endearing in a way.

He drummed his fingers on the tabletop, thinking. He'd managed to polish off his eggs and toast while she took her sweet time with hers. Alice had started playing with her toy computer, which meant the trips to Jenna's side had stopped for now. Noah was beginning to wonder if the food tasted bad, but Jenna finally finished a slice of toast and ate another bite of eggs. Her appetite was improving, and he was glad.

"What about this money thing?" he asked her. "You have any idea what that's about?"

She shook her head, swallowing. "I really don't. I was Sam's assistant, and I saw a lot of paperwork in his office, but nothing about money stood out to me. I dropped deposits sometimes—random checks from people, stuff that wasn't direct deposited to his account. Nothing seemed strange to me."

"But you think he was involved in something?"

She nodded. "He didn't deny he was involved when Fisher confronted him, and he said he knew where the bodies were. I didn't take that literally, though maybe he did mean it that way. He clearly got on the wrong side of the Flanagans, and they wanted their money back, which he probably did steal if he was part of their criminal activities. He'd just bought a huge new house, and he said he was planning to get married. I didn't know he was dating, but knowing him it was a showgirl he'd met in one of the casinos. He liked those type of women a lot."

"So it wasn't odd that you hadn't met her?"

"Not really. Sam was a nice guy and a good boss, but he was very private. He didn't work with associates, and he didn't have a bunch of legal staff. Just me and a detective he kept on retainer."

"A detective?"

"He needed investigations done sometimes. If he took a client on who'd been accused of a crime, he'd send the investigator digging for information. The guy would tail people too, then report back. I wasn't a part of that stuff. I answered phones, typed, did errands, made calls, and fetched things like lunch, dinner, and coffee. I was trying to earn enough money to go back to school and finish my degree." Her gaze dropped. "When my parents died, I quit college so I could deal with their stuff and figure things out."

"You said you'd thought about majoring in early childhood education but didn't. What was your major then?"

"Sociology." She shrugged. "I thought I might go to law school after, which is how I ended up with Sam. One of the girls who worked at the day care dated him for a little while—his clean-cut phase, I liked to call it. Anyway, I met him one day, we got to talking, and a few weeks later he offered me the job. The pay was better, and he promised I could go to night classes after I was trained and settled. Seemed like a no brainer to me."

"Did you ever get to start?"

"No. I was getting ready to, even had the schedule of classes at UNLV, but then Sam was shot, and that was the end of that." She let out a sad sigh. "I liked Sam when I thought I knew him. He was nice to me, and he did what he said he would do. I've spent the past few months wondering how I didn't know what he was really up to."

"Because he didn't want you to," Noah said. "Probably a good thing."

"Yeah, probably. Except for this money crap, because I don't know how much we're talking about, or *where*. And when the Flanagans figure that out, I'm as good as dead."

His gut twisted at those words even as his protective instincts flared. "No," he growled, "I'm not letting that happen."

She reached over and wrapped her fingers in his. "You're a good person, Noah. Anyone who ever treated you as less than wonderful was an idiot and a fool. I hope you realize that."

Though he knew he made a difference in the world, and that he'd helped people before Jenna, her words still meant a lot. "Thanks for saying that. I appreciate it."

"You're welcome."

They smiled at each other for a long moment. He was about to lean forward and kiss her when Alice toddled over, stuffed dog in hand.

"Dog have booboo."

"Oh no," Jenna said in an exaggerated voice, turning all her attention to Alice. "Let me see. Maybe we can get Dog a Band-Aid. Would that help?"

Alice nodded, her little pigtails shaking. "Yeah."

Jenna stood, flashing him an apologetic smile as she took Alice's hand. "Let's go see what we have."

Noah got busy cleaning up the dishes, but not until

he'd watched the two women in his life disappear into the hall bath. He could hear Jenna talking to Alice about Dog, hear them discussing Band-Aids, and he grinned to himself as he washed the pan he'd cooked the eggs in. A few short weeks ago, he'd been alone in this house and he'd been convinced it was exactly what he wanted.

After the muck and blood, and the sleeplessness and pain of a mission, he wanted quiet. He wanted to be alone where he could sleep as long as he liked, reset his brain, and veg out. He wanted delivery food, movies and shows on streaming, and nothing but his own company.

Yet the thought of Jenna and Alice not being there, not chattering in the hall bath about Dog's booboo or sitting in the backyard while Alice splashed in the pool, left him feeling emptier and lonelier than he'd thought possible.

It would be an adjustment to return home to them when he'd been on a mission, especially one where there was a lot of fighting and killing. He wouldn't be able to veg out with two women waiting for him. He'd have to smile and hold Alice and acknowledge all her toys and drawings, and he'd have to take Jenna to bed and make her come as many times as possible.

Oddly enough, the thought of doing all those things felt pretty damned appealing.

———

JENNA COULDN'T BELIEVE it when Noah's teammates showed up later that afternoon. They were all there. The women too. Brooke took Alice outside to play in her splash pool while Haylee and Scarlett joined her. Bliss stayed inside with Hacker, both of them on laptops as they typed like mad and bent toward each other to talk. Jenna was a little confused at Bliss's presence, but the woman definitely wasn't sitting around and doing nothing.

Jenna stayed at Noah's request, though she felt a bit out of sorts. She couldn't stop thinking that these men were giving up their weekend to help her, or that they ultimately were no match for the Mafia. If they were at full strength, meaning with the full backing of their organization and all their military might, then sure. But as a group of off the clock mercenaries?

She just didn't know. She tried to imagine everything she knew about Delta Force and Green Berets—Navy SEALs, too—but she couldn't imagine those entities without their night vision gear, assault suits, and high tech weaponry. Not to mention the helicopters, airplanes, and warships they used to infiltrate conflict zones.

These guys weren't rappelling down the side of the Flanagans' office building and crashing into their suite to threaten them with death if they didn't leave Jenna and her aunt alone, much as that image delighted her.

Still, she was grateful they wanted to try. So very grateful. When it was time, she told them what she'd told Noah. He'd relayed it when he'd asked for their help, but they needed to hear it from her.

"Charlie and Billy Flanagan," Bliss said, tapping her computer. "Irish ancestors, third generation American.

Charles is the oldest. William is two years younger. They inherited a lot of property from their father, who was a big player in the building trade in Las Vegas. They've tried to build the empire bigger and better, but they've made some costly moves and lost money. Current project is the Venus Casino and Resort, which is projected to cost 2.5 billion to build. They're deep into it, and they've gotten loans from various investors. They might be starting to panic a bit."

"Mafia connections?" Saint asked.

"It's an open secret," Bliss replied. "But a lot of the heavy hitters in Vegas are connected in one way or another. The Flanagans are the top of the heap at the moment, but they're heavily leveraged. Baby," she said, looking at Hacker, "tell them about Fisher."

"Owen Fisher. Mafia enforcer, just released from prison when the judge threw out the case due to a technicality. The rumor is that the Flanagans made that happen. Bribing witnesses, that kind of thing. Fisher is their chief enforcer, but they have others. Cold-blooded, cruel, never stays in prison long. Willing to do anything, which is what makes him valuable to people like them."

"Why would a guy like that come looking for Jenna?" Noah asked. "Why not send someone else?"

Hacker shrugged. "Not sure, really. Except that he's the one who did the hit on Sam Baxter, so maybe it's personal? If the Flanagans sent him to collect their money, which he clearly didn't get, and they think Jenna has it, who better to send? If you send someone else, you have to read them in."

"True," Noah said.

Jenna knew the term because of her mother. Reading someone in meant giving them access to the information. Owen Fisher had the access already. Maybe the fewer people who knew, the better. Maybe that's what the Flanagans were thinking.

"I wish I knew how much money Sam stole," Jenna said.

Noah reached over and squeezed her hand. She didn't miss that a couple of the guys looked at their hands, then at Noah, then at her. Mal grinned at Wolf and lifted a brow. Wolf nodded back. She didn't know what that was about, and she didn't really have the energy to think about it at the moment.

"That would help," Saint said. "But it's not one hundred percent necessary. Can you think of *anything* you didn't tell us already? Any minor thing that might tell us where Baxter funneled the money?"

"No. I'm sorry. He bought a new house—a big one —but I was only there once. I'm sure it's been sold by now anyway."

"It hasn't," Hacker said. "The estate has been contested by his two ex-wives and a fiancée named Tiffany who swears he bought the house for her and that she has proof. It's unlived in while the courts decide."

Jenna frowned. "I was there once, like I said. Sam was kind of proud of a Joan Miró surrealist painting he'd bought from Sotheby's, but that's about it. A minor Miró, he said. The house was huge. Standard rich people stuff. I was there to help catalog his possessions for insurance purposes. I wasn't all that impressed, really. Sam's taste ran to tacky nouveau riche stuff like gold-leafed cherubs on pedestals and heavy silk drapes. Except the Miró, which seemed a bit classier, albeit very modern artsy."

"This Miró," Bliss said. "Where was it hanging?"

"The dining room," Jenna said. "Not prime safe space, if that's what you're thinking."

Bliss looked thoughtful. "Unless one wanted to buck the trend and put the safe somewhere unexpected."

Jenna's heart jumped at that thought. She remembered Sam striding into the dining room, ignoring the huge marble and glass table, and pointing at the painting with a flourish. *"Voilà,"* he'd said. *"My most prized possession."*

But Sam was tacky and glaring in his displays of wealth. A Miró, however delightfully odd, was a little out of character. It was the kind of thing that only people who knew art understood. Maybe the Miró was there for another reason. It was weird, yes, and noticeable, but maybe that was the point. If someone thought the Miró was the focal point, they wouldn't consider that he'd hidden a safe behind it.

If, indeed, he had.

"What, Jen?" Noah asked softly.

"I... He said it was his most prized possession when he showed me the house. But I never got the impression that Sam knew a Miró from a Picasso, so why he would care about it that much might be a little odd. It also might mean that he'd spent a lot of money because someone told him it was important, so that's why he prized it. He didn't come from wealth, though. His idea of being rich was more ostentatious than modest."

"Can you get a blueprint of the house?" Noah directed the question to Hacker and Bliss.

"I've got it," Bliss said. "The house was built ten years ago. There's no safe in the dining room on this plan, but the wall butts up to a closet on the other side, so it's entirely possible he could have had one put in. He could have had the closet wall moved back to hide it."

Saint was frowning. "Okay, so somehow we have to get into a house in Vegas and find out if there's a safe behind a painting in the dining room. Except that none of us can do it because we're too close to our deployment window."

Jenna's stomach squeezed as she glanced at Noah. They were leaving soon? And he hadn't told her?

He met her gaze evenly, confirming it. She gave him a slight nod, wanting him to know she understood. It was still terrifying to her that he could be called away at any moment. If these guys left, then what?

"We can't go to Vegas," Noah said, still gazing at her. "But maybe we can ask Ian Black for some assistance."

"I'll do it," Bliss said, and every head swung around to look at her. "What? I've got skills, y'all. And connections. I'll fly to Vegas, get inside the house, and have a look around. I know a safe cracker or two. I'll reach out."

Jenna was gaining a new appreciation for Bliss. She'd thought the woman was a bit of a diva, though not in a bad way. Just expensively dressed and maybe high maintenance. She was learning that wasn't the case at all. Bliss was a skilled operator, and Jenna was a little ashamed of herself for letting appearances make her think otherwise.

"Not comfortable with that, babe," Hacker said. "Who are these people—and what's to say they won't hit you over the head and steal the money, if there is any?"

Bliss caressed his cheek. "I'm not an idiot, baby. I know what to do and who to work with. I had an entire career before you, remember?"

"I know, but I don't like you doing this shit without me."

"I don't want anyone risking their lives for me," Jenna said. "It's my problem, not yours."

"You're one of us now," Wolf said. "We take care of our own."

"But—"

"No buts," Gem piped in. "You're family."

Jenna had to bite the inside of her lip to keep the tears she was holding in from falling anyway. She missed her family every day. Other than Aunt Maggie, she'd had no one. She hadn't realized how lonely and lost she'd been until now.

But though these guys were on her side, she reminded herself it wasn't permanent. She was family so long as she was with Noah and Alice. How long would that last? He'd said he wanted her to stay, but he hadn't said why. There'd been no expressions of deeper feelings from either of them.

She met his gaze and swallowed the sudden lump in her throat as fresh emotion welled inside her. He'd called this meeting for her. To help her. Instead of throwing her out of his house for lying to him about something so incredibly important, he wanted to help.

And maybe it was all because of Alice and that he didn't have other nanny prospects, but she knew deep down he had resources to call on if he had to. He wasn't helping her solely because it was more convenient for him to keep her.

So why *was* he? That's what she didn't know, and what she wanted to find out.

"That's right," Saint said. "No buts. We're doing this. I want to circle back to the house in Vegas later. For now, we need a plan to get Jenna's aunt and bring her back here."

The conversation moved on to Aunt Maggie. Gem, Zany, and Muffin—such an odd name for a grown man —peeled off as soon as the plan was made and hopped into Zany's SUV to make the trip to Delaware. The rest of them stayed to discuss getting into Sam's house and finding the money he'd stolen.

Jenna didn't know how they were going to do it or if there was any money left to find, but it was the only hope she had of getting out of this mess. By the time the meeting was finished, it'd been agreed that Bliss was going to call on her contacts and head to Vegas. Hacker didn't like it, but he accepted it.

Bliss gave Jenna a hug as they were leaving. "Don't worry. I'm good at what I do. If there's anything in that safe, I'll find it. And if there's not, then we'll find another way. Everyone has pressure points, Jenna. Remember that. We'll find the right lever and apply enough pressure to make it too painful for them to continue. Have faith."

"Thank you," Jenna whispered, her throat tight. For the first time since this nightmare had started, she was actually beginning to believe it might end and her life could return to normal.

If she was lucky, that meant a life with Noah and Alice. If he didn't want the same thing, well, at least she'd be free to choose what came next.

It was a nice thought, but the pit in her stomach said otherwise.

Chapter Eighteen

JENNA CRASHED ON THE COUCH AFTER EVERYONE LEFT, drained, as Alice played on the floor. Noah had gone outside to see them off, still talking with Saint and Hacker, and the house was strangely quiet with only Alice's little voice talking to her toys.

Jenna blew out a breath, thinking over everything that'd happened. She felt hopeful for the first time in months, but a part of her was stubbornly filled with anxiety despite the confidence and plans of Noah's team. She'd been scared for so long that it was hard to let that go.

She wanted to sit and think, but she had to get up. It was almost time for dinner, then it would be Alice's bath time, a little more play time, and bed.

Not that Jenna thought she'd be able to sleep a wink tonight while she waited for the guys to return with her aunt. They hadn't called yet, but they'd only been gone for about two hours.

When Noah came back inside, a surge of fresh

emotion flooded her, leaving an ache inside that she didn't understand. She had so many feelings, and she didn't know how to sort them out right now.

Noah dropped beside her and put an arm around her. She burrowed against his side, happy that she could do that now. "How you holding up?" he asked.

"I feel like Lola's battery."

He chuckled. "Depleted? Yeah, I understand. That was intense, I know."

"I'm so grateful, Noah. You have no idea. I'm still scared it's not going to be enough, but I want to thank you for trying."

He hugged her a little tighter. "Have faith, Jen. It's going to work out."

"I'm trying." She sighed. "I need to fix dinner. Alice will be hungry soon."

"Let's order pizza. Make it easy."

She loved that he knew she needed a break. "I think that's a great idea. I need to take care of so many things before Aunt Maggie arrives. I can sleep in Alice's room, but I'll need to gather up some blankets and make a pallet, unless you have a cot tucked away somewhere."

Noah reared back. "What? No way, babe. You aren't sleeping on the floor."

"I have to give my bed to Aunt Maggie."

"I know, but I thought you'd sleep with me if I'm being honest here. Unless you think your aunt will be scandalized, then you can take my bed and I'll take the couch."

She gaped at him. "You would do that?"

"Yes."

"But—why?"

"Because you have enough to worry about. You don't need to sleep on the floor or the couch. I'll do that. Or I'll sleep with you, because that's where I want to be."

Her heart was never going to recover from the tender way he treated her. Never. She wasn't sure if it meant anything or if he was just that thoughtful, and she didn't want to read anything more into it than was truly there.

"I didn't want to assume since we slept together once that you'd want to share a bed. That's a little relation-ship-y, and I didn't want you to think I expect that from you."

"I know you don't. But it's what I want."

"A relationship?"

"Yes, ma'am. Does that shock you?"

She could only blink at him for a long moment, her heart hammering. "Yes."

"Why?"

The heat of embarrassment warmed her. "Well, uh, we haven't known each other long, and you just found out I hid something pretty big from you. I feel like you could do better, Noah. Honestly."

There, she'd said it. He had too much going for him, and she was little more than an itinerant nomad at this point. Maybe she really would get her life back soon, or maybe she'd always be hiding from the Mafia, but either way it was a lot to deal with at the moment.

"All I know," he said, gently tipping her chin up so their eyes could meet, "is that I feel differently than I used to. A month ago, I wasn't the same man I am now. I want to keep Alice. I want you to stay with us. I want to see where we go."

He hadn't said anything about love, but that was a mighty big word for what might only be a shared connection because of Alice. "And if we don't go anywhere?"

She was always waiting for the sky to fall. Since her parents had died so suddenly and unexpectedly, her perspective about what could happen had altered. She knew that life changed in an instant, and she wasn't ever going to forget it.

"Then we'll figure it out, won't we?"

He made it sound so easy. Maybe to him it was. His life had been filled with uncertainty since he was a child. And with unspeakable cruelty. He'd endured, and he'd made something of himself. Something amazing.

It hit her that she could love this man, and not just because he was so damned gorgeous and sexy. He was a good man, despite what he'd been through. That kind of abuse could have twisted him, but it hadn't.

"My dad would have really liked you," she murmured. She hadn't meant to say it aloud, hadn't realized that she had until he grinned at her.

"I'm glad. I wish I could have met him."

Jenna turned toward him and put her arms around his neck and her legs across his lap. He leaned toward her, pressing his forehead to hers. "My mom would have liked you too," she whispered, her heart pounding, feeling a bit shy but also like she had to say it since she'd said it about her dad.

"Is that a yes, Jenna?"

"Yes, Noah, I want to see where this goes. And I want to sleep in your bed. With you. I don't think Aunt Maggie will be scandalized. She never married because she didn't want to be told what to do. Back then, a woman couldn't even have a credit card or a checking account without her husband's permission, and she said no effing way was she doing that. So I'm pretty sure a little sex outside of marriage won't offend her."

"I can't wait to meet your aunt. She sounds awesome."

"She is. She's not your typical eighty-one year old. She's very active. She looks at least ten years younger than she is."

Jenna realized, telling him about her aunt, just how much she'd missed seeing her. The idea that her aunt would be here in a few hours was suddenly more exciting than worrisome. Aunt Maggie wasn't going to like having to leave her home, but she wasn't a stupid woman. She would do it, and they'd spent the next few days catching up again. Jenna didn't want to think about what would happen if Noah and his team didn't find the money or put a stop to Owen Fisher's threat. She couldn't imagine Aunt Maggie agreeing to hide out for the rest of her life.

Noah kissed her, his tongue delving into her mouth for a hot second, sending her body into a deep pool of need. "I have to order the pizza. I hope we can get Alice to bed a little early tonight. I want to do hot, dirty things to you before the guys get back with your aunt."

Jenna's nipples tightened. Her pussy ached with the

desire to be touched. She wished it was eight o'clock and Alice was in bed, but it was still nearly three hours away. "I want that, too," she whispered, kissing him, dragging his tongue into her mouth and sucking on it.

"Denna," came a little voice. "Dog hungry."

Jenna pulled away from Noah and looked down at the child, who stood next to the couch with her toy. She looked between Noah and Jenna then held out her dog.

"Oh goodness, Dog is hungry? Would he like pizza? Uncle Noah is going to order pizza."

Alice nodded in that exaggerated way little kids had. "Pizza good."

"Do you think Dog needs a snack now? Something to tide him over until the pizza gets here?"

"Yes," she said very seriously. "His belly growl."

Jenna stood to take Alice to the kitchen. Before she could walk away, Noah glided his hand over her ass and under the leg of her shorts, his fingers skimming the line of her panties. "Something to think about," he said.

She'd be thinking about it all right. And then, the minute Alice was asleep and they were alone, she was going to make him do it again—with his tongue.

NOAH WAS a lot less certain than he let on about how his team was going to find the money—or find where the money went—and stop the Flanagans from coming after Jenna, but he wasn't going to let her know it. She was worried enough as it was, and he didn't want to make it worse on her.

Besides, if she thought Strike Team 2 didn't have a chance, she'd run away and he might never see her again. He wasn't going to let that happen.

Right now, he was a lot more worried about getting deployed before they'd found a resolution. But at least if Jenna and her aunt were safe in Mystic Cove, he could get through the two weeks or more without fearing Jenna would be gone when he returned. If she had her aunt and Alice to anchor her, plus the HOT women who'd promised to call and come over to help with childcare or just visit if she needed it, then it would be enough to make her stay.

Gem had called shortly after the pizza arrived to tell him they'd reached Dunkirk, Delaware. Jenna had taken a deep breath and called her aunt. Maggie hadn't wanted to leave at first, saying she had a pistol and she knew how to use it, but Jenna eventually convinced her it would be best. Gem, Zany, and Muffin knocked on her door while Jenna was on the phone, there was an agreed upon code word exchanged, and then her aunt sighed and said she needed a few minutes to gather her things. Half an hour later, they were on the road again.

Noah had watched the tension leach out of Jenna once he gave her the message. He could see the exhaustion on her face, the effect of so much fear and worry and adrenaline that she'd been experiencing. He told her to rest on the couch while he bathed Alice and got her ready for bed.

When he brought Alice back down for her hour of play before sleepy time, Jenna was curled on the couch, sound asleep.

"Denna seep," Alice said in a stage whisper.

"Yes, sweetie, she is. Why don't we go play in your room until bed so we don't wake her?"

"Okay."

He carried the toddler back up the stairs, then played with her for half an hour before her eyes started to droop. He put her in the crib, read her a story, and thanked his lucky stars that she was out before he was done. He crept from the room, shutting the door behind him, and went back downstairs to check on Jenna.

She opened her eyes as he hit the last step. It creaked beneath his feet, as it had earlier, but she'd been tired enough she hadn't noticed. This time she blinked awake then pushed herself up, looking adorably confused.

"Where's Alice?"

"Bed."

"It's too early," she said tiredly. "She'll be up at four in the morning."

Noah went over to the couch and sat beside her, pulling her onto his lap. She didn't protest, her body sinking trustingly against his. "It's not early, Jen. It's eight. The guys will be here by ten or eleven. They had to make a pit stop for your aunt. She also wanted a milkshake."

Jenna made a sound that he thought was a laugh but might have been one of frustration. "That's Aunt Maggie for you. She loves a milkshake for a road trip, but then she'll have to stop a couple more times along the way. I tried to tell her it was important not to dawdle."

"It's fine. She's got three big bodyguards who are

armed to the teeth and disinclined to let anyone get close enough to harm her. They'll take a bit of a circular route back here, just in case. That's part of why it's taking longer."

"I hate that I've gotten her into this," she whispered.

His hold on her tightened. "You didn't get anyone into anything. If anybody's to blame, it's Sam Baxter. He's the one who was in league with criminals, then got himself killed for stealing from them."

"I wish I'd gone home that night. But Sam was working late, so I stayed. He didn't ask me to. I just thought he was a good guy, and he did so much for others that I wanted to help. He was always doing *pro bono* work for charity organizations, or for people in need. I think he really cared about those things, despite what was going on behind the scenes."

"I don't think it would have mattered, Jen. These people think you know where their money is. Whether or not you were there that night wouldn't have mattered to them. They'd still be looking for you."

"I've been thinking about it a lot." She lifted her head to look at him. "I didn't leave for a month, and I sometimes thought I was being followed. It was never overt, but I saw the same car a few times in different places. I just… I had enough of a feeling that I kept it a secret I was planning to leave."

"They probably thought you'd lead them to the money if they followed you."

"I think so too. But why would they have that impression? I met Charlie and Billy exactly once. They didn't pay any attention to me. I never met Owen Fisher, though I know I saw him with Sam a couple of times."

"You don't know what Sam told them. Or what he implied. It's possible they believed you had a relationship or that Sam trusted you with everything. You'll never know what he told them about you."

"No, I guess that's true." She yawned and stretched. "Sorry. I didn't realize how tired I was."

"You want to go to bed? Get some sleep before your aunt arrives?"

She nuzzled his throat, and his dick throbbed to life. "I want to go to bed. But I don't want to sleep yet."

He stood with her in his arms and headed for the stairs. "That's what I hoped you'd say."

"But if I wanted to sleep, you'd let me, wouldn't you?" she asked, arms wrapped around his neck as he took them upstairs.

"Yes." He shoved the bedroom door open and stopped so she could quietly close it behind them.

"You're a good man, Noah Cross."

He carried her to the bed and set her down so he could strip her naked. "Not right now I'm not," he growled as he pushed her onto the bed and buried his head between her legs.

"Oh God. Noah…"

Chapter Nineteen

JENNA WAS BONELESS. NOAH MADE HER COME THREE times with his tongue, then rolled on a condom and wrapped her legs around his hips before thrusting into her body. She'd thought she was done moaning his name after he'd licked her clit so thoroughly, but she'd been wrong.

He fucked her slowly, angling his hips to find the right spot. And then he found it, and she shuddered beneath him as the tension inside her began to wind tighter again.

"You feel so amazing, Jenna," he said before taking her mouth in a hot kiss. They strained together on the bed, rocking into each other, until Jenna found her peak. She cried out sharply, then spun apart beneath him as he opened her legs wide and fucked her harder.

She came again as his cock dragged against sensitive nerve endings, shifting her hips to ride the wave. The change in angle soon had him gasping her name in her ear. He stiffened, his cock pulsing inside her as he came.

"Jenna," he said again, his breath hot against her skin. "Goddamn, you feel good. So fucking sexy and sweet."

"You feel good too," she murmured, her limbs useless to do anything except stroke his back rhythmically.

"I need a bottle of water, then I want to fuck you again," he said, nibbling her earlobe. "I've waited all damned day for this. Need anything while I'm going to the kitchen?"

Tingles of sensation tapped down her spine, sliding into her pussy. He was still inside her, and she wanted nothing more than for him to thrust again.

"I'm good."

He kissed her. "Better than good, Jen. So much better than good."

He got up and disappeared into the bathroom to take care of the condom, then he padded downstairs naked before returning with two bottles of water. He set one on the nightstand and downed one, then he tugged her up and on top of him. They were facing each other as he hugged her to him while he kissed her.

When he broke the kiss, he let his gaze glide down her body, lingering on her pussy. "I love eating your pussy," he said, skimming his fingers over her clit. "I love the sounds you make when I do."

He made her feel desirable and needed, and she arched against him happily. "If you must know, I like you eating my pussy too."

His gaze jerked up to hers. "Why, Jenna Lane, you've got a dirty mouth. I love it."

She wished he'd said he loved *her*, but that was a bit of a fantasy. A fantasy she wanted if she was honest with herself. The more intimate they were, the harder time she had separating her heart from her body. She told herself it was just fucking, no matter what he said, but her heart didn't want to believe.

Her heart wanted more.

"I'm full of surprises. But at least this one is a good one."

His hand skimmed down her sides, and then he slid two fingers inside her as he bent to suck a nipple into his mouth. He tugged hard, and she felt the pull in her clit. He had her squirming on his lap in moments, trying to find the rhythm.

"Tell me something dirty now," he said, his mouth against her nipple. "If you can."

"I want to suck your cock," she gasped.

He chuckled again. "I like this side of you."

They touched and kissed and whispered dirty things until they eventually ended up with her knees on either side of his head and his cock in her mouth. Jenna was enjoying herself immensely—and then he thrust his fingers into her pussy, tongued her clit, and she almost forgot to breathe...

"JENNA. WAKE UP, BABY."

Noah shook her gently until she stirred. She blinked into the soft light. He'd turned the bedside lamp onto the nightlight setting so it wasn't harsh when he woke her.

"What?"

He dragged on his pants and a shirt. "The guys are twenty minutes out. We need to get ready to welcome your aunt."

"Oh shit," she said, bolting up faster than he'd have thought possible considering she'd fallen asleep after the last orgasm he'd given her and had barely stirred. That was two hours ago. He'd fallen asleep too, but his internal clock knew they were expecting company, so he woke again right before the text came.

"Slow down, Jen. We've got a little time."

She stopped in the act of pulling on her shorts. "I'm nervous. I need to calm down, don't I?"

He went over and kissed her. "Does telling yourself to calm down usually work?"

"Not really." She looked sheepish.

"Should I tell you to calm down, or will that make it worse?"

She snorted as she finished zipping her shorts and slipped into her bra before tugging on a loose T-shirt. "Worse, I'm sure. In fact, I think it's pretty much guaranteed."

"That's what I thought. Never tell a woman to calm down. It was Lesson Eight in sniper training class."

She gaped at him. "No way."

He laughed. "You got me. No fucking way. One of the best snipers in the business is calmer than still water, and she'd skewer any man who dared tell her to calm down," he said, thinking of Victoria Brandon's legendary reputation at HOT. She was married to Nick "Brandy" Brandon, the Strike Team 1 sniper, and she did contract work for HOT. Together, the husband and wife team were unstoppable.

Jenna finger-combed her hair before twisting it up and wrapping a hair tie around it. "I should brush my teeth and wash my face." She sniffed her T-shirt. "Do you think I smell like sex? I don't want Aunt Maggie commenting on that. I'd die of embarrassment."

Noah blinked. "Would she?"

"Probably." She headed for the bathroom. "I'm spritzing body spray down my shirt and chugging mouthwash."

Noah followed her. "Guess I'd better do the same. Except for the body spray since it smells girly."

"Aw, come on, Noah. It's just your standard cherry blossom scent. You don't want to smell like cherry blossoms?"

He bumped hips with her at the vanity, liking that she was comfortable enough to tease him. "Nope, gonna pass."

"Your loss."

She put toothpaste on her toothbrush, which she'd moved from the hall bath earlier, and he did the same. It was domestic as hell standing in his bathroom together while they brushed their teeth and took turns with the mouthwash. He didn't mind it, though. It felt kind of nice. More than kind of.

It felt right. For the first time in his life, he actually cared if someone stayed with him or left. He'd worked hard not to care when he'd been passed from foster home to foster home. And then he'd worked hard not to care for anyone but Sally when the Parkers were abusing them all.

These days he cared for his team and their women. He cared for the people he helped when he deployed to war zones and other places where terrorists or drug lords held innocent people and threatened them. That was a different sort of caring, but he still cared—about justice and right, and good triumphing over evil.

He cared a lot about a great many things, in fact. But he cared most of all for the tiny little girl in the next room, and for the woman standing beside him at the sink right now. They were wound together in his head as a package, and he couldn't separate them any longer.

Jenna spit out the mouthwash and grinned at him. Then she reached up to smooth his hair. "You've got a cowlick or something."

He took her hand and kissed her fingers. "I got it. Thanks."

"Sure thing, baby," she said before sashaying from the room and leaving him staring into the mirror, wondering how the hell it'd happened. How had he fallen head over heels for a woman he'd only known a short while? How had he fallen when they'd been having sex for precisely two days? How had she scaled the walls around his heart so quickly?

"Fucking hell, dude," he muttered to his reflection. "You're a pretty bad warrior when it comes to protecting your own heart." He cocked a finger gun and fired it. "Boom, dead."

He wasn't telling Jenna. She had enough shit going

on, plus her aunt would be here any second. He also wasn't sure how she'd take it, and the last thing he wanted was to freak her out with a declaration of fresh new feelings that he still wasn't sure how to handle. It would sound desperate and weird if he said it now—plus, he wasn't sure he could say the words. He thought it was what he felt inside, but what if he was wrong?

Shit, he needed to ask Mal. Or Wolf, Hacker, or Saint, though Mal was the latest of their number to fall for a woman. How did you know? What did it feel like? How certain were you?

Good pussy was good pussy, and it'd been a while since he'd had any. Maybe he was just hard up and horny, and Jenna was the right woman at the right time.

Except that's not how it felt. He thought of her climbing into Lola and disappearing in the night, and his gut twisted into a knot. Then he thought of her aunt arriving any moment, and he hurried to wet his hair and smooth it down. The last thing he wanted was to make a bad impression on Jenna's aunt. Though maybe taking Jenna to his bedroom every night would be enough to make her suspicious of him anyway.

He should have thought this out better. Dragged the Army cot from the attic and set it up in Alice's room or simply parked his ass on the couch like he'd said he would.

"I'm going to fix some coffee," Jenna called out.

"It's after eleven at night, babe."

"I know—but someone might want some. Plus, I need something to do or I'm going to crap a brick."

Noah snorted as he left the bathroom and found her

standing by the bedroom door, hand on the knob. "Crap a brick, huh? I thought you said your aunt was progressive in her attitudes toward sex."

"I said I *thought* she was. In truth I'm not sure."

"You could always agree to marry me. Then we'd be engaged, and that wouldn't be nearly as bad, would it?"

"Noah, be serious."

"I am. We never really finished that conversation, did we? I asked you to marry me and help me raise Alice, and you said we didn't know each other. Well, we're getting there, right? We know that we're great in bed, and we know that Alice adores you. I'm growing fond of you myself. I think maybe you're fond of me too."

"I am," she said, dropping her lashes. "But you can't make a life decision based on having sex a few times, or the fact your niece is attached to her caregiver. It could all change in six months or a year."

"Everything can change at any time, Jenna. You know that as well as I do. But that doesn't mean you can't make the most of what you have *right now*. Can't be happy *right now.*" He joined her at the door and ran a finger down her cheek. "Say yes and tell your aunt we're engaged. That's not married, and there's still time to change our minds if it doesn't work out. But *right now*, it works. I like being with you. I like the way you put your heart into caring for a child that isn't yours and the way you treat her as if she's precious. Which she is, no doubt, but some people would see it as just a job and not show her the understanding and care that you do. She loves you and she needs you."

LYNN RAYE HARRIS

He drew in a deep breath and huffed it out. "I thought I could find a family for her. I thought it was the right thing—but I can't do that now. She's Sally's daughter, and I love her. I'm her uncle and I'm keeping her. *You* helped me realize I couldn't give her up. That I shouldn't give her up. And no, I'm not saying that you have to stay because of that. But I want you to stay. With us. If it doesn't work, then it doesn't work. I think it will, though. I'm willing to bet my future on it."

Her eyes were shiny with tears. "Damn you, Noah Cross. I was just going to make some coffee, for heaven's sake. And now you're making me cry with all these pretty words. It's not the most romantic proposal I've ever heard—not that I've been proposed to before, just that I've watched movies and read books." She hesitated a moment, as if gathering her thoughts. "But even if it's not quite how I thought it would go back when I dreamed up a future with someone, I've lived long enough in Las Vegas to know that sometimes you have to take the gamble—"

He caught her to him before she could finish and kissed her thoroughly. "Is that a yes?" he asked. "Tell me it's a yes."

She gripped his arms and laughed. "If you'd have let me finish what I was saying, you'd know, wouldn't you? Yes, it was a yes—but only to being engaged, okay?"

Maybe he was crazy, but hell if he wasn't deliriously happy with the idea of making Jenna his wife. "Yes. And damn it, now I want to eat your pussy again to make you realize why it's a good idea to marry me—but there's no time."

"Not fair, Noah. Don't say shit like that to me when there's no time. Rotten man."

He laughed as he took her hand and pulled her from the room. "Come on. The sooner we get your aunt settled, the sooner we can go to bed again."

Chapter Twenty

AUNT MAGGIE WAS NONE THE WORSE FOR WEAR BUT WAS *very* curious about the circumstances which had brought Jenna to Mystic Cove and why they were both there now. She wasn't judgmental or angry, which Jenna wouldn't have blamed her for if she had been. It was a lot to take in.

"I'm sorry I lied, Aunt Mags. I was worried that if you knew where I really was, it would make you vulnerable. That's why I kept saying I was on the opposite coast. But they found out anyway."

Aunt Maggie sipped her coffee. Noah had found decaf so Jenna had made that instead, which was probably better for everyone. Gem, Zany, and Muffin had dropped Aunt Maggie off with her belongings, and now they were outside with Noah, talking before they left.

Jenna thought maybe Noah had done it on purpose to give her time alone with Aunt Maggie. Whether or not he had, she was grateful to have the time to catch up and explain. She took a nervous sip from her own cup.

Aunt Maggie reached over and laid a gentle hand on Jenna's arm. "I think it's my fault, Jenna. I told you I upgraded the cable. A man came out Friday and said he needed to check everything. I let him in and didn't think anything of it, but I don't think that's what he was there for, really. He didn't go near the cable box, which I found odd, but I admit I was distracted a bit. The reverend came over to discuss the church bake sale, and I was busy with him."

Jenna's neck prickled. "Did he do anything else?"

"He left without telling me he was going. I found that odd, but who knows with people these days? But you said someone called you, and I had written your number on my notebook by the phone. I shouldn't have put your name beside it, but I did. He must have seen it."

"I shouldn't have called you after I left Vegas. Not until this was sorted out," Jenna replied, feeling guilty and a little sick inside. She'd put her aunt in danger by keeping in touch. She'd thought it would be okay, but it hadn't been. She'd never intended to give Aunt Maggie her phone number, but she'd realized she had to. Jenna had asked her aunt to keep it somewhere safe and not to give it to anyone. She hadn't thought that would be a notebook beside the phone, but maybe she should have been more specific.

"Oh, honey. No. If you hadn't called me, I'd have been frantic with worry. I would have spent my days calling everyone I could think of to help me find you. I'd have ended up with an ulcer, make no mistake. Losing your parents was such a blow. You're all that's left of them, and I'd have turned over every stone I could find to look for you."

Jenna's heart glowed with love. "Still, I should have found a better way."

Aunt Maggie leaned forward as if to impart a secret. "Those soldiers you sent are mighty pleasing to look at, especially your Noah. Makes me wish I was a few decades younger. I liked dating soldiers when I was younger. So handsome and strong. One of them asked me to marry him, but I wouldn't do it. I sometimes wish I had. Who knows what might have been?"

"Noah and I aren't in love," Jenna blurted. She'd told Aunt Maggie they were engaged, but she'd already lied about too much to lie about this. "I mean I'm very fond of him, and I think he feels the same, but it's more of a convenience thing really."

Aunt Maggie arched a brow. "Well, dear, it's your life and you may do what you wish. And, really, there was a time when people got married for many reasons besides love. My parents, for instance. They married to unite their families and land, but it turned into a strong, unshakable union that produced three children and much love. They died within minutes of each other, and they were holding hands when they did. I'd say that was a very good marriage, wouldn't you?"

"Yes," Jenna said past the tightness in her throat.

Aunt Maggie winked. "Besides, if you're going to marry someone for convenience, make sure he looks like your Noah does. Not that looks are everything, but it's clear he has a good heart from the way he's taken in his niece and the way he's looking after you. And me."

The door opened and Noah returned inside to find two women staring at him. He hesitated.

"Come over here, Noah," Aunt Maggie said, patting the cushion beside her. "Join us."

Noah did as directed, ducking his head almost sheepishly. Jenna wondered at the change in him, but it wasn't like she could ask him in front of her aunt.

"Jenna tells me you two aren't in love. Is that true?"

Noah shot her a look. She shrugged as if to say, *Hey, you didn't really expect me to lie, did you?*

"Well, ma'am—"

"Aunt Maggie—or Maggie or Mags. Whatever makes you comfortable."

"Well, uh, Maggie… It's true we haven't been together long enough to really make that determination, but I think your niece is one of the best women I know. She's kind and caring, and she makes my little niece happy. It hasn't been easy for Alice to lose her mother, but Jenna has helped her come out of her shell since she's been here. I don't know what Alice would do without her."

"And you? What would you do?"

"Honestly? I don't know. And not just because of Alice." His gaze met hers and he didn't look away. "Alice depends on her, but I do too. I'm endlessly fascinated with her, and I want to know everything about her. I want to take away her fear and uncertainty and make this whole thing go away. I want to crush anyone who would threaten her, and I don't want her to be afraid anymore."

Aunt Maggie put her hand around Noah's and

curled it within her grasp. "That's a very fine answer. If this was still the dark ages and you were asking for her hand, I'd approve it."

Jenna's heart throbbed, but she laughed anyway. "Aunt Mags, there are still men who ask a father's permission to marry their daughter. That hasn't gone away."

"Well, it should. What are we? Sacks of flour? It's a woman's business who she marries and no one else's. Like most things in life. Nosy people want to have a say in things that don't concern them simply because they want to feel superior or be in control. I don't have time for that nonsense."

Noah lifted their clasped hands and kissed Aunt Maggie's. "I hope you don't mind me saying so since we've only just met, but I really like you a lot. You're fuc—fricking cool, Maggie."

She laughed as she patted him. "Thank you, sweet boy. And thank you for attempting to fix the language. Not that I mind a good filthy word for emphasis. They certainly have their place. But the fact you thought it might offend me and changed course endears you to me just a little bit more."

Jenna was shaking her head. Leave it to her aunt to baffle Noah with her special brand of charm. Because she *was* charming. She was a bit of a cross between Dame Maggie Smith and Angela Lansbury. *Downton Abbey* meets *Murder She Wrote*. Sass combined with insatiable curiosity and affability.

"Do you need more coffee, Aunt Maggie? Or would you like to go to bed?"

"Is there a television in my room?"

"Uh, I'm afraid not," Noah said. "But I'll remedy that soon."

Aunt Maggie reached into the giant tote bag she'd set on the floor and pulled out an enormous iPad. "That's all right, honey. Do you have Wi-Fi?"

"I do. Yes. You can use your email, but please don't tell anyone the details of where you are. I have a VPN on the network, so your location won't show. But if you tell someone where you've gone, it'll make you and Jenna easier to find. I cannot emphasize that enough."

"No details. I understand. Truly, I only need to communicate with the reverend and his wife—and maybe one or two others—about the bake sale. I would like to watch Netflix, though."

"You have a Netflix account?" Jenna asked, surprised.

"Of course, Jennie. I may be old, but I'm not a dinosaur. I took computer courses at the library, and while I won't be writing code anytime soon—or ever—I can certainly log into Netflix and watch television."

"Do you mind if I check your settings?" Noah asked. "I'll let you onto my network, too."

Aunt Maggie handed him the tablet. "Certainly."

When it was done, Jenna took Aunt Maggie upstairs to the guest room and showed her the bathroom too. When her aunt assured her she had everything she needed—the guys had taken her bags upstairs when they'd arrived—Jenna left her alone with her iPad and closed the door.

Noah was standing in the living room when she went

down. He looked up worriedly, and her heart skipped. "Do you think she liked me?" he asked. "Or was that just her being polite?"

Jenna went over and put her arms around him, tipping her head back to look up at him. "She likes you. Aunt Maggie speaks her mind, in case you couldn't tell. If she was dubious about you, she wouldn't have held your hand."

"Good to know. I like her, too. She's not what you'd expect, is she?"

"Nope...." She hesitated. "Um, were those things true? What you said about being fascinated with me and wanting to know everything about me?"

"All true. I liked you when I met you at the diner. I like you even more now."

"Because we're having sex, you mean," she teased.

He put his hands on her hips and drew her against him. "Doesn't hurt. But no, it's not the only reason. I like who you are, Jenna. The way you care about people."

"What makes you think I care?"

He snorted. "Don't even try to deflect like that. I see you, Jenna. I see your heart."

Her stomach tightened. She hoped he didn't see *everything* about her heart. If he did, then he'd know it was hopelessly his. "How about I show you some other parts of me?" she purred.

"Mmm, what'd you have in mind?"

She took his hand and led him toward the stairs. "You'll see."

———

"HOW'S JENNA'S AUNT?" Gem asked the next morning as they hit the gym before work.

"She's fine," Noah replied. "She fixed pancakes for me."

Gem stopped lifting the dumbbell he'd been curling. "Wait—pancakes? This morning?"

"Yep." Noah dropped his dumbbell and grinned. "She was dressed and puttering around the kitchen when I got downstairs. She'd already mixed the batter and was just waiting for someone to show up."

"Man, you suck."

Noah laughed. "I have a toddler and two grown women in the house. You willing to take all that on for some homemade pancakes?"

Gem shrugged. "I dunno. Maybe. Well, except the toddler. Can we change it to two nubile women who're crazy for me and sleep naked on either side of me?"

"It's your fantasy," Noah said. "Make it whatever you want."

"I guess the pancakes were amazing?"

"With warm syrup. Yes, amazing. Also the reason I'm doing extra sets this morning." Noah wiped the sweat from his brow. "Between Jenna's dinners and her aunt's pancakes, I think I gotta be careful."

In reality he burned off extra calories easily because of the physical aspects of the job, but it was fun to rub it in Gem's face a tiny bit.

"You suck," Gem said.

Noah laughed. "You asked, dude."

241

Mal sauntered over, towel slung over his shoulder. "Homemade pancakes, huh? And dinner on the table when you get home. Man, better be careful. You'll be domesticated in no time."

"Like you?"

Mal grinned. "Like me. Best feeling ever, my man."

"Both of you suck," Gem said.

"Jealous?" Mal asked.

"Hell, no. I'm looking for busty twins or best friends who cater to my every sexual need. That's better than breakfast and dinner and honey-do lists any day."

"Dream on," Mal said.

Saint walked into the gym. The members of Strike Team 2 could tell from his expression that something was going down. They congregated around him and waited.

"Message from the top, gentlemen. We've got seventy-two hours until we board the plane. Time to get your shit together and prepare to go. Our fun-filled vacation destination this time is Qu'rim, which you are all familiar with. A congresswoman and her staff are going for a little visit, and we get to play protection detail."

Wolf groaned. "Qu'rim? Does anybody else get bad vibes every time we head that way?"

"You mean like that time we caught Ian Black and he still walked free?" Noah asked. None of them would forget that mission a few years back when they'd first met the mysterious Mr. Black and thought they'd ended his operation. Little did they know how powerful he was, or that he was actually one of the good guys. When they'd had to let him go, they'd been filled with impotent anger and frustration at the situation. Now, Black's Bandits were a vital part of their operations from time to time.

"That's what I was thinking of, yeah," Wolf said. "But there was also the time we tried to track down the new leader of the Freedom Force and got nowhere. And now we're on a protection detail for a congresswoman? Greeeaaat. Sounds fun."

"Look on the bright side," Saint said. "This is a quick trip in and out. Unless we get pulled for something else, we'll be home again in a week."

"That is truly a bright side," said Hacker, who'd arrived a few minutes earlier. "Especially since I might not get to say goodbye to Bliss before we go. She flew out this morning at six."

"Did she have any idea when she'd get into the house?" Noah asked, feeling both guilty that his team-mate was giving up valuable time with his fiancée and grateful that she hadn't delayed heading to Las Vegas.

"Bliss is very resourceful," Hacker said. "She expected to get in there sometime tonight. I don't know details because she felt I needed deniability."

"Good woman," Saint murmured.

Hacker grumbled. "Yeah, but I don't like it. Except it's necessary." He shot a glance at Noah. "Wipe that guilty look off your face, Easy. Bliss makes her own decisions, as she reminded me, and it's my job to be support-ive. So I'm supporting her. I just wish it hadn't had to happen *now*."

Mal clapped a hand on Hacker's shoulder. "That's

the job, dude. You know it. She'll be fine, and Easy's woman will be safe."

Easy's woman. Noah liked the way that sounded. He cleared his throat. The guys looked at him. "I asked Jenna to marry me. For Alice. Just thought you guys should know."

Wolf blinked. "For Alice? Not for you?"

Noah shrugged. "A little for me."

Mal slapped him on the back. "Jenna and Easy, sitting in a tree, k-i-s-s-i-n-g. First comes love, next comes marriage, then comes Easy with a baby carriage—except, wait, you sort of got that first."

"You are such a child," Noah said, shoving his team-mate good-naturedly.

Mal hooted. "You would know!"

"Mal, I say this with love—you are *not* right in the head," Noah laughed.

"Dat's what Scarlett says too. I love her anyway."

"Congratulations, Easy," Saint said. "I like Jenna. So does Brooke. I hope, even if you're doing it for Alice, that you find out it's what you want, too."

Noah nodded. "Thanks. I appreciate that."

The other guys congratulated him. It felt awkward at first to tell them he was engaged, and now it felt right. He couldn't wait to go home and kiss Alice on the cheek, say hi to Maggie, and when no one was looking, back Jenna against a wall and cop a feel while kissing the daylights out of her. Not a bad way to spend an evening.

"Okay, guys," Saint broke in. "We've got work to do if we're going to make wheels-up. Let's get moving so we can get this mission done and return to our loved ones."

Chapter Twenty-One

JENNA DRANK COFFEE WITH AUNT MAGGIE ON THE BACK patio while Alice played in her splash pool. It was only about ten in the morning, but the little girl had been begging to get wet since breakfast. Jenna figured why not and filled the pool with a couple of inches of water, added some hot water from the electric kettle to warm it up a bit, and dressed Alice in her swimsuit.

Aunt Maggie was wearing a pink velour tracksuit with white tennis shoes that had rhinestones on them. Jenna thought it was a little too warm to wear all that, but Aunt Maggie said her blood was thin and she needed the extra warmth. Her white hair was cut into a stylish bob with long layers that parted on one side of her face, and she'd put on a subtle layer of makeup. Aunt Maggie was not the kind of woman to give up on primping herself at any age. She'd be putting on eyeshadow and lipstick until the day she died.

Jenna studied her great-aunt as discreetly as she

could. Was Aunt Maggie thinner? Did she look tired? Wan? Was she slowing down?

"Ask your question, Jennie," Aunt Maggie said, her blue eyes focused on Alice. She cut a smile toward Jenna, who blushed a little at being caught.

"That obvious?"

"It is to me. What's bothering you, sweetheart?"

"I was just wondering how you're feeling. It was a long trip, and I was thinking it might have upset you a bit to have to change your routine so suddenly."

Aunt Maggie gave her a look. "You mean my old lady routine?"

"I, uh… Not quite what I meant, no."

Aunt Maggie laughed. "Yes, it is. And no, I'm not upset. I do have a routine, dear, and it comes from living in the same town for so long and from not going on adventures anymore. But I like adventures, and this one was quite fun. Three handsome military men came to my door to whisk me away. They bought me a chocolate shake and snacks and took me on a road trip. And now I'm here, with you and this precious little girl, and while it's different, it's not unbearable." She patted Jenna's arm. "No, I'm quite enjoying myself. It's like going on vacation. And I haven't seen you in so long that it's lovely to be sitting here with you now. I could wish you'd come to Dunkirk, and that you were safe and well, but I'll enjoy our time regardless. Your handsome young man and his friends will fix everything. I know they will."

Jenna smiled. "I think so too."

"He's a good man, your Noah. I like him."

"He is a good man." Jenna warmed with happiness. "I told him you liked him, but he was worried that you didn't."

"Was he? Goodness, I should have been clearer."

"It's okay. I like that he worried about it. Means he cared what you thought. It was sweet."

Aunt Maggie sipped her coffee. "I know I told you that you didn't have to be in love to get married because love could come later, but be sure my darling that you really can love this man. Your happiness is very important to me. Your dad said that when he met your mother, he knew right away she was the one. He never doubted it, and neither did she."

Jenna's heart squeezed. "They risked a lot to be together."

"I still don't quite understand, but apparently romance between enlisted and officers are frowned upon. Still, it didn't stop them, did it?"

"No, it didn't." Jenna smiled a little sadly. Not because her parents got together, but because they were no longer with her. "I miss them, Aunt Mags."

"I do too, honey. I thought Luke would inherit the house, but it'll be yours someday."

Jenna blinked. "But your brother had children too. What about them?"

She was Aunt Maggie's only family who'd stayed in touch, but there were other relatives out there who had not. Jenna had never asked, but she knew her great-uncle Beau had children. Her father's cousins.

Aunt Maggie waved a hand dismissively. "Beau's kids have never contacted me. Not once. Beau wasn't interested in the family heritage and neither are his children. There's only you, sweet girl. I've left it all to you. You may sell it or live in it. Doesn't matter, but the house and land are yours when it's time."

"I want you to live there forever, Aunt Maggie," Jenna blurted.

Her aunt laughed. "I do too, honey. But that's not how it works. Oh, don't you start getting paint and wallpaper samples anytime soon. I intend to live to one hundred. In fact, it may be your children who inherit. Perhaps even little Alice there." She smiled at the child in the pool who was happily singing and splashing. Alice smiled back and splashed a bit more.

Jenna's heart ached with so much love. For her aunt. For Alice. And for Noah, who wasn't even there. She wanted to wrap her arms around him and hug him tight.

"Maybe so," Jenna said, her eyes stinging just a little bit. Of course Aunt Maggie wasn't wrapped up in blood relatives and rightful inheritances. She cared about who loved whom and who would love her house. Her family's house. It was over a hundred years old now, and it deserved someone who would treasure it.

"She's a sweet little girl," Aunt Maggie said. "Such a tragedy about her mother. But I think you will be a good mother to her if that's the path you choose. Of course you'll raise her to know about Sally, but don't feel guilty about letting her think of you as her mama here on earth."

Jenna reached for her aunt's hand and held it. "I love you, Aunt Maggie, and I've missed you like crazy."

"Me too, honey. I'm happy to be here with you, even if I would have preferred it be under different circumstances. I'm treating this like a vacation, though, so don't you worry about me. It's nice to get away for a change. Perhaps that Nora Burtle will stop pushing everything about the bake sale on me and actually do her part this year."

Jenna laughed. "You sound a bit militant there, Aunt Mags. Does Mrs. Burtle leave you holding the bag a lot?"

"She does indeed. The bake sale, the flowers for the Ladies Auxiliary. You name it, she volunteers for it and then expects others to do the work. And don't even get me started on her disastrous turn as Regent of our DAR chapter. Everyone else had to do the paperwork every month while she swanned around to events in her sash and played like she was a queen. Annoying woman."

The sound of the doorbell echoed through the house. Jenna thought about letting it go, but she'd told Mrs. Barlow she'd be home today if the woman needed her to watch her grandchildren while she went to her hair appointment.

Jenna went through the house to the front door and pulled it open. It wasn't Mrs. Barlow. A man in a shirt with the name of the local power company stood there, smiling. "Hi, ma'am. I'm here to check the fuse box. Is it in the garage?"

"Yes, it is. I can open it for you."

"Sure. I'll go around and meet you there."

He turned away and Jenna started to close the door, but the man's foot was suddenly between the door and the jamb. He pushed his way inside as Jenna tried to hold the door. She finally let go, intending to grab her phone from the charger in the kitchen and run into the backyard to scream and dial 911. But what the man said next stopped her in her tracks.

"Run and I'll shoot. Then I'll shoot the old lady and the kid. Your call."

———

TOO LATE, Jenna recognized Owen Fisher. She hadn't at first because she'd never seen him up close, plus he'd had on a ball cap to hide his thinning hair and a pair of sunglasses that he'd now removed and tucked into his pocket.

"Well, Jenna Lane. Here you are. Finally."

He didn't look like a Mafia enforcer, but maybe that was the point. "I don't know what money you're talking about, and I don't have it," she blurted.

He strolled toward her, grinning evilly, the gun held loosely in his hand. "Not sure I believe you, sweetheart. Where's the old lady and the kid?"

Alice's little voice drifted in from the backyard, and Owen lifted an eyebrow. "Okay, that problem is solved. Get them in here. Quietly."

Jenna held up both hands. "Please, just leave them alone. I'll go with you. I'll try to find this money you're talking about, but I honestly don't know where it is. I didn't even know about it."

"Yeah, that's what you'd say if you wanted it for yourself, right? It's a fortune in Bitcoin, sweetheart, and I'm here to get it back."

Jenna blinked. Bitcoin? She knew what it was, and she knew it was currently very valuable, though also volatile. If Sam had stashed stolen money away in Bitcoin, it made a perverse kind of sense. It was easy to store and wasn't accessible by others unless they knew the password. Didn't help her much though. She didn't know where he kept it, and she didn't know how to access it.

Bitcoin was typically stored in a digital wallet, which could be a physical device like a memory stick, or it could be in the cloud or in a mobile app on his phone. Sam had been dead for over six months, and while she remembered seeing him with a memory stick that he kept his work files on, he would have had it with him in his office when Owen shot him. Owen could have grabbed it then, unless he hadn't known to look for it. If he hadn't taken it, then the police probably had it in an evidence bag.

"Sam didn't give any Bitcoin to me or access to Bitcoin. I don't know anything about it. I was just his assistant."

"Right, right. You were his assistant and he trusted you with many things. Maybe things you don't even realize. But you're gonna figure it out, aren't you?" He took a menacing step toward her. "I know you were there that night. Didn't know it at first, but I figured it out later when I tailed you. Your Nissan was on the street when I left Baxter's office, and there was no one in it. Which means you were inside."

She shook her head, but he aimed the gun at her with deadly accuracy. "Don't fucking lie to me, sweetheart. The engine was warm. If I'd realized it was yours instead of some rando visiting the dentist next door, I'd have gone back inside and found you. Where were you hiding?"

"B-bathroom." There was no use in pretending she didn't know what he was talking about. It would only make him angrier. "I didn't see anything. I heard voices, but I couldn't make out what they were saying. I didn't know anything until I heard the shots. I perched on the toilet and stayed there for a long time before I found him." Her eyes filled with tears. "You killed him. Why did you do that?"

"He wasn't a good guy, if that's what you're thinking. He played both sides, stole from the Flanagans *and* from the government. The government might turn a blind eye, but you can't steal from the Flanagans and get away with it. That includes you." He lowered the gun to his side, but she knew he could aim again lightning quick.

"Why did you follow me for a month? Why not just kill me?"

Her heart hammered, but she had to know. She wasn't sure he would answer. He did, though it wasn't much of a reply.

"Because that's what the boss ordered." He waved the gun. "Go get the old lady and the kid. Now."

Jenna couldn't figure out how to warn Aunt Maggie or

how to get her and Alice out of the backyard before Fisher could catch them. The privacy fence was high, and the gate was stiff. You had to lift it to get it open because it was older and the wood had warped. Aunt Maggie was quite spry at her age, but the gate might be too tough. And even if it wasn't, it required more speed than Aunt Maggie would have while carrying a wet, squirming toddler.

Jenna walked to the door, bypassing her phone on the counter. Owen palmed it and tucked it in his pocket, and despair swelled inside her. She started to step out the door, but he was there, his cold pistol against her back. "Ask her to bring the kid inside. You aren't going out there and trying anything."

Jenna swallowed. "Aunt Maggie," she called. "Could you bring Alice inside? I'm a little tied up."

Aunt Maggie swung her gaze around to look at Jenna. Owen Fisher lifted the gun and put it against her cheek. The color drained from Aunt Maggie's face as she got to her feet and went to get Alice from the splash pool. Aunt Maggie wrapped the child in a towel and lifted her up. Alice pitched a fit as the older woman carried her toward the kitchen door.

"I'll take her," Jenna said as Aunt Maggie stepped inside.

Owen didn't stop her as she grabbed the sopping wet toddler from her aunt. "I need to change her into dry clothes," she said.

"If you've got them within reach, go for it. But I'm not letting you out of my sight."

Jenna frowned. "The laundry room. Can you walk

with me to the laundry room? I'll just grab something from the basket and—"

"No. I don't care if you change the brat or not. Just shut her the fuck up."

Alice was wailing mightily now, probably a combination of being taken from the pool and encountering an angry man who she didn't know in her home. He wasn't exactly giving off good vibes, and kids were no fools.

"She'll quiet down if you let me change her and give her a snack. Please."

Owen grabbed Aunt Maggie's arm and hauled her to him, jamming the gun against her side. "All right, let's go to the laundry room then. Try anything and I'll shoot your aunt."

"I'm not going to try anything," Jenna growled before carrying Alice to the laundry room and rooting around in the clean clothes for a little T-shirt and pants. Owen held Aunt Maggie close while Jenna found what she needed. She dried Alice off and changed her on the dryer, thankful she had a box of diapers in the laundry room so she could add a fresh diaper as well. Alice was getting so good at using her potty chair, but Jenna didn't want to have to worry about the little girl needing to pee and being unable to make it because of the stress—or if Owen didn't let Jenna take Alice to the potty.

Once Alice was changed, she started to simmer down a bit. Jenna walked them into the kitchen and got Alice a cheese stick and some apple slices. Once she was in her high chair with her food and her sippy cup of water, she whined a bit but she didn't cry.

"Sit down," Owen said, pushing Aunt Maggie toward a chair. "You, too," he told Jenna.

They sat. Jenna glanced at her aunt, worried that the poor woman was terrified since she hadn't said a word yet. She wasn't terrified, though. She was furious. Her eyes crackled with fire and her cheeks were red. Jenna prayed that her aunt didn't say or do anything to piss this man off.

"Now you're gonna tell me where that Bitcoin is, or I'm going to start cutting," he said very coolly, dragging a switchblade from his pocket and flicking it open as he tucked the gun into a hidden holster at his waist. He glanced over at Aunt Maggie. "Starting with her. It won't be easy though, I promise you that. I'll cut off fingers and toes before I go for the big stuff. Gonna be messy, and it'll hurt like hell."

"How dare you," Aunt Maggie spat. "How dare you threaten us this way."

"Watch it, grandma, or I'll gag you," he replied with a growl.

"It's okay, Aunt Maggie. Just let me handle this."

"Yeah, handle it, Jenna. Tell me where the money is and you can get back to your lazy morning hanging by the kiddie pool."

Jenna didn't believe him for a second. If she told him where the money was—if she *knew* where the money was—he'd kill her and Aunt Maggie both. He might let Alice live because she was a toddler and couldn't ID him, but then again maybe he wouldn't.

"I don't know where it is," she began. Owen's eyes narrowed as he made a move toward Aunt Maggie. He grabbed her hand and jerked it forward, then pressed the knife against her middle finger. A line of blood welled up and spilled over, but Aunt Maggie didn't so much as flinch.

Jenna shook so hard she thought she would rattle apart. She swallowed down the scream that threatened. "I might be able to find it," she blurted. "I have an idea where to look."

Owen didn't let go of Aunt Maggie's hand, but he lifted the knife and leaned back. "Oh yeah? Where?"

"I can't tell you." He started to move the knife back to her aunt's hand and Jenna let the words tumble out. She didn't know if she was brave or stupid, but she knew he'd kill them all if she gave him the information. "If I tell you where, you'll kill us."

"I need to make sure I have access to the account. I can't do that if you're dead."

"And I need to make sure my aunt and my friend's baby stay alive."

He assessed her. Then he let go of Aunt Maggie's hand and leaned back in the chair, all cocky and superior. "Okay. Tell you what. I'll give you twenty-four hours—in fact, I'll be generous and give you until noon tomorrow. That's an extra hour." He got to his feet, and relief started to melt her spine. But then he grabbed Aunt Maggie's arm and tugged her up, and Jenna's spine stiffened again. "Grab the kid, grandma. We're going for a ride."

Jenna shot to her feet. "Wait, no—you can't take them."

"Honey, be glad I'm not killing them. I'm taking the

old lady and the kid, and you're going to get that money for me. You don't get it by noon, I'm going to send you a finger. And I'll keep sending fingers and toes until they ain't got any left. Call the cops, they die. I see a cop sniffing around or hear anything on the scanner, they die. Better make that clear to your boyfriend, too. Got it?"

"Yes." She swallowed. "You should take me with you instead. I'm the one who knows where to look. They don't know anything at all—"

"Doesn't work that way, girl. If I take you, you might decide to get all brave on me or lead me on a wild goose chase for the hell of it. It's amazing what kind of resistance people are capable of when they set their mind to it. But if I take people you love…" He shrugged. "Different story. You'll do anything to save them, though you might not do it to save yourself."

"Please," she begged. "I want to live. I'll do my best for you—"

"I know you will, which is why I'm taking granny and the brat." He took a small envelope from his shirt pocket and handed it to her. "Swallow that."

Jenna opened the envelope. There was a small pill inside, but it wasn't filled with powder. It looked… metallic. "What is it?"

"GPS device. I want to know where you are at all times, sweetheart. I don't know where you are, they die."

"And if the signal craps out?" she asked as fresh anger surged in her veins.

"Guess you'll have to take that chance."

"How do I know it works? You could be lying."

"How do you think I found you? There's one in her wallet. Put it there when I checked the cable. Led me right to you. Stupid broads, the both of you. Now swallow it and don't try to stick it under your tongue."

Jenna gritted her teeth. Aunt Maggie looked a bit more scared than she had before. "Fine," Jenna said. She grabbed a bottle of water and swallowed the pill.

"Open your mouth and show me the underside of your tongue."

She did and he pushed her head back, tugged her jaw open wider, and peered inside to make sure she hadn't hidden the pill anywhere. "How am I supposed to get in touch with you? You have my phone," she grated when he let her go.

"I'll be in touch." He grinned. It wasn't a nice grin. "I'll know where to find you, won't I?"

"Take me," Aunt Maggie blurted. "I understand why you have to. But leave the child. She'll be more trouble than you want."

"Nice try, but I'm taking you both. Grab the kid and let's go."

"I need to get her diaper bag," Jenna said on a rush. "She needs snacks and clothes and some toys—"

"The kid doesn't need anything. I don't care if she shits herself, and she looks healthy enough to me. We're only talking twenty-four hours here, not a weekend retreat."

"Please," Jenna said. "She'll be quieter that way."

"Fucking hell. Get the brat's stuff, and be quick. Again, if anybody shows up to follow me or tries to interfere, I got no problem blowing heads off."

"I know, and I'm not trying to do anything but make sure she's comfortable. But I have to go upstairs to get it. Do you want to come with me?" She hoped he didn't because she had an idea.

His jaw tightened. "You've got one minute. I hear a siren, I start shooting. Now run."

Chapter Twenty-Two

"EASY, YOU'VE GOT A PHONE CALL. IT'S YOUR NANNY. Patching it through now," said the voice over the intercom.

Noah and the guys were in their ready room in the secure area of HOT, which meant no personal cell phones allowed. They were planning the mission to protect Congresswoman Fairhope on her journey to the middle east, and the clock was ticking down until go-time.

But if Jenna was calling him at work, then something was going on. He shot to his feet and jogged over to the desk where the phone was located.

"Jenna, what's happening?"

"Noah," she blurted, and he could hear her teeth chattering. The hairs on the back of his neck prickled in alarm. "He took them. Owen Fisher took Alice and Aunt Maggie. He broke in and he took them."

A shard of ice dropped into his stomach. "Wait—what? Owen Fisher abducted your aunt and Alice?"

He turned when he said it, speaking as much for the guys as for himself. Everyone shot to their feet and waited.

"Yes. He… He thinks I have the money. Sam's money."

"Wait a second, Jen. Calm down. I'm putting you on speaker so the guys can hear, okay?"

"Y-yes."

He hit the speaker button and dropped the phone in the cradle. "Go ahead, honey. Tell us what happened."

He was trying to be calm, but inside he was a boiling mess of fury and ice. The fucking Vegas Mafia had taken his niece along with Jenna's sweet aunt. He'd kill them. Every last one of them. The look on his team-mates' faces said they felt the same way.

"He put a tracker in Aunt Maggie's wallet when he pretended to be with the cable company. He followed her here. He had a utility company shirt on and I thought he was legit—" Her voice choked off, and Noah gritted his teeth.

"It's okay, Jenna. Tell us the rest."

"He shoved his way inside, then he threatened to cut off Aunt Maggie's fingers if I didn't give him the money. He said it's a Bitcoin account. I panicked and told him I might know where it is, but I refused to tell him the location because I said I knew he'd kill us all."

"That was good thinking, Jenna."

"H-he gave me twenty-four hours to get the money. He took Aunt Maggie and Alice and threatened to send me fingers and toes if I didn't. He also said he'd kill them if we called the police. He said to make sure you understood that too. I need help, Noah. Please."

Her voice broke, and his heart felt like it was breaking too. He wanted to be there with her. Right fucking now. But all he could do was listen.

Saint looked grim. The other guys did too. Hacker shoved a hand through his hair and swore under his breath. They were wheels-up in less than seventy-two hours. The last twenty-four would be spent in isolation before they deployed. They had no time. No fucking time.

For the first time in his life, Noah considered what it would mean to go AWOL. He couldn't do it, of course, because he'd end up in prison for abandoning his post. For deserting.

But, *fucking hell*, what was he supposed to do now?

"I know, honey. We're going to fix it. Somehow."

"Noah, he made me swallow a GPS tracker. He wanted to know where I am at all times. He said if the signal quits, he'll kill them both."

Noah wanted to growl. Fucking Owen Fisher intended to follow Jenna to the money and eliminate her once he had it. He'd kill her aunt and Alice too. He wasn't a nice man, and he didn't give a flying fuck about anyone's life or future. He wanted to motivate Jenna to get the money, but he didn't intend to let her live.

"I did something," she continued. "I convinced him to let me get a diaper bag for Alice. I didn't have much time, but I upended Aunt Maggie's wallet into the bottom of the bag. I didn't want to put the whole wallet in there for fear he'd find it."

Noah's heart thumped. "Did you check her wallet after they were gone?"

"Y-yes. I didn't find anything like the pill he made me swallow. I hope it's in the bag, but I don't know. Everything was so fast it could have rolled under the furniture. I don't know."

God, she was brilliant. Brave and brilliant despite being scared out of her wits. It wasn't an easy thing to geolocate a tracker you didn't have the software for, but it wasn't impossible either. Especially when you had another like it. "You did good, Jenna. I'm coming home. Don't go anywhere."

Her voice broke again, and this time she sobbed. "I don't have anywhere to go. I t-tried to follow him. I ran to Lola, but she wouldn't start. I tried to get a jump, but it was too late."

He hated hearing her cry. Fucking hated it. "Don't give up on me, honey. We aren't helpless, and you might have tagged him. We'll find the money, or we'll make him think we have. I gotta go now, but I'll be there as soon as I can, okay?"

"Okay," she said, her voice sounding weak and small. "Hurry."

"I will. I'll call you once I'm in the car."

"He took my phone. I had to borrow Mrs. Barlow's. She had your work number because of Alice."

"Okay, honey. I'm on my way as soon as we hang up. Stay with Mrs. Barlow and I'll come get you."

"I want to go home. I'll be okay, but I need to be by myself. Mrs. B can tell something's wrong, and I don't want her calling the police."

"All right. Go home, lock the doors, and don't open them for anyone."

"I will."

Noah ended the call and looked at his guys. His eyes were gritty, and his throat was dry and tight. Anger ate him up from the inside out. He felt as helpless as he had when the Parkers had abused him and the others. He'd been powerless to stop them, and he felt powerless now.

"We're coming with you," Wolf said, giving Saint a significant look. "We know as much as we need to for this mission at the moment, and we'll finish it when we go into lockdown. Right now, we've got a limited amount of time, and we have to save your family."

"Amen," Saint said. "We fucked up. We should have taken the time to get the equipment so Gem and the guys could've scanned Maggie's belongings more thoroughly."

It wasn't like Strike Team 2 personally owned the sophisticated scanning equipment, or that they carried it with them at all times. It was HOT property, not theirs. Detouring to HOT when they needed to get to Delaware would have taken another hour or more, and they'd assigned it a lower priority. That's what you did on missions. You calculated the risks and made decisions.

They'd made the wrong one, and they were paying for it. They'd used a cheaper, hand-held scanner that could be obtained over the counter to scan for cameras, listening devices, and magnetic GPS trackers. It wasn't sophisticated enough for what Fisher had used.

"It wasn't a high probability that he'd tagged her

with anything other than a magnet on her car," Hacker said. "We didn't even know how he'd gotten Jenna's number until her aunt told her about the cable guy."

"We can debate it later," Saint said. "Let's get over to Easy's place. Head home and change into civvies since we aren't on the clock for this one, but get to Easy's ASAP."

"Bliss should be on the ground in Vegas soon," Hacker said. "Maybe she'll find something in Sam Baxter's house."

"Hack, bring the HOT scanner to Easy's," Saint replied. "We need to scan Jenna and see what kind of tracker Fisher is using. If we're lucky, her aunt's tracker landed inside that diaper bag."

"Copy," Hacker said.

"Saddle up, pardners," Mal said, doing his best cowboy impersonation. "We got work to do if we want to clean up this here town. Yippee ki-yay, motherfuckers!"

"You're mixing your movies again, buddy," Gem said in a stage whisper.

Mal aimed a finger gun and fired. "Bang-bang, mofo."

Noah wasn't in a laughing mood, but he appreciated the effort. "I need to go prepare Jenna for what's coming," he said. "I'll see y'all in a bit. Bring the ladies if they want to come. And maybe grab some food on the way. If somebody can bring dinner for me and Jenna, too, I'd appreciate it. We've eaten pizza recently, so I'd like to give her something else if possible."

"You got it, buddy," Gem said. "I'll stop for subs and wings. Will that work?"

"Works great. Thanks."

Noah badged out and headed for the parking lot. His stomach was in knots, and his heart hurt worse than it ever had before. He'd do whatever it took to get Alice and Maggie back again. No one threatened his family and got away with it. Not even the Mafia.

———

WHEN NOAH WALKED through the door an hour later, Jenna threw herself into his arms. She'd thought he might be angry, might push her away, but he clasped her in his arms and held her tight while she cried.

She hated crying, hated feeling so helpless, but for once she had someone strong to hold her while she did so. Soon enough, she dried her eyes and pushed away from him, feeling guilty for breaking down. "Sorry, sorry."

"For what? Crying? You're entitled to cry, Jenna."

She sniffled and grabbed a tissue from a box on the end table. "I know… But I feel helpless and stupid. And doomed. Definitely doomed." She threw her arms wide as frustration and fear pounded her. "I don't know where Sam kept his Bitcoin wallet, or even if it was a physical device or an app on his phone! I don't have any USB sticks or SD cards or anything like that. I've always used the cloud. I don't have anything I need to hide. All the important papers from my parents are in a lock box in a bank in Vegas."

She'd been racking her brain, trying to stay focused, because if she didn't she'd break down at the thought of Alice and Aunt Maggie being scared or hurt. She'd told Owen Fisher she had an idea where Sam's Bitcoin was, but she'd been stalling for time.

She hadn't expected him to take them instead of her. She'd been trying to save their lives, but she'd gotten them into worse trouble.

Noah rubbed her arms. "Bliss landed. She can't get into the house yet, but she's working on getting access earlier than we'd planned. There may be a clue in that safe."

"Assuming there really is a safe behind the painting," Jenna wailed. She hated the idea that she might have sent Bliss off on a fool's errand. What if she was reading too much into Sam's glee about the Miró? Maybe he'd gotten a sudden appreciation for art that she hadn't been aware of. He hadn't told her everything about his life. She hadn't known about Tiffany, the fiancée.

Jenna had been his assistant, and she'd often wondered why he didn't have anyone else working with him, but she'd come to the conclusion he was just eccentric enough that he didn't work well with others. He'd clearly been doing well, though she now chalked that up to stealing money from the Flanagans more than legal fees and good investments.

"If there isn't, she'll search the house and see if she finds anything. Can you think of anywhere else he might have kept a physical e-wallet?"

"The obvious places. His desk, his briefcase. Maybe

his bedside table. But the Flanagans would have had those places searched already."

"They might not have realized it was being held in Bitcoin at first. They must have thought he had an offshore account, or maybe even had some cash stashed somewhere."

Jenna hugged herself and shivered. "I'm glad they didn't think I had it right away. If they had, I don't think I'd have made it out of Vegas alive."

Noah frowned. "Probably not."

"Even if Bliss miraculously finds it," Jenna said, "I don't know how to get in. There's a password, and probably a pin if he enabled two-factor." She'd looked it up while waiting for Noah.

"Can you think of a word or combination of words he would have used? Special numbers?"

"I don't know." The pin could be anything. His birthday. Tiffany's birthday, which left Jenna in the dark entirely. As for the password? Good God, how was she supposed to figure that out?

Joan Miró? Moneybags-R-Us? Stealing-from-the-Mafia-never-felt-so-good?

She didn't mean to make light, and yet if she didn't she'd start screaming and never stop.

"The guys will be here soon, Jen. The ladies might come, too," Noah added. "They're bringing food, and we'll work on this until we figure something out. We'll try to find Fisher, and we'll try to find the Bitcoin. If we have to invent a fortune instead, we will. Won't be the first time we did something like that."

Her heart thumped. "Really? You could fake it?"

He nodded. "We can with time." He looked troubled for a moment.

Jenna's belly squeezed tight. "What aren't you telling me?"

He was silent. Then he sighed. "We're deploying soon. In forty-eight hours, we go into lockdown for the mission."

"Oh Jesus," she breathed.

He hugged her to him, stroked her hair. "Hey, calm down. It isn't over yet. We've got time, and we'll work this out. We have until tomorrow at noon, right? We'll focus everything we have on this, and we'll solve it. I swear."

Jenna appreciated his conviction, but she knew the confidence was for her benefit. She squeezed her eyes shut and breathed him in. Aunt Maggie and Alice were gone and she didn't know when she'd see them again. And now Noah was leaving her too.

It was too much. Too much like losing her parents all over again. She couldn't go through that, couldn't lose the people she loved most in this world ever again. Because she did love him. Loved him, his niece, and her aunt like crazy. They were her people, even if they didn't know it.

Well, Aunt Maggie knew. Alice was too young. Was Jenna brave enough to tell Noah? Could she say the words and deal with his reaction if it was anything other than complete acceptance and mutual agreement?

The answer was a resounding no. She couldn't. Not right now. She was feeling fragile enough as it was.

Noah gently tipped her chin up and studied her face.

"You didn't do anything wrong, Jen. In fact, you did a lot right. Dumping that tracker into the diaper bag was a stroke of genius. Hacker will find the signal to the one you have, then he'll know how to find Maggie and Alice. We'll get them back."

She nodded because she didn't trust herself to speak.

"What is it, honey?"

"Even if you find them, even if you kill Owen Fisher, the Flanagans will still think I know where the wallet is. They'll never stop hunting me, Noah. If I don't find that money, they're never going to stop."

He hugged her tight again. "I'll stop them. I promise."

Chapter Twenty-Three

"I've got the signal," Hacker said, tapping on his computer as he looked at the screen on the scanner.

Jenna's eyes met Noah's. He smiled to reassure her. She smiled back, but he knew she was still scared. He wasn't scared, but he was worried. Alice had been through so much already. She didn't deserve yet more crap. The knot in his stomach hadn't gone away, but he managed to push it deep and focus on the job. Because that's what he did.

The guys had arrived about an hour ago, dragging in bags of chips, subs, wings, and soda. No beer this time. Haylee and Scarlett were still at work, but Brooke was there. Noah had checked with the neighbors to find out if anyone saw anything earlier, but most of them worked or were out running errands when Fisher pushed his way inside and abducted Maggie and Alice.

Mrs. Barlow had been turning onto the street when she saw a white Chevy Tahoe with a man in a baseball cap and an older woman who held a child on her lap.

She'd noticed because she'd been shocked that anyone would drive around without a car seat. She hadn't realized the child was Alice though, because her face had been buried against the old woman's shoulder. She was positive the car was a rental because she'd seen the sticker in the window that identified it as such.

Hertz, she'd said. Or maybe Budget. Or Avis.

Didn't matter because the information was still golden. A white Tahoe rental was a lot more specific than he'd expected. Noah could have kissed Mrs. Barlow, but he'd settled on thanking her instead.

Hacker did a few more things then looked up. "I have the type of tracker and the frequency, but I'm not getting anything other than Jenna's. It's possible they're out of range, or the tracker is dead now. They aren't designed to last more than a few days."

Jenna made a noise and Noah put his hand on her shoulder. "It's okay. We've got other tricks up our sleeve."

Hacker nodded. "Yep, searching up white Tahoes that have been rented lately. I've checked the flights from Vegas over the past few days, prioritized the non-stops, and I'm running a search on the rental databases for any matches. It'll take a bit of time, but I should be able to narrow it down and get a plate number—or several."

"I thought it was such a good idea to try and get the tracker in the diaper bag," Jenna said sadly. "I didn't realize it would be so difficult to find."

"It was a good idea," Noah told her. "When we find the Tahoe, we'll track it down using the GPS system onboard. If the other tracker still works when we're in range, it'll help us pinpoint where they are."

They'd already tried to find the number that Fisher was calling from by hacking into Jenna's phone records again, but he'd been smart enough to block it. If they'd gotten it, they could have tracked his cell phone. No such luck, though. They'd tried to track Jenna's phone since Fisher had taken it, but they weren't getting anything there either. He must have been smart enough to stash it inside a metal container to block the signal.

Hacker's phone rang with the special tone that he used for Bliss, and everyone went quiet. "Babe," he said. "Got you on speaker."

"Hey, gang. I'm outside the house having a look around. It's a big mother—"

"Bliss," Hacker interrupted with a growl. "Be careful."

"Calm your tits, sweetie. There's a realtor sign on it. Someone's coming out to show me in a few minutes. I'll have a look inside, see if there's a safe, and come back later with Bernie—"

"Who's Bernie?"

"Bern is an old friend. He's seventy-five, if you're worried, and an excellent safecracker."

"Not worried about that. Worried about *you*."

It would have been fun watching Hacker have a meltdown over his very competent fiancée's plans if this was just a job and Noah wasn't personally involved. As it was he could appreciate it, but he was impatient for everything to get moving. He needed answers, and he needed his niece and Maggie back safely. Which he knew everyone was trying like hell to do.

"I thought there was a dispute about who got the house," Jenna said. "Sam's ex-wives and Tiffany were fighting about it, right? It was sitting empty until the courts decided?"

"True," Bliss said. "But all three women apparently agreed to sell. The money will go into trust until the court determines who gets it, though I'm not sure how much there'll be after the mortgage is paid. Sam Baxter didn't pay it off before he died, but that's not surprising. So many of these guys hold onto the Bitcoin, thinking it'll keep appreciating. It's the ultimate gamble, really. But the market's hot and the women want to unload it while they can get the most bang for the buck. Whatever's leftover will go to the winner of the court case." Bliss called out to someone. Then she was back. "Showtime, y'all. I want to stay on with Jenna while I walk through, but we'll go off speaker. I don't think we'll need it. I'll pretend like she's my husband back home. If anything comes up, she can tell you about it."

"Love you, baby," Hacker said.

"Love you too, Sky. Now let me work and I'll get back home to say a proper goodbye before you head out on that business trip."

Hacker handed Jenna his phone and she went out the back door to stand on the patio while Bliss took a tour of the house. Hacker gave one last longing look in the direction Jenna went, but Noah knew it was really for Bliss. Then Hacker sat down, expression grim, and got to work finding the Tahoe while the guys made plans on how to rescue Maggie and Alice when he did.

Twenty minutes later, Jenna came back inside. She didn't look as beat down as she had before. Instead, she seemed excited as she handed Hacker his phone. That was a good thing.

"What is it, Jen?" Noah asked, going to her side.

"There's a safe," she said. "Behind the painting in the dining room. He had one installed."

"That's good. Really good."

"I know. But we have to wait until tonight before we know if there's anything in it. I'm not sure how I'm going to do that."

Noah blew out a breath. He was closer to feeling like she did than he cared to admit. "It's part of special ops, babe. We wait and wait and wait—and then we go, adrenaline flooding our bodies, and we get the job done. This time will be the same. You'll see."

"I appreciate that you're so positive." She frowned. "It's been four hours since Owen Fisher was here, and I haven't left the house. He's going to wonder, isn't he?"

"Probably. But he gave you until tomorrow, so he's not likely to do anything yet."

She nibbled her lower lip, and he found himself wanting to kiss her to reassure her. And himself.

"You're right. I guess we wait."

He put an arm around her and hugged her to his side. "We wait."

———

JENNA CONSIDERED HERSELF A PATIENT PERSON, but this time the waiting was torture. After the initial success of learning what kind of vehicle Owen Fisher was in and finding the type of GPS tracker he'd used on her and Aunt Maggie, there was no progress. Hacker had narrowed down the flights and potential rentals, but he was still going through them.

By the time Bliss called, it was nearly midnight. Hacker put her on speaker again.

"We're in the safe," she said. "But there's no device in it. There's nothing except a sealed envelope."

"Open it," Jenna said. "Please."

Paper rattled and then Bliss whistled. *"If you're reading this, you might be looking for my fortune. You won't find it. If I'm gone, it's gone. 3000 Bitcoin. You do the math. If you know me well, then you know what my most prized possession is. Maybe that will help. Maybe not. If I'm dead, which is a real possibility, then I'm laughing right now because they won't get the money back. I did what I had to do, and I took what I had to take. That's all the explanation you get. ~ Sam"*

"Goddammit, Sam," Jenna growled, her heart throbbing. "Why would you do that?"

"I'm sorry, Jenna," Bliss said. "But at least we know what we're looking for. Sky, better get busy faking an e-wallet for Jenna. How much is that, anyway?"

"Today?" Sky asked. "About ninety million dollars."

"Good God," someone muttered.

"That's a fuck-ton of money. No wonder they want it back," Noah said. He reached for Jenna's hand and squeezed. "Sorry."

"Bliss," Jenna said before the other woman hung up. "Can you look at the painting, specifically the frame?"

"Sure can. What am I looking for?"

"A USB device, or something like that." Excitement began to bubble inside her. "Sam once said to me that the painting was his most prized possession. I don't know if it means anything or not, but what if he hid something in the frame?"

"Okay. This will take a little time. It's a big painting."

They waited while Bliss spoke to someone in the background. The minutes ticked by excruciatingly. Jenna couldn't help but think that the clock was running down and she was no closer to having the money than before. Ninety million dollars. No wonder the Flanagans had noticed. If Sam had taken a couple hundred thousand, they might not have realized it. She would never know his reasons or how he got the money in the first place. It was useless wondering.

But she was still angry about it. She had every right to be since he'd dragged her into it without her knowledge. Just being there with him, being his assistant, had been enough.

"Bingo," Bliss said. "There's a USB stick wedged into a hollowed-out notch on the back of the frame. Nothing else, though. No more paper anywhere."

"Good work, babe," Sky said. "Please get your cute ass out of there and come home."

"On my way, darlin'. I should just make the red-eye."

The call ended and everyone seemed to let out a

collective sigh. Haylee and Scarlett had arrived earlier, then left again after a couple of hours because they had to work tomorrow. Brooke was still there, and all the guys, including Jake "Harley" Ryan and his fiancée, Eva Gray, who was a gorgeous, heavily tattooed woman with a kind smile. Jenna didn't think she'd been at her best for meeting new people today and she'd apologized for it, but Eva told her not to worry and they'd have plenty of time to get to know each other later. Then she'd hugged Jenna and said, "Welcome to the family."

It'd been comforting at the time, though nothing comforted her for long. There was too much at stake.

"Now what?" Jenna asked tiredly. "I have to get the money to him by noon, and time is running out. I don't even know where it's supposed to happen, or what I have to do."

Fisher said he'd be in touch, but how was he going to do that? She had no idea.

Hacker rubbed a temple. "I don't know what we're dealing with until we get that e-wallet, but you should all know that it's impossible to fake Bitcoin. It's a blockchain transaction, and it's incredibly secure. We could possibly mock up something to show a flush account, but the moment you try to transfer it, nothing's going to happen."

"Can you crack the password to the e-wallet?" Saint asked.

Hacker shook his head. "No. You only get a few tries, then you're locked out forever. It's happened to legit owners before. They lose the credentials and the money is gone. Nobody gets it."

"Then we're going to need another plan," Noah said. "We have to find that son of a bitch, and we have to get the drop on him."

"I'm working on it. I've got it narrowed down to three white Tahoes. One's at a residential address in Clinton, another's at a hotel in Laurel, and the third is at an apartment complex in Edgewater. My money's on Edgewater since it's the closest. None of the Tahoes were rented by an Owen Fisher, but I don't suppose we expected that."

"Nope," Saint said. "Maybe we need to take a ride and see if we can't pick up a signal from Maggie's transmitter. What's the name on that Tahoe?"

"Patrick Morgan."

Jenna felt a tickle of recognition. "I've seen that name on some of the contracts that Sam had me type. Patrick Morgan is a contractor for the Flanagans. Oh sweet Jesus, a contractor. That's not even subtle, is it?"

"Not really," Hacker said. "Okay, so that's probably our guy. He's at the Palms in Edgewater—though all I can do is track the Tahoe. I won't know which apartment unless Maggie's device is still transmitting when we get close."

"I want to go," Gem said.

"Me too," said Muffin and Zany at once.

Jenna teared up. They were the ones who'd gone to get Aunt Maggie only yesterday, so the fact they wanted to be there to save her aunt and Alice now was touching.

"I'm going, too," Jenna said. "I can't stay here and wait any longer."

Noah's expression was filled with empathy. "You

can't go, Jen." She started to say something in protest, but he went on before she could. "He knows where you are. If he's monitoring the transmitter and sees you approaching, it's over."

"Oh. Right. Shit."

"Gem, Muffin, and Zany—you three go stakeout the place," Saint said. "See if you can get a signal. Hacker, start work on a fake account just in case. Maybe it'll be enough to distract him with. The rest of you, bed down for now. If Gem and crew get a signal, we'll go to Edgewater. If not, we've still got a lot left to do. Time's running out on us."

It wasn't the immediate action Jenna wished for, but it was something. Noah took her up to his room. They lay together fully clothed, her back to his front, the occasional tear running down her cheek to drip onto the pillow. He hugged her tight.

"Jenna. Baby. We'll get them back." His voice sounded strangled, and she thought maybe he was working to believe it too. He had to be frantic for Alice. He'd only just gotten her in his life, and now she was gone. In danger. Because of Jenna. "There are nine of us. We're highly trained and lethal. This is what we *do*."

"I know," she whispered, "but you usually have assault equipment. You aren't going to have it when this isn't an official mission."

His breath was soft against her ear as his lips feathered over her skin. "We have what we need. You don't think we do what we do and don't buy our own stuff, do you? We got this."

"It's all my fault," she whispered, her throat tight. "If he hurts them, I'll never forgive myself."

"No. It's not."

The tears started to fall in earnest now. Noah put a leg over hers and wrapped her up in his embrace. Then he held her through all the long hours of the night.

Chapter Twenty-Four

Noah was pouring his first cup of coffee when there was a knock on the front door. Wolf pulled it open and Bliss sailed in. It was a little after six a.m. She dropped her computer bag on the table and went to kiss Hacker.

"How in the hell did you get here so fast?" he asked.

She grinned. "I might know people with private jets, sweets. Then I might have asked for a ride once I found out they were in town." She produced a small cylinder from her purse. "*Voilà*, boys and girls. Ninety mil worth of what is essentially pretend money if you think about it."

"Wait a minute," Hacker said as he took it from her. "Why didn't you text me and tell me you were coming?"

She patted him. "I wanted to surprise you."

He looked like she'd beaned him with a heavy object. "I'm surprised. Very surprised."

"A girl needs some mystery. Is there coffee for me?"

"I'll get it," Noah said. "What do you want?"

"Just cream. Thanks."

He handed it to her, suppressing a yawn. "Thanks for going out there and taking the risk to break into the house."

She shrugged. "All in a day's work, Easy. Where's Jenna?"

"Sleeping. She didn't sleep much last night, so I didn't want to wake her when I got out of bed."

All eyes turned to him, and he realized what he'd said. Oddly enough, he felt hot color creeping into his cheeks. "What?"

Mal snorted. "Told ya."

Wolf groaned and took out his wallet. He handed Mal a twenty.

"Wait—did you bet on Jenna and me?"

"Yes. Is that a problem?" Mal pretended innocence.

"It's not like that, Mal. Jenna's not, um...."

Mal rolled his eyes. "Dude, it's not the fact you're sleeping with her. It was the way you blushed when you realized what you said. Which you wouldn't have done if she was the usual Easy thing. You care about her."

His face was still hot. "I said I asked her to marry me, didn't I? Of course I care."

"Okay, guys," Bliss cut in. "Enough of the heart-warming girl chat. I just flew across the country twice in twenty-four hours, and I'm feeling a little cranky. Let's get this show on the road and take this Fisher asshole down, okay?"

They could all agree on that.

It was another couple of hours before Jenna came downstairs. She'd twisted her hair up and her face looked freshly scrubbed, but her clothes were the same and there were bags under her eyes. "Any news?" she asked.

"No signal from Maggie's transmitter, but the guys are still watching the Tahoe. And Bliss is back," Noah said. Bliss waved. "Hacker plugged in the USB. It's definitely what we were looking for. But we don't have the password or the pin to the digital wallet app."

"How many tries do we get?" Jenna asked.

"I didn't try any," Hacker said. "But I'd guess five to ten. Once we try something, it'll tell us how many more guesses we get."

"Do you have an idea?" Noah asked.

Jenna shook her head. "Not yet," she whispered. "I keep trying to think of something, but I don't know. It could be anything, right?"

"Pretty much."

"Great," she said, frowning.

"Here, have some coffee. There are donuts, too."

"Thanks. I'm not hungry."

Noah didn't like the shadows under her eyes or the way her hands shook when she lifted the coffee cup. Stress was eating her alive. "Jen, please eat. You won't be any good to Maggie or Alice unless you do."

She looked at him with that wounded expression that threatened to rip his soul in two, but then she nodded. "Okay."

A delivery truck pulled up outside. Saint peered out the window to confirm. "FedEx coming this way."

The driver rang the bell, and Noah answered. The man looked up and swallowed, and Noah knew he must look pissed. He tried to look friendlier.

"Uh, I have a delivery for a Miss Lane. She has to sign for it."

Noah exchanged a look with Saint. What the fuck?

"I'm Jenna Lane," she said, coming forward.

The driver held out a digital reader for her to sign, then handed her an envelope. Noah shut the door and they went to the kitchen table. Jenna still held the envelope, and her face was white.

"What if he started early? What if it's a finger?"

"I'll open it," Noah said gently, taking it from her. He unzipped the tab and peered inside the foil-lined envelope. "It's a phone."

"That's mine," Jenna said as he pulled it out and held it up.

A moment later, it rang. Jenna started, then stared wide-eyed at Noah. "You should answer it, Jen. It's got to be Fisher. He'll have instructions for you."

"What do I say when he asks about the money?"

"Tell him you're still working on it. You have until noon, so he needs to chill."

Easier said than done when a cold-blooded killer had your niece and your woman's aunt as hostages. Jenna nodded.

"Hello?" she said, hitting the button to put the call on speaker.

"Do you have my money?"

"I'm working on it. Are my aunt and Alice safe?"

"You don't ask the questions here. I do. You haven't

gone anywhere since I left you yesterday. How the fuck are you getting the money if you don't go anywhere?"

"I'm looking online. Through Sam's accounts. He had some offshore accounts, and—"

"I'm sending you an address. Be there at noon with access to the account, or the old lady and the kid are dead. Bring anyone with you, they're dead. Try to run, they're dead and so are you. I'll track your ass down and I won't make it easy or quick. You got me?"

"Loud and clear."

"Good. Time's wasting, girlie. Better find that money."

The line went dead. Jenna closed her eyes and sucked in a deep breath. "I've never been a violent person, but I swear if I got a chance to kill that man, I wouldn't hesitate."

"None of us would," Noah growled. "We've got a little over three hours to go. We need to figure out where this address is, and we need to come up with a plan."

———

IT WAS ALMOST GO-TIME, and Jenna was feeling the stress. Hacker had plugged in the USB drive, and Jenna had tried to guess Sam's e-wallet password. There were other files on the drive, also password protected, but she didn't care about those. Her first two tries failed. There were three left, and she'd been too on edge to guess again. She'd begged for a break, they'd taken one, and then Gem called and said they had a faint signal from Maggie's transmitter.

That was an hour ago. They'd discussed the team hustling to Edgewater and breaching the apartment, but it was broad daylight and there were civilians around. Someone could get hurt, and that might give Owen Fisher enough warning to kill Maggie or Alice—or both —and make his escape.

Instead, they decided to wait for Fisher to leave. If he didn't take the hostages with him, then Gem, Zany, and Muffin would rescue them. If he did, they would follow him to the meeting and take them when there was opportunity.

Owen Fisher was one man, and he seemed to be working alone. There would be opportunity. Even if he had help, Strike Team 2 was confident they could master the situation. It was what they trained for and what they did countless times over the course of their careers in the military. They were elite soldiers, and Jenna needed to believe them when they said they were going to bring her family home alive.

Eva and Brooke were going to wait in Noah's house in case they were needed afterward. Bliss would ride with Hacker, Saint, and Wolf. Noah would ride with Harley and Mal. Jenna had to go alone, though Noah promised they'd be nearby. Hacker also had the signal to her GPS transmitter and would keep tabs on her at all times.

The meeting location was a warehouse complex a little south of Annapolis. The guys pulled up a schematic of the building Fisher had indicated and went over it thoroughly, making plans for the mission. A check of the address had revealed that it was a Flanagan-owned property, which made Jenna's stomach curdle. She'd been this close to their property and hadn't known it. What if they'd had people there who'd seen her before? And what if those people had come to the diner and then called Charlie and Billy once they recognized her?

She shuddered. Nowhere was safe when the people hunting you were rich enough to stretch their web from coast to coast. She'd been lucky, and she hoped she stayed lucky. Just a little while longer.

Noah and his team had to get Alice and Aunt Maggie back. Hopefully, they'd take down Owen Fisher while they were at it. That still left Charlie and Billy, but maybe Jenna would figure out the password to the digital wallet. She could transfer the money to them, and they'd leave her alone.

It was a long shot, and she needed time to make it happen. Time was something she didn't have right now. Not while her aunt and a sweet little girl were in danger.

Hacker gave her the USB, folding her fingers around it and pressing just enough to convey his belief in her. "You've got this, Jenna."

They'd discussed giving her a mockup but decided there was a chance that Fisher had seen the USB in Sam's possession and would know if it wasn't the same distinctive superhero logo that Sam had been a fan of. It was entirely possible Fisher knew *exactly* how Sam's Bitcoin account was stored. Just because she'd lied about researching offshore accounts didn't mean he'd fallen for it.

"Thank you." Her eyes stung, but she didn't cry. She felt like family with these people. She hadn't had that in so long now, and she'd missed it.

One by one, the guys gave her a fist bump as they headed outside to get into their vehicles. They were wearing urban camouflage, and she already knew they had tactical vests and weapons stashed away. They were mic'ed up, each of them wearing a tiny transmitter in his ear that let him communicate with the team.

Noah walked her to his Jeep. He'd insisted she take it since Lola wasn't reliable.

"I'm a little nervous about taking your Jeep," she said as they reached the vehicle.

He pulled the driver's door open and turned to look at her. "Don't be. I'm not."

"It looks new."

He smiled. He was so handsome with his dark hair and blue eyes, so intense with the way he looked at her right now. "Newish. Doesn't matter though."

"I don't want to scratch it."

"I don't care if you do. I really don't."

"I should have gotten that battery already. I should have just gone to the auto parts store when the garage Mr. Pruitt sent me to said they didn't have it in stock. I shouldn't have waited for them to order it just because it was cheaper there."

Noah put an arm on either side of her, caging her in. Her butt and lower back were against the seat. There was nowhere to go, so she tilted her chin up to gaze at him.

"Don't worry about the battery, Jenna. Don't worry about anything but getting to that warehouse and doing what you have to do to keep yourself alive. If you have to give him that USB, give it to him. Ninety million bucks doesn't matter if you can't find the password anyway. Let him plug it in, whatever it takes. Stall him, and we'll attack when the moment is right. He won't get away with anything."

"I hope you're right," she whispered past the ache in her throat.

He put his hands on her face and kissed her, his tongue delving inside to stroke against hers. She wanted to melt, wanted to forget, but she couldn't. She kissed him back, knowing this might be goodbye. Knowing this might be the last time ever.

"I am right," he growled after he broke the kiss, his forehead pressed to hers. "We're getting married, Jenna Lane. You can be Jenna Cross or Jenna Lane Cross or Jenna Lane or Jenna Jenna Bo Benna. Don't care which one you choose, okay? I just want to be with you."

Jenna's heart throbbed. "Jenna Lane Cross? Sounds like a video game."

What she really wanted was to ask what he meant about wanting to be with her, but she couldn't bear the answer if it wasn't exactly what she wanted it to be.

"That's what you picked up on in that speech?"

"Um, yes. Was there something else?"

His gaze dropped for a moment. When he looked at her again, his eyes were filled with emotion. "I loved my mother. I loved Sally. They were the only family I ever had. Okay, my team is my family too, but not the same kind of family. That's not what I meant." He swore, then put his hands on her shoulders and squeezed. "I'm not saying it right. My mother and Sally were the only people I loved, the only ones who loved me. Now I love Alice, and I think I might love your aunt because she's awesome—and I fucking *know* I love you."

Jenna's jaw dropped and her heart raced and the world felt suddenly brighter and more colorful than it had before. "You do?"

"Yes, I do. Maybe I'm nuts, maybe it's all too fast, but I don't fucking care. I know myself and I know when I feel something like this, it's not typical for me. I love you because you're amazing, because you make me want things I never knew I wanted, because I have an endless need to know you and learn everything about you—and right fucking now, I need you to go into that warehouse and let me do my job so I can bring you home again. I want to marry you for real. I want to raise Alice with you, and maybe have our own kid too. We can talk about that, but—"

Jenna threw her arms around him and pressed her mouth to his, kissing him with her whole heart. "I love you, too."

Noah squeezed her as he set her away from him. His eyes were glassy, and he dragged in a breath. His voice, when he spoke, was raspy. "We have to go, Jenna. There's no more time. Hold onto that thought, okay? I want to explore it fully in the near future."

"Okay, yes, definitely."

"Get in the Jeep."

He stepped back, and she climbed in and pressed

the button to start the vehicle. They touched hands one more time, then she closed the door, sniffed away her tears, and backed out of the driveway. Once she was on the street, she waved at Noah. He waved back.

It was all they had time to say. For now.

Chapter Twenty-Five

NOAH FELT LIKE HIS HEART WASN'T IN HIS BODY. IT WAS driving down the road with Jenna, and it was with Alice and Maggie. The people he loved were in danger, and there was nothing he could do except wait until the right moment to pull them out of it.

"I was an orphan," he said to no one in particular. He knew the guys in the other car could hear him too because they were miked up and able to communicate back and forth. "You guys know that. I have a hard time with showing emotion because my sister—who was my foster sister, by the way—and I were abused for five years by our foster family. She was sexually abused by the asshole husband who's in prison now. The wife is there, too, but she won't be there as long as he will. There were ten of us in their home, and we were punished with cages and chains and withholding food. It was a prison, and it was hell, and I learned to keep my feelings to myself because nobody was going to fix my life but me.

"I know y'all stuck with calling me Easy when I first joined the team because of the coffee thing—thanks again, Mal, for convincing me that new recruits had to memorize everyone's coffee order—but I got the name in Special Forces training because I kept saying the Army was easy whenever the guys would ask why I didn't ever complain about how hard they pushed us. Sleep deprivation, not eating for hours on end, running with a full pack—didn't matter. It was fucking *easy* compared to being a kid in that house."

He clenched his fists and jaw and told himself it was good to say it. Good to share his secrets with the men who were as close to brothers as he'd ever get.

"I never said any of this to you guys because I've spent my life burying my feelings down deep or pretending they were a lot less intense than they were. Easy likes it easy, right? No messy entanglements, no chaotic emotion. But I love Alice and I might love Maggie too—and if anything happens to Jenna, I'll fucking lose my mind. She's it for me, which I know you guys all get." Gem, Zany, and Muffin weren't on the frequency yet, but they would be when they reached the warehouse area. It occurred to him that Bliss was listening because she was part of the computer team, but that was okay.

Mal—crazy Mal—reached over and put a hand on Noah's shoulder. "We're going to save her. We're going to save them all. You guys were there for me when Scarlett needed us. I thought she was probably dead—but she wasn't. We aren't going to fail."

"Thanks," Noah said, his throat tight.

"Thanks for telling us," Saint said. "I'm fucking sorry you went through that, but damned glad you're on this team."

Noah sucked in a breath. "I feel like a fucking girl right now—no offense, Bliss."

"None taken, honey," she said. "Emotions are rough sometimes."

"I'm not saying they're bad, not at all, and women are pretty scary when they cry because they're pissed off, but I don't want to cry. And I don't want to feel like my heart is bleeding out all over the place, but this shit is new for me and I've realized that I don't control a damned thing. It won't take much to break me. I'll survive if they don't, but I'll wish I was dead too."

"That's pretty much how it works," Wolf said. "When you fall in love, it's fucking amazing. And terrifying too because you no longer own your heart. She does."

"Just so you guys know," Bliss said, "you own her heart as much as she owns yours. We die a little bit every time you guys go on a mission. Now, is it too nosy to ask if you told Jenna how you feel?"

Noah couldn't help but laugh. "I told her."

"Okay, *aaaaand?*"

He felt the heat of happiness glowing inside him. "She feels the same."

"Awesome," Bliss replied. "I like her."

"Me too," Hacker said.

The guys all chimed in, and Noah tried to hold onto the happy feeling he got from thinking about Jenna and how great life would be with her. But the tension in the car notched up as the miles ticked by.

Noah could see the Jeep ahead. They were trailing Jenna at a good distance, but at least he could see the tail end of the vehicle. Hacker had outfitted her with a small microphone, but it wasn't hooked into the team's comm system. It was intended to capture the things Fisher said. Bliss would be monitoring the conversation from the car just in case.

"Gem called in," Saint said in their ears. "Fisher is on the move, and he's got the hostages with him. No one else in the car, no other cars appear to be following. He's a lone wolf."

That was good news. Or would have been if Noah didn't have a knot in his stomach the size of an asteroid.

Maybe that was normal for the situation since he'd never been so personally invested before. Or maybe it was his gut telling him bad things were coming. He closed his eyes and willed the apprehension away. This was a job, like all the other jobs he'd done.

He had to dig deep, find his focus, and do the work. It was the only way to free his family and secure their future together. A future he'd tried to avoid but now wanted more than he wanted his next breath.

"Getting close to the warehouse," Wolf said in their ears a short while later. "Let's get this done like we planned it so Easy can take his ladies home and spend time with them before we gotta take that desert trip."

"Roger that," Mal said. "Yippie ki-yay, motherfuckers! Let's go kick some mafia ass."

———

THE WAREHOUSE where she was supposed to meet Owen Fisher sat at the backend of a complex of warehouses. Chain-link fencing surrounded the compound, but the gate was open and there were no guards. Trucks sat at the loading docks to the first couple of warehouses, loading or offloading, but no one paid attention to a woman in a Jeep.

Jenna drove slowly through the complex. When she spotted a white Tahoe sitting empty in front of one of them, she knew she'd found the right place. Noah had told her that Fisher would likely get there first. He wanted the tactical advantage of already being inside when she entered the warehouse.

Jenna parked nearby and sucked in a breath to slow her racing heart. She didn't know what was going to happen, but she knew she would do anything to get her aunt and Alice back safely. She just had to go inside and make Fisher believe she had what he wanted.

Bliss was listening, but there was no way Bliss could speak to her in return. The guys had debated giving her full comm but decided it was too risky. The small microphone was positioned in the bun on top of her head and blended perfectly with her hair color. The hope was that Fisher would incriminate himself and the Flanagans, but Jenna thought he might be more cautious today.

"Going in. Wish me luck." She turned off the Jeep and pulled the emergency key out of the fob. Her heart hammered and blood rushed in her ears. She wanted this to be over, but she was also terrified by all the ways it could go wrong.

The bright side, though, was she had an entire Black Ops team at her back. Which she never would have had if she hadn't met Noah. Her belly tightened at the memory of kissing him and telling him she loved him. She wanted to do that again. And again. She prayed she got the chance.

"If anything happens to me, tell Noah I love him, please. And tell him I'm sorry I got him into this. I'm sorry I got all of you into it. But thank you for helping me." She sniffled. "Okay, enough of that. I'm going to think good thoughts and get this over with."

Jenna stepped out of the Jeep and shut the door. She didn't lock it because Noah had told her not to in case she had to run. She kept the key in her hand because it was a weapon. Noah had told her that, too, but she'd already known it. He'd seemed relieved when she demonstrated how to use it.

Jenna went up the steps to the loading dock and over to the door. It opened with a rusty creak. It was dark inside. She thought the guys might like that info, so she said, "Wow, it's dark in here," in a low voice.

The warehouse smelled old and rusty. The ceiling soared above her head, and dim light filtered in through a few panes of glass high up on the sides of the building. As her eyes adjusted, she realized it wasn't quite as dark as she'd thought. But it was still dark.

She made her way into the building, trying to hear beyond the hammering of blood in her ears. Crates were stacked up in one section of the warehouse, and there were piles of debris scattered randomly across the floor.

"Up here," a voice said.

Jenna looked up to see a man in shadow standing on a catwalk that ran across the back of the warehouse. Behind it, she could just make out doors and what seemed to be rooms. Offices?

"Where are Aunt Maggie and Alice?"

"They're here. Come up and we'll talk."

"I need to know you have them with you," she said, fear crawling up her spine.

He pushed open a door behind him. It was utterly dark inside the room, but a moment later Aunt Maggie called out, "We're here, Jenna."

Alice wailed then, and Jenna's insides liquefied. Her legs were shaky as she pushed them forward. The stairs were metal and they clanked as she walked up them. She hoped Bliss was relaying all this to the guys. She wanted to describe everything she saw but she couldn't figure out how to do it and not make Fisher suspicious at the same time.

Alice was still crying when Jenna reached the top of the steps and stopped. Owen Fisher was leaning on the railing, watching her with an intense expression. "Did you get my money?"

"Your money?" she asked as anger and hatred swirled in her belly. "I thought it was Charlie and Billy's money."

"Answer the question. Do you have it?"

She took the USB stick from her jeans pocket and held it up. "Yes, I have it."

Fisher did something and then yellow light flared on the catwalk and inside the room where Aunt Maggie and Alice were. "You won't mind plugging it into a computer and showing me then."

"Let Aunt Maggie and Alice go first."

"You come plug that thing in and show me you have access. I better see a Bitcoin account. I better see that you can get into it. We'll transfer the money. Once I verify it's in the account, I'll leave."

"Sounds too easy."

"Maybe it is. Don't see what choice you have though." As if to emphasize her utter helplessness, he lifted his hand and pointed a gun at her. "Either way, you're going inside the office and proving you have the dough."

Jenna swallowed her fear and moved forward slowly, hoping something was about to happen. But nothing did and she reached Fisher's side. He grabbed her arm, digging his fingers into her flesh until she yelped before shoving her into the room. Horror rolled through her at the sight of Aunt Maggie and Alice. They were inside a big metal dog crate with a padlock on it. Aunt Maggie's pink velour was streaked with black dirt and rust. Alice held the bars and wailed while Aunt Maggie tried to soothe her as tears tracked down her own cheeks.

Jenna whirled, clenching the key in her fist with the point barely sticking out between her fingers. He hadn't noticed it, which made her feel at least a little bit like she had some protection. "You let them out right now," she grated. "I'm not giving you anything until you do."

Owen Fisher raised the gun and aimed at her head.

Then he smiled evilly before slewing it over to point at the cage. "You don't want to cooperate? Which one should I shoot? The brat, probably, so she'll shut up."

Jenna shook with rage and fear. She told herself to calm down and narrate what was going on for Bliss and the team. That hadn't necessarily been what they'd intended, but she could do that much if it helped. "Fine, I'll cooperate. But you put them in a cage like dogs. It's old and rusty, and it's in a dark corner of the room. What kind of person are you?"

"The kind that doesn't let sentimentality stand in the way of the job." He jerked the gun toward a desk with a laptop computer on it. "Get over there and access that account. Now."

"I'm going."

She couldn't figure out how to say the desk was on the opposite side of the room from the cage without it seeming patently obvious that she was narrating everything, so she didn't. Fisher stood beside her as she pulled out the squeaky chair and sat. He flipped open the lid to the laptop.

"Now, sweetheart, or I start shooting."

Jenna pushed the USB into the slot with shaking hands. *Anytime now, fellas. Please.*

If Noah and his guys didn't burst in here soon, Owen Fisher would know she couldn't get to the money. And then he'd kill Aunt Maggie or Alice—or both.

"Why didn't you get the money from Sam before you killed him?" she asked. "Wouldn't that have been easier?"

"Didn't know how much he'd really stolen. Charlie

and Billy wanted an example made of him. It wasn't about the money so much as the disrespect, which he displayed right to the last."

"I don't understand."

"You don't have to. Open the account."

They could both see the files sitting there when the USB connected. An e-wallet app and the other files Sam had put there. All were password protected—and Jenna didn't know any of them. She clicked the app, her heart lodging in her throat. Alice wailed as Aunt Maggie tried to shush her.

The password box came up. Three more tries. That was it, and the ninety million was gone forever. Locked up and encrypted so no one could ever access it again. Not that Jenna felt like it mattered, really. It wasn't her money, and she wasn't going to keep it even if possession was all that was needed for Bitcoin. It wasn't like a traditional bank account that belonged to a specific person. It belonged to the person with the password and the pin. End of story.

"Type," Fisher grated. "Or the kid goes first. Maybe once I splatter her brains all over granny, you'll believe I mean business."

"You're making me nervous!" Jenna cried. "If my hands shake too much, I'll get it wrong. Do you want me to get locked out?"

He looked confused for a second. And then he looked murderously angry. He whirled toward the cage.

"No, I'm doing it! I swear! Stop! Please!"

Fisher whirled back, eyes flashing. "Type the fucking password, bitch."

Jenna lay the key on the chair beside her leg and typed with both hands. It was her third guess, and she'd been thinking about it since the last one failed. She just wanted to get in and buy them a few more seconds. If it worked, she'd still need the pin. She was clueless about what it could be, but she'd worry about that if the prompt came up.

Jenna hit enter and held her breath.

Access Denied. Two Attempts Left.

"What the fuck?" Fisher growled. He grabbed her hair and yanked her head back, and Jenna grasped the key, slotting the edge between her fingers as she clenched it in her fist. She was about to swing it toward Fisher's groin as hard as she could.

Until the ceiling caved in.

Chapter Twenty-Six

Noah, Mal, Gem, and Zany burst through the ceiling where the office was located. They'd gotten Bliss's updates from Jenna, and they'd confirmed it was a suspended ceiling on the schematic. They'd scaled to the warehouse roof using the outer stairs and a fire escape ladder, then infiltrated through the windows nearest the office. From there they'd been able to crawl onto the rafters and skirt along to where the office was located directly below. The ceiling tiles were secured using a drop system, which meant they weren't solid like drywall.

All they had to do was kick the tiles in and drop to the floor. They were counting on the element of surprise to disorient the gunman just long enough to take control of the situation. On Noah's mark, they collapsed the ceiling.

The rest of the team was coming up the stairs as well as securing the perimeter from any interference, should Fisher have outside help in the complex. Since this was a Flanagan property it was possible, though they'd seen no sign of anyone heading in this direction since they'd arrived.

Noah, who was closest to a shocked Fisher, got off a kick from above. It glanced off Fisher's shoulder, and his gun skittered away as he fell to the floor. He scrambled for it as the team landed with a mighty thud. Noah took in Jenna's frightened face as his feet hit the floor. He couldn't focus on her right now, but he was overjoyed she was alive.

Her chair had turned over when she'd jumped out of it and pressed herself to the wall. Fisher was closest to her as he rolled, coming up with the gun in both hands, ready to fire. Noah launched himself at Fisher as the gun went off, booming in the small space. The bullet went wide, but the next one might not.

Noah didn't care. He was taking this motherfucker out, or he would die trying. He was almost there when Jenna moved. She was closer than he was, and she screamed as she threw herself at Fisher. Noah yelled, but it was too late.

Jenna landed on the Mafia enforcer's torso and the gun went flying. He wrapped his hands around her throat and started to squeeze—and then he screamed as Jenna's hand came up and slashed downward. Noah reached Jenna and jerked her backward, off Fisher.

The Jeep key fell to the floor, covered in blood and tissue.

Fisher kept screaming, his hands over the socket where his eye had been. Blood gushed. Jenna whirled into Noah's arms as Gem rushed by and secured Fisher's wrists and ankles with zip ties.

The rest of the guys appeared, and someone got bolt cutters to free Maggie and Alice. Noah felt frozen inside as he watched. His emotions had chilled the instant he got the news from Bliss that Maggie and Alice were in a cage. Like dogs. One of his childhood nightmares had returned, and it made the bile rise in this throat.

Not for himself this time. He was more than capable of stopping anyone who tried to do that to him ever again. He was enraged for the woman and child who'd had to suffer the fear and indignity and helplessness of being caged.

Fucking Owen Fisher. Fucking asshole who cared more about money than about a human life. He'd threatened to kill Alice for crying. If the man wasn't in agony already, Noah would've taken pleasure in breaking a few limbs. It wasn't necessary, though. He'd never see out of that eye again. Too bad the key hadn't been longer and sharper. Jenna could have penetrated into the man's brain and killed him.

Then again, Noah didn't wish that burden on her. As it was, she'd probably have nightmares about what she'd done.

As soon as the cage door was open, Zany reached in and took Alice, who was sobbing. Gem helped Maggie to her feet. She clung to him as she emerged from the cramped position of sitting inside the cage.

"Thank you, sweet boy," she said.

"Anytime, Mags," Gem said gently.

Zany took Alice out of the room and downstairs. As much as Noah might want to hold her, he had Fisher's blood on him from where Jenna had clung to him with it on her hands. They both needed to clean up before they could hold Alice. Saint and Wolf were there, looking pissed off as the others grabbed Fisher and took him from the room.

"You okay, Jenna?" Saint asked.

She was still clinging to Noah. "Y-yes. I'm okay. Aunt Maggie, I'm so sorry."

Maggie looked over at them and smiled a little wearily. "You can't be responsible for evil people, child. Now hush up, tell that man you love him, and I'll hug you when I'm not so dirty." She glanced down at her pink tracksuit. "This was my favorite. Stupid jerk."

Noah thought he might love her for saying she was too dirty to hug Jenna instead of pointing out the blood on her grandniece's hands.

"We'll get you another one," Gem said. "If we have to comb through every store between here and Dunkirk, we'll find it."

"Oh honey, it'll launder. I'm just feeling mighty pissed off about it is all."

Gem led Maggie from the office and Noah put an arm around Jenna to escort her down the stairs and to the restroom. He hoped the water was still on in the building so she could wash her hands.

She stopped him on the landing. "Are you okay, Noah?"

He blinked. "Me? You're asking me if I'm okay. Baby, I'm worried about *you*. How are you?"

She sniffed. "I'm fine. I think. I mean he didn't really hurt me, but my throat is a little sore."

"We'll have to check that out when we get out of here. Make sure everything's okay."

"I understand. But what about you, really? Are you all right?"

He was still processing everything, but he could feel the thaw happening inside, which meant his emotions were starting to churn again. He glanced back at the room, at the cage with the door hanging open and the padlock dangling uselessly from the latch. "I'm okay. It was a shock when Bliss told us they were caged, but I'm glad you were able to relay that. We knew they were safer inside there than if they'd been free in the room the way you were. We didn't know if we'd be coming down on top of you or not, but we had to do it."

"Okay, Noah. I just thought... maybe it brought up old feelings."

He swallowed and nodded, amazed that she was worried about *him* right now. "It did, but they were nothing compared to the thought of losing you."

He pictured everything since the moment he'd dropped through the ceiling—and nearly froze again as he replayed it. Jenna had *thrown* herself onto Owen Fisher when he'd been firing at Noah.

He hugged her tightly to him, and she melted in his arms. He pressed his mouth to her hair and choked back an overwhelming urge to cry. Where the fuck had that come from?

"Never do that again, Jenna. Never put yourself in danger like that. Not for me, and not for anyone."

She tilted her head back to look up at him. "I was closer, and he could have killed you. If he'd gotten a head shot—" She sucked in a breath, and hugged him tighter. "I had the key, Noah. He wasn't expecting it."

He wanted to chastise her some more. Sit her down and lecture her about all the reasons she shouldn't have done it. But he didn't. He lay his cheek on top of her head and held her, letting the rightness of it flow through him and make everything better.

"You would have done the same," she whispered when he didn't speak.

"Yeah, I would have."

"I love you, Noah."

"I love you, too."

"Can we go home now?"

"Yeah, we can go home."

She went down the stairs in front of him. They went over to the restroom and turned on the sink. It worked, and she washed the blood off, muttering the whole time. He figured that was a good sign, though he expected her to react hard at some point. He cleaned up as well as he could, then he put his arm around her as they walked through the warehouse.

"How do you feel about a vegetable garden?" she asked.

"If you want one, I want one."

"What about a cat or a dog? Or both? I always wanted a pet, but we never had them because we moved so much."

"Get them both if you want." He stopped her before they reached the Jeep. "I want what makes you happy,

Jenna. If it's a cat or a dog or a vegetable garden, I'm down for it. If you want to paint our bedroom pink and put in rose curtains, I'm there. I'll help you hang them. All I need is for you to smile at me every morning and every night, and tell me you love me at least once a day. I'm *easy* to please."

And he was. So long as he had her and Alice, and even Maggie, his life was going to be better than he'd ever expected. He would always miss his mom and sister, but he was going to live every day to its fullest with the family he had now.

With the family who'd saved him and shown him what he could have if he let himself feel all those emotions he'd worked hard to suppress over the years.

Being in love was messy and scary and awesome and amazing, and so many fucking things it would take him a lifetime to figure it out.

But it was going to be *so* worth it.

"We're going to have fun together, aren't we?" Jenna asked a touch shyly.

He smiled. "Yeah, we really are."

———

FIVE DAYS LATER...

JENNA'S PHONE WAS RINGING. She reached for it, bleary-eyed, and picked it up. A glance at the time told her it was only three in the morning.

"Hullo?"

"Jenna, it's me."

She scrambled upright in bed, her heart racing. "Noah? What's happened? Are you okay?"

"I'm fine." She could hear the drone of an engine. Or so she thought. "We're coming home."

Happiness bubbled inside her. "You are? Really?"

"Really."

"When will you be here?"

"About an hour, I think."

"I—what's that sound? I thought you were on a plane or something."

Noah laughed. "It's Gem's Corvette. He's giving me a ride since you have the Jeep."

"Oh no, he's going to be annoyed with me. Why didn't you call me? I could have come to get you."

Lola was finally in the shop getting her new battery, which was why Jenna had kept the Jeep. Lola was getting a brake job, too. Turned out she needed that pretty badly. Jenna might sell her, but she wasn't selling her with shitty brakes.

"I didn't want you to have to wake Alice."

"Aunt Maggie is still here," she said, feeling guilty that he hadn't known. She hadn't texted him because he was supposed to be out of contact for at least a week, maybe more. By then Aunt Maggie would've been home again. "We went to Dunkirk for a couple of days, but then she came back with me and Alice because she decided to let Nora Burtle see what it was like when *she* had to handle the church bake sale for a change."

Noah chuckled. "Giving Mrs. Burtle a taste of her own medicine, huh?"

"Yep."

"I missed you, Jenna."

Happiness was a warm flame inside her. "I missed you, too. I guess you'll tell me when you get home why you're back early."

"It won't be the first thing I do, but yeah, I'll tell you."

"Should I put on some coffee?"

"Nope. How about a robe with nothing under it?"

She laughed. "I can do that. See you soon."

———

JENNA'S entire body tingled with satisfaction. Noah had been home a little over an hour, and they'd taken advantage of every moment. She rolled over in bed as Noah returned from the kitchen with two cups of coffee. She pushed up on an elbow and watched him. He was so damned handsome, so strong—and all hers.

"I should be the one fetching coffee for you," she said, yawning. "You were out there on a mission while I was here lounging around in the backyard with Alice and Aunt Maggie."

He perched on the side of the bed and leaned over to kiss her. He was mighty awake for someone who'd just spent five days on a mission only to return when extremists attacked the congresswoman's convoy. The congresswoman had been shaken enough to cancel the visit, and everyone had boarded a plane home. Noah said he'd slept then, so that's why he was awake now. Plus, it was midday where he'd just come from.

"It was a short one. I'm not complaining."

"I saw it on the news, but I didn't know that's where you were," Jenna said as she took a sip of the hot liquid.

"No one was hurt, but they were shaken up a bit." He sighed. "The congresswoman has a daughter. Everly Fairhope. She's on her mother's staff. I think Gem was interested."

Jenna lifted an eyebrow. "Really? Hmm, think we can get Everly Fairhope to come to dinner sometime?"

Noah laughed. "If anyone has her number, it's Gem. Maybe you can tell him to invite her. Or strongly hint he should bring a plus one. That should prod him to ask."

"Okay… But do you think maybe you're a little too hopeful here? Seeing connections where there might not be any?" Jenna teased.

Noah leaned over to kiss her. His free hand slid beneath the covers to cup her breast. "The only connection I'm interested in is with you, Miss Jenna Lane. I want to make love to you again."

She sighed. "Alice will be up in about twenty minutes, and I need to get dressed."

Her body was already responding, softening in all the right places. He tweaked her nipple and pulled his hand away. "I could take you to the shower and rock your world in ten, but I think maybe I'll save it for later when we have more time. I don't feel like a quickie with you. I feel like a long, slow, languid fuck with lots of kissing and touching and sighing."

God, she loved this man. "We just did that, Noah."

"I know. It was great, right?" He grinned.

She grinned back. "Yep."

"Get in the shower, babe," he said, standing and adjusting the hard-on that was clearly visible in his shorts. "I'll go start breakfast."

She watched him go, feeling happy and slightly sleepy. She hadn't fallen asleep until eleven, and he'd called at three. She'd gone back to sleep until he walked in a little after four, then spent the next hour curling her toes while Noah made her come again and again. Another short doze, and she was about to shower and start the day.

But that was okay because she wanted to spend as much time with Noah as she could. There hadn't been much of it after the warehouse. Bliss had contacted her friends in law enforcement and given them the audio of Owen Fisher confessing to murdering Sam and to being ordered to do so by the Flanagans.

It might not be enough to put him away for good, or to do much to the Flanagans, but it was enough for now. Fisher was being charged with kidnapping, extortion, and threats with a deadly weapon in Maryland, and he would probably be extradited to face murder charges in Nevada.

Jenna sat up suddenly, a cold chill washing over her skin. She jumped out of bed and threw on her robe then ran downstairs. Noah turned, alarmed. "What's wrong?"

"The USB," she blurted, hurrying to the table where her laptop was plugged in. She took it from its hiding place and inserted it into the slot then waited as the files came up.

"Do you think you know?"

"Maybe. I don't know. There are only two tries left on the app."

Noah stood over her and leaned down to kiss her on the temple. "Does it matter?"

She gazed up at him. "Maybe not—but I think the files *do* matter," she said, pointing at the folder with the documents in it. "I want to find out what's in them."

He nodded. "Okay. Go for it."

Jenna double-clicked the folder and a password prompt came up. Sam hadn't liked memorizing passwords, so whatever he'd used for the digital wallet app, he'd probably used for the documents. He'd always used the same password on his computer and all his files at work, but she'd tried that one. This one was different.

"My most prized possession is Miró," she said, typing in the first letter to every word. She added the two digits for the year he'd bought the painting. It was the way Sam did his passwords. He thought up basic phrases then used the first letter for each word. Then he added a number, like a year or an age. Sometimes a birth year. She chose the year of acquisition.

The document folder opened, revealing pages of files labeled with the Flanagan name.

"Oh my God," she said. "It's all here. All the dirt on the Flanagans."

"Wait a minute, you don't know that for sure."

She clicked a random file. It was a record of a conversation between Sam, Charlie, and Billy about padding invoices for the Venus Casino. "Say again," she said, feeling suddenly light inside. This was it. There was enough here to bury the Flanagans for a long time.

"I'll call Hacker a little later and get copies to him. Bliss can pass it to her FBI contacts and whoever else can use it."

"This means more to me than the money."

"What about the money? Think you know that password, too?"

She shrugged. "I might. But I'd need a few tries at the pin, and we don't have that."

"Let's get these files to Hacker for peace of mind. Then I think you should try it when you're ready. Why not?"

Why not indeed? All she had to lose was ninety million dollars she'd never had in the first place, and wouldn't keep anyway. That was a drop in the bucket compared to how she felt about Noah and Alice and Aunt Maggie. People were more important.

Her people. Her family.

As if on cue, Aunt Maggie walked into the kitchen. "Noah! You're back."

"I'm back, Maggie," he said, holding out an arm so she could go and give him a side hug.

"Well, now, sit yourself down and let me fix up some pancakes," she said after giving him a squeeze. "Won't take me but two shakes of a dog's tail."

"You don't have to, Maggie."

She waved him off. "I know that, sweet child, but I want to. Now sit. Jennie, can you pass me that flour?"

"Of course, Aunt Mags." She brought the flour over. "I better go get Alice. It's almost time for her to wake."

"You go on, Jellybean. There will be plenty of pancakes, don't you worry."

Jenna kissed Noah on his beautiful mouth, laughed at his somewhat stunned expression—big bad Black Ops soldier taken down by a little gray-haired old lady—and headed upstairs.

Her heart was full. Her life had taken a turn she hadn't seen coming, but she was so damned grateful she hadn't left town when Allison fired her. She'd taken a chance on Noah and Alice instead.

And she'd won. She'd beat the odds, and she'd won the jackpot.

It was the only jackpot she ever needed.

Epilogue

Six months later....

"I'M NERVOUS," Jenna said.

Noah had his arm wrapped around her shoulders and he gave her a squeeze. Alice was perched on his hip, her arms around his neck. "Nothing to be nervous about. We're already Alice's guardians. Adopting her is a formality, isn't it?"

She nodded. "I wasn't this nervous when we got married at the courthouse. Why not?"

"I don't know, but if you think you aren't the perfect mom for Alice, you're wrong."

"I think it's because of your sister. I never met her. Would she approve?"

Noah could honestly say, "Yes, she would. She would have liked you and Aunt Maggie a lot."

Jenna smiled softly. "I'm glad."

Noah smiled back. Maggie—he'd graduated to

calling her Aunt Maggie now—was a regular fixture in their lives. Noah, Jenna, and Alice drove over to Dunkirk a couple of times a month, and Maggie came to stay with them often. She'd helped Jenna plant her vegetable garden, and they'd taken Alice to the shelter to pick out a cat.

They'd come home with two, and Jenna had informed him a dog was next. She hadn't gotten around to the dog yet, but she would.

Noah loved coming home to a house filled with living, breathing creatures—and Tom Petty blaring more often than not. Jenna was always cooking something marvelous. Alice had progressed to using the potty and talked almost all the time.

She was rarely clingy these days. They'd taken her to the Early Bird Diner, and she'd happily gone with Vicki while the woman made her rounds.

Allison hadn't said a thing to Vicki about it, because she wouldn't dare according to Jenna. She'd also come over to congratulate him and Jenna on their marriage, though it was a fake congrats if he'd ever heard one. More like she was jealous. Barnyard Tami had been more sincere, though she'd winked at him as if letting him know she was still available.

Jenna had laughed her ass off when he told her about it after Tami walked away.

"You've still got a chance for the wounded chicken squawk," she said, giggling.

"No. Hell no."

A few days after Noah had returned from the aborted congressional escort mission, he'd gotten a package in the mail from Sally's bank. She'd had a safety deposit box, and she'd filled it with mementos. Photos, a lock of Alice's hair, a journal about her pregnancy and Alice's birth, her thoughts about healing and her love for Noah. She'd called him the best brother she could have hoped for, and that had made him tear up as he read it.

There were pictures of her during her pregnancy, and of Alice from birth to about a month before Sally's death. She'd had some printed, and she'd had a hard drive with photos and documents. She'd even written a letter about why she'd put those things in a safety deposit box and what she hoped would happen in case of her death.

It had shocked him at first, but it was just like Sally to think of those things. She knew how precarious it was to be a single parent, and she'd wanted to make sure that Alice had the important things if something ever happened and Sally was no longer there.

Noah and Jenna had a plan for sharing everything with Alice as she grew up. Sally would always be her mother in heaven, but Jenna was going to be her mother here on earth and Noah would be her dad. They wouldn't let Sally be forgotten.

Noah had thought it would take Alice time to start calling them Mommy and Daddy, but she'd taken to it like a fish to water. Except sometimes she called him Daddy Unk No, which was kinda hysterical.

Kids.

When it was time to go in for the hearing, Noah and Jenna held hands while Noah carried Alice. The judge asked questions, they answered them, she spoke to Alice

—and then it was over. They were legally Alice's parents as they walked out of the courtroom.

As they emerged from the building into the cold December air, Noah thought he might explode from the happiness coursing through him. It was almost Christmas, and he had a wife and child he adored. He also had an aunt for the first time ever, and he adored her, too. He felt like he'd undergone an adoption as well. It was something he'd desired when he was stuck with the Parkers, but it had never happened. No family had wanted him.

Now he had his own family, and he planned to spoil them.

"Christmas is in three days, Alice," he said. "Have you been a good girl for Santa?"

"Yes! Very good."

He hugged her. "You have. Are you excited about going to Aunt Maggie's for Christmas?"

She nodded so hard her brains were probably scrambled.

"We're leaving tomorrow," Jenna said. "With Titus and Cornelius and lots of presents for everyone. I can't wait."

Noah couldn't wait either. Except for the part about taking two cats on a road trip. They meowed indignantly every time they went to the vet, so he couldn't imagine how much racket they'd raise on the journey to Delaware. Still, they were family, and you didn't leave family at home alone during the holidays.

They reached the Nissan Armada he'd traded the Jeep in for and Noah put Alice into her car seat. Then he caught Jenna before she could escape and tugged her into his arms for a quick kiss.

"I love our life. I love you. Thank you for marrying me."

She pressed her gloved hand to his cheek. "I love everything about life with you, so thanks for asking."

"Have you thought any more about school?"

She shrugged. "A little. But honestly, I'm enjoying what I'm doing right now. Between taking care of Alice and you, and posting cooking and lifestyle videos, I'm happy. When we drive out to Vegas to get my stuff out of storage, I'm going to do a travel vlog about the whole thing, too."

He'd been surprised when she'd told him it was possible to make some money doing those things. But she had a small income going from it. People liked watching videos about other people cooking and taking care of a household, which was fine with him.

"Sounds good. But if you ever want to go back to school, we'll make it happen."

She kissed him. "I know. You're the best Christmas present I ever got."

He grinned. "It's not Christmas yet."

"It is for me. Every day since I walked into your house."

"*Our* house."

"Our house," she echoed softly.

———

CHRISTMAS MORNING, Jenna woke early. Noah was still asleep when she crept from the room, grabbing her laptop as she went. It was before dawn, and Jenna turned on the tree. Aunt Maggie and Alice were still asleep too, but soon the house would be filled with a little girl's delightful squeals and the laughter of adults. Then there'd be the cooking smells. She couldn't wait.

Jenna had one thing she needed to do, though. She opened up her laptop and inserted Sam's USB. She hadn't tried to guess the password or pin to the e-wallet app since she'd successfully opened the incriminating files on the Flanagans.

Files which had helped bring them down. They were no longer major players in the building trade in Vegas. The Venus Casino and Resort was broke and looking for investors to salvage it. Charlie and Billy were awaiting trial on fraud charges, and Owen Fisher was dead. He'd died under mysterious circumstances in prison, though Jenna figured that was the Flanagans' doing.

Hadn't done them any good though. Sam had kept thorough records of every misdeed and bribe. When he said he knew where the bodies were buried, he'd literally meant it.

The bodies and *all* the secrets.

Jenna dragged in a breath then pulled up the app. She typed the password she'd used on the documents folder. She held her breath as she waited for the pin prompt. She'd been thinking about that, too. She was going to use Joan Miró's birthday. If that failed, she'd use Sam's.

And if that failed, the Bitcoin was gone forever.

When the pin prompt appeared, she hesitated—and then she changed her mind and typed four digits. Zero. Seven. Zero. Four. Sam's birth month and day. He'd always been proud to be a July Fourth baby.

The account opened.

"Oh my God," Jenna breathed. Three thousand Bitcoin, just like he'd said. Ninety million dollars, give or take on any given day.

Tears sprang to her eyes. She couldn't keep it and wouldn't keep it, no matter that possession was all it took. Under any other circumstances, the money could be returned to those who'd been defrauded. But there was no way of knowing who to return it to.

"Hey."

She looked up through teary eyes to find Noah looking down at her.

"Noah. I did it."

"Did what, baby?"

"The e-wallet. I'm in."

His eyebrows climbed up his forehead. "Holy shit."

She nodded. "Yeah."

He sat beside her and looked at the balance. "That's amazing."

"We can't keep it."

"No, we can't."

"I don't want to give it to the government and hope they do the right thing with it, either."

"Agreed." He took her hand. "There are a couple of guys on another team in HOT whose wives are wealthy. They have charitable organizations they run to help people. We can ask them for help if you want."

"That would be great… You aren't mad I don't want to keep it?"

"Mad? No, why would I be?"

"It's life-changing money. Like winning the lottery."

"Except it was stolen, right? From criminals who probably stole it from decent hard-working people. And from the government, which means they stole it from all of us."

"That's pretty much what I was thinking. I know there are people who would call me crazy, but I can't keep what is essentially stolen money. And I can't *not* try to do some good with it."

He put an arm around her and they snuggled into the couch, watching the blinking lights on the tree. "That's why I love you, Jenna. You care about people, and you're going to do great things for those who need it."

"We'll start with scholarships for orphans," she mused. "And programs to help abused children."

Noah took the computer from her lap and set it on the coffee table. Then he dragged her across his lap and kissed her senseless. He'd just unbuttoned the first two buttons of her Christmas pajamas when a little voice squealed, "Santa was here!"

"He certainly was," Aunt Maggie said as Noah and Jenna scrambled upright and fixed their clothes. Her eyes sparkled as she looked at the two of them knowingly. "Well, who's going to start handing out presents? This little girl needs something to open."

It was a long while later, after presents had been

opened and breakfast consumed, that Alice fell asleep beneath the tree.

"I'll watch her," Aunt Maggie said from her chair. She was busy knitting a blanket, and both Titus and Cornelius were trying to attack the thread. "You two go upstairs and get your showers."

The way she said it told Jenna that her aunt wasn't fooled in the least about what they were going to do when they were alone.

"You're one in a million, Aunt Maggie," Noah said.

"I know, dear boy. Now scram, both of you."

They scrammed.

Bonus Epilogue

Six months later...

Today was his wedding day.

Correction, today was his *let's have a big ceremony wearing his Army dress uniform while Jenna wears a white dress* wedding day. They'd been married for a year, but Noah had always felt bad about not having the big day with pictures and cake.

They'd gone to the courthouse and said their vows with Aunt Maggie and a couple of friends, but it wasn't quite the same. Not that he cared, and Jenna said she didn't, but he had a burning desire to have the photos for his children someday.

They'd found the perfect white church set in the woods, complete with a red door, and as soon as the minister said yes, they'd started planning. The church was halfway between Annapolis and Dunkirk, so that meant everyone could drive to it in under two hours.

It was summer, a warm breeze blew, and Noah was

sweltering in his dress blues. So were his teammates, but they'd all agreed it was worth it.

The church was packed with friends and family who'd made the trek. The women were beautiful in their colorful dresses, some with matching hats, and the men who weren't in the military wore their Sunday best. Old Mr. Pruitt was there, and Mrs. Hanley. Allison had surprisingly RSVPed that she was coming. And there she sat, looking as if she'd sucked a lemon.

Vicki dabbed at her eyes, and the ceremony hadn't even begun. A few other of Jenna's old coworkers were there, too. Even Tami, who'd been threatened on pain of death not to bring weed, had squeezed herself into a red dress that looked like a second skin. She was making eyes at the soldiers and SEALs, and it was fricking hilarious.

Noah had asked Jenna if she was sure she wanted to invite Tami. She'd said yes. Her reasoning was that it would be unkind not to, plus it might provide some comic relief. Jenna wasn't one to worry about her big day being overshadowed by barnyard sounds coming from the restroom, should the occasion arise.

Besides, she'd said, all the guys she knew in HOT had better sense than that.

He wasn't so sure, but whatever.

"You gonna make it?" Gem asked. Gem was by his side as they stood at the back of the church, just outside the sanctuary.

"I'm already married. I'll make it. What about you?"

Gem shrugged. "My wedding isn't for another

month. I'm looking at this like a dress rehearsal. Except for the part where I don't actually say vows."

Noah had asked Gem to be his best man because they'd always been tight. And now that Gem was about to get married, it seemed like the thing to do. Noah would have been happy with any of his teammates as his wingman, but Gem was the one who'd come to mind immediately.

Jenna had asked Bliss Bennett-Kelley to be her maid of honor. The two had grown close over the past year. Jenna was close to all the women, but Bliss was her bestie. It had seemed an odd pairing in a way. Bliss was always impeccably groomed in designer clothing, and her hair and makeup were always perfect. Jenna wore her hair in a messy bun much of the time, and her clothing often consisted of jeans or yoga pants with T-shirts. In summer, it was cutoffs and T-shirts.

But the two of them were close, and that made Noah happy.

Aunt Maggie was in the front pew, dressed in her finest pink floral dress, and she'd brought several members of the Ladies' Auxiliary with her. The ladies had taken over the reception preparations, which was happening in a tent on the church lawn after the ceremony, and Noah knew he was in for a treat when he got to eat the things they'd prepared. There was nothing like good food made by women who'd gotten the recipes from their grandmothers and great-grandmothers. He supposed that was true of men, too, but there were no men in the Ladies Auxiliary.

Though Reverend Smith and his wife were there,

too, and the reverend was reputed to make a very fine pound cake. Maybe it'd be on the dessert table when this was over.

When the signal was given, Noah and Gem went into the church and stood on the dais at the front. The organist played something soft and sweet as Alice appeared at the rear of the aisle with Brooke Rodgers. Brooke's baby bump was prominent, and the look she gave her husband was filled with happiness as she walked behind Alice.

Alice did her job well, scattering pink rose petals from her basket. Brooke was there to keep her on task should she need it, but she didn't. She got to the end and dumped the basket, which made everyone laugh.

"I did it, Daddy," she practically yelled to Noah as Brooke took her hand and led her to sit by Aunt Maggie.

"You did, baby," he said proudly as Bliss came up the aisle, looking pretty in a pale lavender dress that was surely made by some fancy designer. Not that it looked fancy, but knowing Bliss, it had a fancy price.

The organist launched into "The Wedding March" and Jenna appeared at the rear of the church on General John "Viper" Mendez's arm. Noah's breath stopped. Just stopped. His bride—his wife—looked incredible. She'd refused to let him see the dress she'd picked out, and he was glad.

Because in that moment, he'd never seen a more amazing bride in his life. Her beautiful hair was piled on top of her head with soft spiral curls that framed her face. He thought she wore more makeup than usual, but that's probably because he wasn't used to seeing her in lipstick. He figured Bliss had done her makeup. Whatever she'd done, it was perfection.

Jenna's dress was satin, and it skimmed her form like one of those dresses in a Jane Austen movie. He knew what that meant because he'd watched a few with her during their TV nights. She'd wanted simple but elegant. She'd definitely gotten it. There was no lace, no fussy appliqués, just satin and Jenna's feminine figure.

Perfection.

Noah managed to close his mouth by the time she got to him. The minister asked who gave this woman in marriage, and the general answered that he did. Old-fashioned, but whatever. Jenna had asked the general if he would do the honors because he reminded her of her dad more than anyone else she knew. He'd graciously accepted, which had kind of shocked Noah because he'd thought the HOT commander would be too busy.

"Never too busy for my HOT family," Mendez had said.

Now, he placed Jenna's hand in Noah's and stepped back. Noah trembled as he held Jenna's hand. His eyes prickled. This was supposed to be for show. For her. For memories. Yet he was the one getting emotional.

"Hey," she said softly.

"Hey," he said past the tightness in his throat.

"Today's the day it stops," she whispered.

"What stops?" he asked, confused.

"The day you stop dragging my heart around," she answered with a grin.

A Tom Petty reference. At their wedding. Total

proof she was meant to be his. He wanted to laugh, but managed not to. And he didn't get emotional either, because she'd successfully defused that bomb.

"I'm free-fallin' into this marriage with you," he told her, throwing Petty back.

Her smile made his heart skip.

The ceremony continued, the light shined through the high window behind the altar, and Noah was at peace in his soul. His life. His woman. His future. All of it perfect.

Books by Lynn Raye Harris

The Hostile Operations Team ® Books
Strike Team 2

Book 1: HOT ANGEL - Cade & Brooke

Book 2: HOT SECRETS - Sky & Bliss

Book 3: HOT JUSTICE - Wolf & Haylee

Book 4: HOT STORM - Mal & Scarlett

Book 5: HOT COURAGE - Noah & Jenna

Book 6: HOT SHADOWS - Coming Soon

———

The Hostile Operations Team ® Books
Strike Team 1

Book 0: RECKLESS HEAT

Book 1: HOT PURSUIT - Matt & Evie

Book 2: HOT MESS - Sam & Georgie

Book 3: DANGEROUSLY HOT - Kev & Lucky

Book 4: HOT PACKAGE - Billy & Olivia

Book 5: HOT SHOT - Jack & Gina

Book 6: HOT REBEL - Nick & Victoria

Book 7: HOT ICE - Garrett & Grace

Book 8: HOT & BOTHERED - Ryan & Emily

Book 9: HOT PROTECTOR - Chase & Sophie

Book 10: HOT ADDICTION - Dex & Annabelle

Book 11: HOT VALOR - Mendez & Kat

Book 12: A HOT CHRISTMAS MIRACLE - Mendez & Kat

———

The HOT SEAL Team Books

Book 1: HOT SEAL - Dane & Ivy

Book 2: HOT SEAL Lover - Remy & Christina

Book 3: HOT SEAL Rescue - Cody & Miranda

Book 4: HOT SEAL BRIDE - Cash & Ella

Book 5: HOT SEAL REDEMPTION - Alex & Bailey

Book 6: HOT SEAL TARGET - Blade & Quinn

Book 7: HOT SEAL HERO - Ryan & Chloe

Book 8: HOT SEAL DEVOTION - Zach & Kayla

———

HOT Heroes for Hire: Mercenaries
Black's Bandits

Book 1: BLACK LIST - Jace & Maddy

Book 2: BLACK TIE - Brett & Tallie

Book 3: BLACK OUT - Colt & Angie

Book 4: BLACK KNIGHT - Jared & Libby

Book 5: BLACK HEART - Ian Black!

Book 6: BLACK MAIL - Tyler Scott

Book 7: BLACK VELVET - Dax's story! Coming soon!

———

The HOT Novella in Liliana Hart's MacKenzie Family Series

HOT WITNESS - Jake & Eva

———

7 Brides for 7 Brothers

MAX (Book 5) - Max & Ellie

7 Brides for 7 Soldiers

WYATT (Book 4) - Wyatt & Paige

7 Brides for 7 Blackthornes

ROSS (Book 3) - Ross & Holly

Filthy Rich Billionaires

Book 1: FILTHY RICH REVENGE

Book 2: FILTHY RICH PRINCE

———

Who's HOT?

Strike Team 1

Matt "Richie Rich" Girard (Book 0 & 1)
Sam "Knight Rider" McKnight (Book 2)
Kev "Big Mac" MacDonald (Book 3)
Billy "the Kid" Blake (Book 4)
Jack "Hawk" Hunter (Book 5)
Nick "Brandy" Brandon (Book 6)
Garrett "Iceman" Spencer (Book 7)
Ryan "Flash" Gordon (Book 8)
Chase "Fiddler" Daniels (Book 9)
Dex "Double Dee" Davidson (Book 10)

Commander
John "Viper" Mendez (Book 11 & 12)

Deputy Commander
Alex "Ghost" Bishop

Strike Team 2

Cade "Saint" Rodgers (Book 1)
Sky "Hacker" Kelley (Book 2)
Dean "Wolf" Garner (Book 3)
Malcom "Mal" McCoy (Book 4)
Noah "Easy" Cross (Book 5)
Jax "Gem" Stone (Book 6)
Ryder "Muffin" Hanson
Zane "Zany" Scott
Jake "Harley" Ryan (HOT WITNESS)

SEAL Team 1

Dane "Viking" Erikson (Book 1)
Remy "Cage" Marchand (Book 2)
Cody "Cowboy" McCormick (Book 3)
Cash "Money" McQuaid (Book 4)
Alexei "Camel" Kamarov (Book 5)
Adam "Blade" Garrison (Book 6)
Ryan "Dirty Harry" Callahan (Book 7)
Zach "Neo" Anderson (Book 8)
Corey "Shade" Vance

Black's Bandits

Jace Kaiser (Book 1)
Brett Wheeler (Book 2)
Colton Duchaine (Book 3)
Jared Fraser (Book 4)
Ian Black (Book 5)

Tyler Scott (Book 6)
Dax Freed (Book 7)
Thomas "Rascal" Bradley
Jamie Hayes
Mandy Parker (Airborne Ops)
Melanie (Reception)
? Unnamed Team Members

Freelance Contractors

Lucinda "Lucky" San Ramos, now MacDonald (Book 3)
Victoria "Vee" Royal, now Brandon (Book 6)
Emily Royal, now Gordon (Book 8)
Miranda Lockwood, now McCormick (SEAL Team
Book 3)
Bliss Bennett, (Strike Team 2, Book 2)
Angelica "Angie" Turner (Black's Bandits, Book 3)

About the Author

Lynn Raye Harris is a Southern girl, military wife, wannabe cat lady, and horse lover. She's also the New York Times and USA Today bestselling author of the HOSTILE OPERATIONS TEAM ® SERIES of military romances, and 20 books about sexy billionaires for Harlequin.

A former finalist for the Romance Writers of America's Golden Heart Award and the National Readers Choice Award, Lynn lives in Alabama with her handsome former-military husband, one fluffy princess of a cat, and a very spoiled American Saddlebred horse who enjoys bucking at random in order to keep Lynn on her toes.

Lynn's books have been called "exceptional and emotional," "intense," and "sizzling" -- and have sold in excess of 4.5 million copies worldwide.

To connect with Lynn online:
www.LynnRayeHarris.com
Lynn@LynnRayeHarris.com